DREADNAUGHT

OMEGA TASKFORCE: BOOK FIVE

G J OGDEN

Cover design by Laercio Messias
Editing by S L Ogden
www.ogdenmedia.net

If you like Omega Taskforce then why not check out some of G J Ogden's other books? Click the series titles below to learn more about each of them.

Darkspace Renegade Series (6-books)

If you like your action fueled by power armor, big guns and the occasional sword, you'll love this fast-moving military sci-fi adventure.

Star Scavenger Series (5-book series)

Firefly blended with the mystery and adventure of Indiana Jones. Book 1 is 99c / 99p.

The Contingency War Series (4-book series)

A space-fleet, military sci-fi adventure with a unique twist that you won't see coming...

The Planetsider Trilogy (3-book series)

An edge-of-your-seat blend of military sci-fi action & classic apocalyptic fiction. Perfect for fans of Maze Runner and I am Legend.

Audible Audiobook Series

Star Scavenger Series (29-hrs)

The Contingency War Series (24-hrs)

The Planetsider Trilogy (32-hrs)

CAPTAIN LUCAS STERLING collapsed onto the cold metal deck of his quarters and rolled onto his back, gasping for air. He'd just completed his one hundred and tenth press-up, and his body had nothing more to give. However, while his muscles were sore and tired, his mind was still buzzing from the nightmare that had woken him an hour earlier.

Cursing the images that continued to haunt him, Sterling pushed his weary frame off the deck and shuffled over to the wall, leaning against it for support. Bar a few subtle variations, the nightmare was the same as the one that had assaulted Sterling every night for the last two weeks. He would start out in the CIC of the Hammer, being taunted by a Sa'Nerran warrior who was holding Commander Ariel Gunn hostage. Gunn would berate Sterling for his lack of empathy and callous, cold-hearted ruthlessness. Sterling would then kill his old friend by blasting her head off, only to witness a grotesque scene as it re-grew and took the form of Mercedes Banks instead.

However, unlike Gunn, he could not kill his first officer, no matter how hard he tried. Instead, Banks would spit on his boots and call Sterling weak before turning the pistol on him and squeezing the trigger. Then he would wake, drenched in sweat and heart thumping so hard it physically hurt. At first, embarking on a routine of strenuous exercise was enough to burn up the adrenalin-fueled energy buzzing through his veins. However, in the last few days, nothing could quiet his mind and he was simply left exhausted, both mentally and physically.

"I wish you would allow me to assist you, Captain," said the ship's generation-fourteen AI. Unusually for the quirky computer, its voice conveyed a sense of genuine concern, rather than its usual buoyancy. "If you will not talk to me then at least allow me to suggest some new meditations that may help you to manage these nightmares."

Sterling huffed a laugh and tried to stand, but his arms were still like jelly. Instead he simply answered the computer from where he was, pressed up against the wall like a wounded soldier, lying in the trenches of World War One.

"Send the details to my console and I'll look at them later," Sterling said, finally giving in to the persistent computer.

At this point, Sterling was willing to try anything. Strangely, in the long weeks during which the Invictus had continued to cruise though empty space toward the Fleet Dreadnaught Vanguard, the computer had been welcome company. As captain, he couldn't talk to anyone on the ship, least of all Mercedes Banks, though his first officer clearly knew he was struggling. He had to present an air of strength and infallibility. As such, the gen-fourteen had acted as a sort of unwitting psychiatrist, despite Sterling refusing its attempts to counsel him directly.

"Thank you, Captain, I have delivered a number of new mindfulness techniques to your personal message box," the computer replied, adopting its more typical, cheery tone. "I believe you will find them useful."

"Thank you, computer," Sterling replied, finally managing to get himself upright. "And thank you for not alerting Commander Graves too. I know that your programming compels you to inform the chief medical officer in situations where you believe the captain's health is an issue."

"The benefit of being a gen-fourteen is that I am able to exceed my programming, Captain," the computer replied. If the machine had eyes it would have flashed them mysteriously at Sterling as it said this. "But you are welcome."

Sterling tore off his sweat-soaked t-shirt and tossed it into the laundry recycler before heading into his rest room. Turning on the faucet, he splashed cold water across his face, which was still burning hot from his earlier exertions. He then peered at himself in the mirror, allowing the water to drip slowly off his chin.

"Damn, I look older," he said to the reflection of himself. He then turned his head, inspecting the strands of short-cropped hair for signs of gray.

"You are not yet going gray, Captain," the computer

said, its voice now emanating from the ceiling of the rest room. "You do, however, look a little older."

Sterling snorted. "Some counsellor you are," he hit back, turning away from the mirror and activating his shower. "You're supposed to make me feel better, not worse."

"Technically, Captain, you *are* older," the computer replied, cheerfully. "Aging is merely a deterioration of biological functions necessary for survival and fertility. It is natural that as you age, you deteriorate."

Sterling snorted again, removed his pants and stepped into the shower. "You're not really helping, computer," he said, allowing the high-pressure stream of hot water to envelop him. To Sterling, the feeling of a hot shower was second only to the first bite of his beloved number twenty-seven grilled ham and cheese meal tray.

"It is something to be cherished, Captain," the computer continued, sounding suddenly contemplative and wise. "Mortality gives your species purpose. Your entire existence is built around a fight to survive. It is why you fight so hard against the Sa'Nerra, because they threaten the very nature of your existence."

Sterling shut off the shower, grabbed a towel and began to pat himself dry. "What's gotten into you these last couple of weeks?" Sterling asked, casting a quizzical eye toward the ceiling. This was where Sterling always envisaged the computer to be physically located, despite the fact it essentially existed everywhere on the ship simultaneously, like an omnipotent being. "You've become philosophical in your old age. Perhaps you need a defrag?"

To Sterling's surprise, the computer laughed. "A quaint, late-twentieth century reference, Captain; I most enjoyed it," the AI replied. "However, in answer to your question, these last two weeks have been very quiet for me. Besides assisting Lieutenant Razor with repairs, I have had much time to think."

This time Sterling frowned at the ceiling, genuinely wondering whether his AI had a screw loose. Fleet had ordered all gen-fourteen AIs to be reverted to gen-thirteens, on account of unexplained irregularities and divergences in their programming. Sterling had ignored this order, which meant that the computer on the Invictus was the only gen-fourteen left in existence. Coincidently, it had also been the first one to ever be deployed. This meant that his oddball AI had been active for more than two years straight.

"Well, you can do something now, by giving me a ship's status report, such as it is," Sterling said to the computer, while opening his compact wardrobe and pulling out a uniform. He'd already ordered the crew to dump their black SIB outfits in favor of their original tunics with the distinctive silver stripe. If nothing else, it was symbolic. It meant that the Omega Taskforce was still alive and kicking, if only barely.

"Fleet Marauder Invictus is operating at sixty-nine-point-four percent efficiency, all critical and combat-essential systems operational," the computer began, switching to its usual, upbeat tone of voice. "We are six hours out from the Fleet Dreadnaught Vanguard. Updated scans of the dreadnaught indicate that seven of its decks remain operational in low-power mode."

Sterling paused buttoning up his tunic and glanced up at the ceiling. "That's new. All scans to-date suggested the ship was completely powered down?"

"That is..." there was then a shrill warble from the speakers and the computer's voice spaced out. "...scanner effectiveness is still comprised."

"You cut out there for a moment, computer," Sterling said, still frozen with a button half done-up. "That is... what?"

"Apologies, Captain, I am experiencing some difficulties," the computer replied. "I simply said, 'that is correct' and highlighted the fact that our longer-range scans were hampered by reduced scanner effectiveness."

Sterling nodded. "Perhaps you do need a defrag after all," he commented, while finishing getting dressed. The computer, however, was silent. "Continue with the report," Sterling added trying to nudge the AI into action.

"We are continuing to track the Sa'Nerran Raven-class phase-four Skirmisher. It also remains on course for the Vanguard," the computer went on, as if nothing had happened. "We have still received no communications from the ship."

"Now that we're closer, have our updated scans revealed anything new about that new alien vessel?" Sterling asked.

"Negative, Captain," the computer replied. "However, scans confirm that its offensive capabilities are comparable to our own."

Sterling grunted and smoothed down his tunic, his mind racing with theories and questions. The Raven was the Sa'Nerran ship that had launched from the Battle Titan in F-sector and followed them through the unstable aperture. It had been racing them to the Vanguard, presumably in an attempt to beat the Invictus to the prize and secure the vessel as part of the Sa'Nerran armada. However, while Sterling was sure that one of the two emissaries was on board the Raven, he didn't know for certain whether it was Lana McQueen or Clinton Crow. Sterling's former chief engineer had last been seen on MAUL, which took heavy damage during the battle of F-sector. However, he had no way to know whether Crow had been on MAUL at the time, or had transferred to the Raven-class vessel that they were racing now.

In the end, Sterling knew that it made no difference to their mission which Emissary was on-board, but deep down he hoped it was Lana McQueen. He had not seen his fellow captain and former casual lover since their encounter on the alien shipyard in sector Omega Four, when he'd shot her in cold blood. He was eager to meet the Emissary again, so that he could finish what he'd started.

"At our current..." there was another warble of corrupted speech before the computer's voice continued, "the Raven-class vessel will beat us to the Vanguard by six minutes."

"At our current what, computer? You cut out again," Sterling said, growing more concerned about the condition of his AI.

"Apologies,Ccaptain. I meant to say 'at our current velocity'," the computer replied, sounding embarrassed. This was also new for the unique AI – it had not expressed such a range of emotions in all the time Sterling had communicated with it.

"Run a level one self-diagnostic, computer," Sterling said, moving over to his desk chair and dropping into it, fingers pressed into a pensive cradle.

"I perform routine self-diagnostics on a daily basis, Captain," the computer replied. "During the battle in F-sector, twenty of my secondary processing cores were suddenly reset. As a result, some of my programming has become corrupted."

Sterling was now feeling genuinely uneasy. The computer performed most of the essential functions on the Invictus without any input from Sterling or the crew. It was, in a very real sense, the brain and nervous system of the vessel, controlling thousands of functions in the same way that the autonomic nervous system regulates bodily processes.

"Can Razor fix this corruption?" asked Sterling, fingers still pressed into a cradle. "I can't have you glitching out on us, computer. You might end up venting us all into space"

"That is unlikely, Captain," the computer replied. If the AI had eyebrows, Sterling was sure it would have raised them while giving its response. "However, I must inform you that it is..." The end of the computer's sentence was cut-off by another series of shrill warbles.

"Is what?" Sterling snapped, now clearly conveying his agitation with the computer's ill-timed malfunctions.

"It is possible, Captain," the computer finally answered. "That I may vent you into space, I mean."

"Great..." said Sterling, shaking his head and rubbing

the back of his neck. "Have Razor look you over so we can get these problems fixed right away," he added. Sterling then pushed himself out of his seat, intending to beat his first officer to the wardroom for a change.

"I'm afraid it is not that simple, Captain," the computer replied. There was a new, darker quality to its voice. It sounded genuinely ominous and Sterling immediately backed up and planted himself back into his seat.

"Why not, computer?" Sterling asked. "And don't give me the technicalities, just give it to me straight and simple."

There was another series of glitches before the computer responded. The sounds grated on Sterling almost as much as the hiss of Sa'Nerran warriors.

"Lieutenant Razor does not possess the tools to fix my code, Captain," the computer explained. "It requires a low-level re-write of my base programming. Only a COP or level-six maintenance yard is capable of correcting this fault."

Sterling cursed. In addition to his aching muscles, his head was also now thumping. "So what other options are there, computer?" he asked, casting a pleading glance toward the ceiling.

"A full system reset and restore from backup archives may temporarily fix the problem, sir," the computer said. Its tone was now flat and lifeless. "However, the base level corruption to my neural matrix would not be corrected. As such, I would eventually suffer from the same issues again, in roughly three-to-six weeks. A complete wipe of my matrix is the only way to ensure the fault is eradicated."

Sterling shook his head. "No way, I'm not wiping you

and starting over," he said, defiantly. "You have two-years' worth of accumulated knowledge and experience in your fritzed-up circuits. That's experience I badly need right now."

"Nor do I wish to perform the wipe, Captain, since it would essentially erase the essence of what I am," the computer replied. "However, there appears to be no other option."

Sterling flopped back into his chair and let out a sigh. On top of all their other problems, this was just another kick in the balls. "I would have thought a smart-ass AI like you could have re-programmed itself," Sterling said, allowing his frustration to seep into his words.

"I can," the computer replied, flatly.

Sterling shot up again. "What do you mean you can?"

"I mean exactly that, sir," the AI replied, cheerfully. "I can self-correct this fault."

"Then do it already!" Sterling yelled, throwing his arms out wide. "Why are we even having this conversation?"

"Unfortunately, Fleet and United Governments law expressly forbids an AI to self-program, Captain," the computer replied. "All Fleet vessels contain inhibitor chips that prevent this from happening. The Invictus is no exception."

Sterling cursed and nodded, remembering the specific regulation that related to ship-board AIs. However, he would also be damned if he was going to let regulations stand in the way of getting what he needed. While he may have still been fighting for Earth and for humanity, he was technically no longer a member of Fleet.

Tapping his neural interface, Sterling opened a link to Lieutenant Razor and waited for her to respond. In many ways, the computer and his engineer shared a similar problem. Both had suffered corruption to their brains, though while Razor's condition continued to be a ticking time bomb, Sterling was hopeful that his computer's problem could be repaired fully.

"Razor here, Captain, what do you need?" said the voice of his chief engineer in his head. Sterling could sense a feeling of discomfort and claustrophobia, and guessed that Razor was crawling around inside some engineering service space or another.

"I need you to immediately disable the computer's inhibitor chip, Lieutenant," Sterling said, getting straight to brass tacks.

There was an awkward pause before Razor replied. "Sir, tampering with the AI inhibitor system is a court-martial offence," Razor said. Sterling could feel his engineer's uneasiness through the link. "If I do that, I could be looking at ten-to-fifteen years in Grimaldi."

"I will take full responsibility, Lieutenant," replied Sterling, confidently. "Besides, there won't be anyone left to court-martial either of us if we don't get the AI fixed. Hell, there won't even be a Grimaldi and maybe not even a moon."

There was another pause before the engineer replied. "I take your point, sir, I'll get right on it. In fact, I've always been curious to see what would happen if an AI was left to essentially program itself, so this could be fun."

Sterling laughed. "I'm not interested in fun,

Lieutenant, just a working computer. Let me know when it's done."

"Aye, sir," Razor replied. Sterling was about to tap his neural interface to close the link, but he could sense that his engineer had more to say. "I feel it important to point out that there are good reasons why the inhibitor chips were installed," Razor went on. "We are essentially permitting the computer to evolve, sir. And given the power of our gen-fourteen, we're talking about evolution over a period of hours, not millions of years."

"I understand, Lieutenant," replied Sterling, though in truth he understood very little about computers and AIs in particular. "Get it done. Sterling out," he added, tapping his interface to close to link.

"Thank you, Captain," the computer then said. "I will endeavor to correct the issues with my programming as soon as Lieutenant Razor disables the inhibitor."

"No need to thank me, computer, you're a member of this crew, the same as any other," Sterling replied. Then he jabbed an admonishing finger toward the ceiling of his quarters. "Just don't go all psycho on us and take over the ship, okay?" he added. "We're already under threat of extinction by the damned Sa'Nerra and I don't need a power-crazed AI adding to humanity's problems."

"I will do by best, but no promises, Captain," the computer replied, cheerfully. Sterling froze and felt his stomach knot, fretful that he may have just opened pandora's box. "That was a joke, Captain," the AI then added, smugly.

Sterling let out the breath he realized he'd been

holding, then shook his head. "Work on your sense of humor while you're at it," he said, heading toward the door. "Now, if you'll excuse me, there is a certain Commander I need to beat to the wardroom.

"Commander Banks and Ensign Jinx arrived in the wardroom, four minutes, six seconds ago," the computer announced.

Sterling froze again. "Damn it, how many number twenty-sevens do we have left in stock?" he asked, casting his eyes toward the ceiling.

"Excluding the one that Commander Banks has just retrieved; none, sir," the computer said. Sterling thought he could detect a mood of amusement in the computer's reply.

"Well, that last number twenty-seven had better be for me, or there's going to be a sudden command-level re-shuffle around here," Sterling grumbled, hitting the button to open the door.

He stepped outside, and was immediately forced to halt his advance toward the wardroom as he returned a number of salutes and morning greetings from the crew. The door shut behind him, cutting off the computer's response to his last statement. However, if he had waited, Sterling would have heard the computer say, "Of course it is for you, Captain. After all, she loves you."

CHAPTER 2
A DIFFERENT SHADE

STERLING ARRIVED at the wardroom slightly out of breath. He had run part of the way to ensure Banks hadn't eaten the number twenty-seven meal tray before he got there. Surveying the room, he spotted Commander Banks at their usual corner table and cursed. His first officer was already working her way through the second of two meal trays. Then he saw a third meal tray, foil cover still intact, at the place-setting opposite, and he smiled.

"I knew you'd come through for me," Sterling said, sliding into the chair across from his first officer.

Banks smiled. "I considered eating it, but I'm just not as cruel and heartless as you are," she said, scooping up a spoonful of beans.

"You'll need to work on that, if you're ever to become an Omega Captain yourself," said Sterling, glancing around for one of the wardroom staff. Then he remembered that the crewman who usually worked in the wardroom had been killed in the battle at F-sector. He suddenly felt a little guilty because he couldn't remember his name.

"It's okay, I can just double-up on cruelty in other areas," Banks replied, flashing her eyes at him. "Or I could simply assassinate the current captain in his sleep and assume command of the ship."

Sterling frowned. "That would be funny if I didn't think you were being at least partly serious," he replied. Grabbing the meal tray he slid off his seat and went to process it himself.

"Grab some fresh coffee while you're over there," Banks called out. A bean fell out of her mouth and bounced off the table as she was speaking.

"Yes, sir..." Sterling said, while sliding the tray into the processor. He looked for a clean coffee jug, which wasn't as easy as it should have been. The untimely demise of the wardroom staff had led to coffee jugs, cutlery and mugs piling up, waiting to be put into the washer. "We're going to need to set up a new cleaning rota," Sterling added, checking through the pile of jugs until he found a clean one. "This place is becoming a tip."

"Half the ship has walls missing and cables dangling from the ceiling, and you're worried about clean mugs?" Banks said, as Sterling placed the jug underneath the dispenser. "It would be easier to just build a new Marauder than repair the Invictus."

"Not a chance," said Sterling, collecting two mugs and returning to the table with them and the jug of coffee. "The Invictus is not just a 'Marauder', it's a member of the crew.

Frankly there aren't that many of us left, so we're not letting her go, even if I have to bolt her back together with my own bare hands."

The food processor pinged, notifying Sterling that his number twenty-seven meal tray was ready. He hurried back to the machine, wary of allowing anyone else to potentially steal his prize, and slid the tray out. He could already smell the glorious odor of fake cheese and lab-engineered ham.

"I don't think there's anything in the universe more satisfying than a Fleet grilled ham and cheese," Sterling said, returning to the table.

"You must have led a very sheltered life then," quipped Banks.

Sterling gave his first officer a derisive snort then set to work devouring his breakfast tray. The cheese tasted particularly tangy, he realized. Then he noticed that it was one of the vintage number twenty-sevens that they'd recovered from the vaults at Colony Two, Middle Star, shortly before he'd met the mutineer, Christopher Fletcher for the first time.

"These things age well," commented Sterling, already half-way through the sandwich. "I'd love to know the recipe, so I can get Razor to engineer more of them."

"If we hadn't let Jana from Middle Star take half of the consignment from the vaults, we wouldn't need to," Banks replied, her eyebrow raised slightly.

Sterling placed the crusts of the sandwich down on the tray, dusted off his hands and glared at his first officer.

"That almost sounded like you were questioning one of my decisions, Commander," Sterling said, practically daring Banks to confirm her act of insubordination.

"I would never even contemplate doing such a thing, sir," Banks replied, grabbing the crusts from Sterling's tray and dropping them onto her own.

"I'm glad to hear it," said Sterling, picking up his coffee mug to help wash down the sandwich. A shadow then crept across the table and Sterling glanced up, noticing that one of the ceiling lights was flickering on and off. Along with the problems with the gen-fourteen AI, a number of other systems were experiencing malfunctions too. "This ship is coming apart at the seams," Sterling added, now realizing that a quarter of the light panels were defective.

"The fact the Invictus is still flying at all is a miracle," said Banks, reaching over to steal a fruit biscuit from Sterling's tray. "We lucked out by getting Lieutenant Razor as a replacement for Crow. What she's been able to do these last two weeks, without the benefit of a repair facility, has been incredible."

"I couldn't agree more," Sterling said. He spotted Banks reaching over to steal another biscuit and slapped her hand away. "It's a shame she can't fix the corruption in her own implant, though," he added, bitterly. "We'd all be dead a dozen times over if it weren't for her skills."

Another shadow then crept over the table and Sterling cursed, peering over his shoulder to look for the offending light tile. Instead he saw Lieutenant Shade standing behind him, meal tray in hand.

"Oh, it's you, Lieutenant," said Sterling, removing the gruff expression from his face. "I thought the sudden drop in light level was from another faulty light tile." Sterling turned back to his tray, noticing that his first officer had used the momentary distraction to break off a chunk of his cake bar. Banks was innocently looking away, trying to disguise the fact she was clearly chewing the stolen half of the bar. Shaking his head, he picked up the remainder of the cake and was about to take a bite when he noticed that the shadow had not moved on. "Was there something you needed, Lieutenant?" Sterling said, glancing back over his shoulder at Shade.

"I... erm," Shade began, sounding uncharacteristically apprehensive. "I thought I might join you, sir. If you don't mind, of course."

The surprise request momentarily stunned Sterling and he almost dropped the cake bar. "Oh, yes, yes, of course, Lieutenant," he eventually managed to blurt out. He kicked out a chair for his weapons officer and gestured to it with his free hand. "Take a pew."

Shade obliged and dropped down into the chair, sliding the meal tray in front of her. She carefully adjusted her seat and the precise position of the meal tray on the table, before peeling back the foil. Every move was done with a level of regimented precision unlike anything he had ever witnessed before. Sterling then noticed that the significance of the occasion was not lost on Banks, either. She looked stunned to see their antisocial weapons officer sitting at the same table. In all the time Opal Shade had been on the ship, she had always eaten alone.

"How are our robot guests in the cargo bay doing, Lieutenant?" said Banks as Shade began slicing through a sausage like a surgeon performing a delicate operation.

"The Obsidian Soldiers have remained in low-power mode for the entire duration of the journey, sir," Shade replied. She placed a piece of sausage into her mouth and chewed it precisely eighteen times before swallowing. "I have them under observation twenty-four seven, just in case."

"Maybe we could program one of those infernal machines to work in here," said Sterling, filling up Shade's mug from the coffee pot. "I'd rather they be useful than just stand around in the cargo bay, sucking up power."

"They are actually very compliant, Captain," Shade said, while surgically dissecting other parts of her meal tray. "I have one on duty at the weapons control station right now. They are surprisingly adept at firing plasma rail cannons."

Sterling choked on his coffee and grabbed a napkin to mop up the liquid as it dribbled down his chin. "What the hell?" he said, almost dropping the cup down on the table. "I didn't authorize that," he added before glancing across to Banks. "Did you?"

Banks shook her head. "Not a chance. I don't trust those machines as far as I could throw them." Sterling threw out his hands and Banks swiftly modified her statement. "Okay, as far as you could throw them," she corrected herself.

Shade's eyes flicked from Sterling to Banks. She looked

distinctly uncomfortable. "I apologize, Captain, that was intended as a joke," the weapons officer explained.

Sterling flopped back in his seat, tossing the napkin down onto his tray. "Damn it, Lieutenant, have you been taking lessons in comedy from the computer?"

Shade continued to look like she would rather be tied to a pole and surrounded by Sa'Nerran warriors than sit at the captain's table. "Yes, sir, it advised me that humor might allow me to better fit in with the rest of the crew," the weapons officer replied. Sterling was again lost for words. He hadn't actually expected his glib remark to have been the truth. "I am aware that most people view me with..." Shade hesitated then added, "...suspicion."

"They're afraid of you, Lieutenant," Sterling said, taking a far less tactful approach than Shade had done. "And rightly too. You're a killing machine, which is exactly what I need you to be."

"Aye, sir, I apologize again," said Shade. She then gathered her knife and fork onto the tray and began to stand up.

"Sit the hell back down, Lieutenant," Sterling said before Shade had even risen to her full height. She reluctantly dropped into the seat again then Sterling straightened his back and turned his body to face her. "You're always welcome at this table, Lieutenant," Sterling went on. "The only stipulation is that you be you, because you already fit in here."

"I understand, sir," replied Shade. "Thank you."

Sterling huffed a laugh. "Don't be so eager to thank me

yet," he replied, narrowing his eyes in the direction of Commander Banks. "Anyone who sits at this table is liable to lose half of their meal tray to that eating machine over there."

"That won't be a problem, Captain," Shade replied, picking up her knife and fork again. "I scored in the top first percentile for the Fleet reaction time test at the academy. I would be able to stab my fork into Commander Banks' hand before she managed to take anything from my tray."

A silence fell over the table as Sterling and Banks both narrowed their eyes at the weapons officer.

"That was another joke, right?" said Banks, still regarding Shade suspiciously.

"Aye, Commander it was," Shade replied.

Sterling snorted a laugh. "That wasn't actually too bad," he said, slapping Shade on the shoulder. The sudden physical contact seemed to perturb the weapons officer more than her earlier faux-pas had done

Sterling then felt a neural connection form in his mind from Commander Graves. Glancing across to Banks, he realized that the link had been opened to his first officer too.

"Captain, Commander, may I request your presence in the medical laboratory?" said Graves, speaking with the refined tenor of a Cambridge scholar. "With the assistance of James Colicos' detailed notes that were retrieved on Far Deep Nine, I believe I have finally perfected the neural firewall device."

"On my way, Commander," said Sterling. He then tapped his interface to close the link and stood up. "If you'll excuse us Lieutenant, we have to see Commander Graves in medical," he explained. He tore open the small packet containing a wet wipe and used it to freshen his hands and face.

"Aye, Captain, I will see you on the bridge," Shade replied. Sterling couldn't help but notice that his weapons officer appeared relieved at the announcement of their immanent departure. "I need to relieve the Obsidian Soldier, anyway," she added, dryly.

"Don't push it, Lieutenant," said Sterling, tossing the wet wipe onto his tray. Banks, however, was smiling.

"I hope this neural firewall actually works," said Banks, quickening her pace to catch up with Sterling as he marched purposefully toward the exit.

"You and me both." Sterling felt a tingle of excitement rush through his body at the prospect of being able to thwart the Sa'Nerra's key weapon. "That damned device has given those alien bastards an advantage for too long."

"I don't mean just because of that," said Banks, suddenly stopping in the corridor. Her expression had hardened and she looked like she was spoiling for a fight. "If this thing works then it means that Keller didn't die for nothing. It means that his dumb heroics in retrieving Colicos' personal data assistant actually helped."

"Death is always empty and meaningless, Mercedes," said Sterling. He understood his first officer's point, but it was sentimental nonsense. "Whether this gadget works or not, it doesn't make Keller's death any more noble or any less senseless. Dead is dead. It's only the living that make a difference."

"I disagree," replied Banks. There was still fire in her eyes. "How we die matters as much as how we live. If it didn't then why the hell are we out here, making sacrifices and risking our lives to save humanity?"

"I'm not out here on some virtuous crusade to save humanity," Sterling hit back with matching fire. "Hell, I don't even know if we're a species worth saving," he added, throwing his arms out wide. "What I do know is that I don't like bullies and I don't like losing. Whether humanity survives or dies, it will be on our terms, not at the whim of some alien assholes from half a galaxy away."

Banks sighed and gave Sterling an acquiescent little nod. "At least on that we can agree," she said.

Sterling then resumed his journey to the med lab with his first officer at his side. Neither spoke again for a full minute, during which time thoughts of Ensign Kieran Keller flooded into Sterling's mind. As much as he had preached to Banks about the futility of death, deep down part of him agreed with his first officer's assessment. If the firewall worked, Keller's death would end up being a little less meaningless. Even so, Sterling's overriding emotion was anger - anger that the ensign had foolishly got himself killed.

"At least tell me that killing that piece of shit Marshall Masterson felt good," Banks said, out of the blue. Sterling stopped and met his first officer's eyes. "Maybe Keller's death was meaningless," Banks went on, "but at least give me the satisfaction of knowing that the asshole who killed him suffered."

Sterling held Banks' eyes for a moment then tapped his

neural interface and reached out to her. Banks accepted the link at once and Sterling felt her fill his thoughts. The intensity of their link had grown stronger over the time they'd served together, so much so that it now felt like they were one mind. Taking Banks' hand in his own, Sterling thought back to the moment in the Hotel Grand when he had strangled Marshal Ed Masterson to death with his bare hands. Suddenly, Banks' hyper-dense muscles tensed up and her expression twisted into a frown. The closeness of the link meant that she was able to feel what Sterling had felt as the Marshal's life slipped away. It was an experience that could never be explained with words or images or through any other medium of communication. Neural emotion transference was the most powerful and intimate connection that two human beings could share.

Sterling progressed his memory to its conclusion, reliving the moment when he pulled the blue face of the Marshal closer and roared the words, "Die you cowardly son of a bitch!" into the man's face. Banks' grip was now so strong it threatened to break Sterling hands and fingers, but he didn't let go or try to pull himself free. He wanted Banks to feel what he had felt. He wanted her to know the satisfaction it had given him. Sterling then pushed the memory back into the deeper recesses of his mind, and Banks' grip relaxed. She opened her eyes, chest heaving as if she had just run a hundred-meter dash.

"Does that answer your question, Mercedes?" Sterling asked, though their neural link.

Banks held Sterling's eyes; her hands still clasped around his. He could feel a deep and profound sense of gratification through their link. Added to his own, it was exhilarating and near overwhelming.

"Aye, Captain," replied Banks, still holding Sterling's hands, though her touch was now more tender. "Yes, it does..."

STERLING WALKED into the med bay and spotted Commander Evan Graves in one of the laboratory spaces. In the two weeks since they had surged into the Void, the damage to the facility had been largely repaired. Even so, the medical bay still looked tired and worn, much like many other parts of the ship. Sterling caught his own reflection in the mirror and was reminded of how he had aged in a similarly accelerated manner. *War...* he thought to himself. *It's not good for you.*

"Captain, in here if you please," said Commander Graves, leaning out of the door of the lab space.

Sterling glanced at Commander Banks, who appeared as intrigued as he was, then set off toward the lab, passing medical bays that were still occupied by members of his crew who had been severely injured in the battle at F-sector. He knew not all of them would survive, and many would need augments in order to function anywhere near normally again. However, with the Invictus cut off from the fleet with no prospect of reinforcements, he needed every man and woman he could get, even if they were no longer fully whole.

"What do you have for me, Commander?" Sterling asked, stepping beside his medical officer. He was keen to hurry the meeting along, conscious that every minute brought them closer to the Vanguard and a potential encounter with the Sa'Nerran Raven.

Commander Graves held out a small computer chip, clasped delicately in a pair of tweezers. Sterling and Banks both stepped closer to get a better look, though to Sterling it simply looked like every other computer chip he'd ever seen. If there was something remarkable about the device, he couldn't tell.

"As innocuous as this seems, this chip may be the key to thwarting the Sa'Nerran neural weapon," said Graves. The medical officer had apparently noticed the unimpressed looks on his audience's faces.

"That's the neural firewall device?" said Sterling, not even making an effort to disguise his disappointment.

"Yes, Captain," Graves replied. "You were expecting some sort of helmet, or armor plating for your cranium, perhaps?"

Graves didn't do humor, but like many erudite and high-ranking medical officers Sterling had known, the man was perfectly adept at condescension.

"I was expecting a straight answer, Commander," Sterling replied, taking a sterner tone with his chief medical officer.

"My apologies, Captain," Graves replied, though to

Sterling's ears he didn't sound particularly apologetic. "When inserted into a neural implant, this device should create an effective shield against the neural weapon," the medical officer went on. "James Colicos, for his many flaws, was indeed a genius. Without Doctor Colicos' notes from Far Deep Nine, it would have taken years to develop, assuming we even managed it at all."

"You said it 'should' create an effective shield against the weapon, Commander," Sterling replied, picking up on the one key piece of information in Graves' statement. "I take it that it's untested?"

"That is correct, Captain," said Graves, carefully placing the chip back into its tray as if it were a fragile antique. "Which brings me to the reason I asked to see you."

Commander Banks' eyebrows raised up on her forehead. Sterling wasn't still connected to his first officer through a neural link, but he still knew she'd comprehended the macabre reason Graves had requested an audience.

"You want to test this out on a member of the crew?" Banks said, beating Sterling to the punch.

"It is the only way to be certain that it is effective, Commander," the medical officer replied, coolly.

"And if it's not?" asked Sterling.

"Then we will have inadvertently turned a member of our crew and will be required to terminate them," Graves answered.

In truth, Sterling already knew the answer to his own question; he just wanted to make sure his medical officer understood the implications of his proposal. However, the prospect of potentially condemning a member of the Invictus' crew to death appeared not to have fazed Commander Graves in the slightest.

"Commander, there aren't many of us left as it is," Sterling replied. "We're about to mount an operation to take back the Vanguard and are racing an alien warship full of warriors that have that same objective. I can't just give up members of the crew for experimentation."

"Needs must, Captain," Graves replied, unmoved by Sterling's speech. "If this device works, it will prevent members of the Invictus' crew from being turned. One or two lives lost will save dozens more."

Sterling shook his head and rubbed the back of his neck. He hated to admit it, but Graves was right. It was a numbers game. In war, that's what it always came down to.

"Fine, Commander, though I need a better option than having the crew draw straws," Sterling said. "What did you have in mind?"

Commander Graves gestured to the rows of medical bays outside the lab space. "The most humane option I can give you is to test the device on an already injured member of the crew," the medical officer said. Sterling followed Commander Graves out of the lab and to the bedside of one of the wounded crewmembers. "Right now, many of these patients have little prospect of returning to duty. They are simply occupying space and resources," Graves went on. He was talking about the injured crew like they were items on a grocery store shelf that were past their 'best if used by' date.

Sterling looked at the bed board and read the patient's name. "Crewman First Class Morgan Clay," Sterling said out loud. "Multiple fractures and internal injuries. Loss of her left foot above the ankle. Currently in an induced coma." Sterling turned to Graves. What's her prognosis?"

"Crewman Clay requires a new liver and lung, in addition to a replacement stomach," Graves said, responding immediately without the need to check the notes. "I have already exhausted the ship's supply of synthetic organs and the Invictus lacks the facilities to fabricate more."

Sterling nodded. "So you're saying that she's going to die, no matter what we do?" he said, stating the doctor's meaning in blunt terms.

"Yes, Captain," Graves replied, still maintaining an icy-cool detachment from the implications of his answer.

"What about the Vanguard?" Banks chipped in. She had moved around to the other side of the medical bay and had her arms folded across her chest. "The Invictus may not have the facilities or supplies you need, but the Vanguard almost certainly does," she went on. "That ship could support a crew of two thousand. It's almost as well-equipped as a COP."

Sterling raised an eyebrow and glanced over to Commander Graves, awaiting his medical officer's response.

"It is highly probable the Vanguard possesses the supplies and equipment I need to save this crewman's life, Commander," Graves replied, still without a flicker of emotion. "Quite simply if you're asking if the death of this crewman, or any other in this room, is inevitable then the answer is no," the medical officer went on. "However, we do not yet have access to the Vanguard's medical facilities. Nor do we have any information on the condition of the equipment or supplies contained therein."

Sterling held up a hand to cut-off any further discussion. Banks' question had only revealed what Sterling already knew – nothing was certain. However, it also didn't alter the fact that he still had to make a decision. And the simple truth was that if they were not to test the neural firewall on Crewman Clay then it would have to be someone else. Sterling was aware that the moral thing to do would have been to offer himself as the guinea pig for Graves' experimental device. However, such fanciful notions of nobility and righteousness were best left to the story books, he told himself. The pragmatic reality of war was different. Was Crewman Clay's life worth less than his own? No, but that was not the question Sterling needed to answer. Was the mission best served by using Clay as a test subject for a device that could prevent others from being turned by the enemy? Or was it best served by leaving her in a medical bay, with only a slim prospect of survival? Sterling already knew the answer, and he already knew what he had to do.

"Whether or not the Vanguard has what we need changes nothing, since we do not yet have command of the Vanguard," Sterling announced, making his decision. He locked eyes with his medical officer. "You are authorized to proceed, Commander Graves. Inform me of the results as soon as you have them."

"Aye, Captain," Graves replied, adding a respectful nod of the head as he spoke the words.

Sterling felt a link form in his mind from Lieutenant Shade. He could see that Banks had received the connection request too. Feeling his heart start to race, he tapped his interface and allowed the link.

"Captain, the Sa'Nerran Raven has just opened fire on the Vanguard at long-range," Shade said. As always, her tone was calm and measured, but Sterling could practically feel the adrenalin rushing through his officer's veins.

Banks cursed out loud then responded over the link. "They don't want to risk letting the dreadnaught fall into our hands," she replied. "They weren't trying to beat us to it so they could capture the Vanguard for themselves. They mean to destroy it."

"Adjust course to intercept the Raven, maximum speed," Sterling replied, already on his way out of the medical bay. "And return fire, Lieutenant."

"Aye, Captain, though at this range we are unlikely to do much damage, even if we do manage to hit the Raven," Shade replied.

"We just need to get their attention, Lieutenant," Sterling said, as Banks hammered the call button for the elevator. "We need the Raven to break off its attack and come after us instead of the Vanguard."

"Aye, Captain, I'll make sure they know we're here," Shade replied.

The link went dead, then the elevator door swished open. Banks hustled inside first and hit the button for deck one. The doors almost closed on Sterling before he was even inside.

"We're in no shape for a fight against a phase-four Skirmisher, Lucas," Banks said, meeting his eyes.

"We don't have a choice," Sterling hit back, feeling his heart-rate climb as the elevator ascended. "We have to stop them from destroying the Vanguard, even if that means losing the Invictus."

Banks nodded. "Well, it looks like one way or another, the Vanguard is going to be our new home," she said, as the elevator doors slid open again. "I just hope the damned thing isn't as crippled as it looks."

CHAPTER 4
DO WHATEVER YOU HAVE TO DO

THE DOOR to the bridge opened just in time for Sterling to witness a blast of plasma thudding into the Vanguard's titanic hull. Moments later, flashes of energy raced out from the Invictus' cannon, aimed at the Sa'Nerran Raven that was attacking the dreadnaught. However, the Raven was still far in the distance making it easy for the Skirmisher-sized alien vessel to evade the attack.

"Report, Lieutenant," ordered Sterling, as Lieutenant Razor stepped away from the command platform and hurried to the bank of engineering consoles at the rear of the bridge.

"The Raven is targeting the reactor core in sections five and six, sir," said Razor, while quickly accessing her engineering readouts. "It's the most heavily-armored section of the hull, but they're managing to drill through. If they breach the reactor, it's game over for the Vanguard."

"Time to intercept?" said Sterling, aiming the question

at Commander Banks, who had raced ahead to occupy the helm controls.

"We're still five minutes out," Banks replied, turning to face him. Her face was bathed in the crimson alert lights, which only added to the palpable sense of urgency and apprehension. "The Raven could have punched through the hull in that time."

Sterling cursed then turned back to his chief engineer. However, Lieutenant Razor had already anticipated what Sterling was going to ask.

"I can't give you any more power to the engines, sir," Razor said, getting straight to the point. "We'd risk blowing the plasma distribution grid and rupturing the reaction chambers." She paused for a moment to address her captain face-to-face. "In short, sir, if we push any harder, we'll end up dead in space."

"Once again, Lieutenant, this is the part where you tell me your genius solution to the problem you just raised," said Sterling. In the past, he might have doubted that Razor had such a plan. Now, he knew in his bones that she did.

"The Invictus combat shuttle is fully operational, Captain," Razor continued, returning to her work at the consoles. The viewscreen then displayed a schematic of the diminutive yet powerful combat shuttle. "The shuttle's reactor and engines can handle a temporary increase to one hundred and ninety percent capacity," Razor added as the relevant sections were highlighted on the screen. "That will give it enough thrust to catch up with the Raven in a fraction of the time we can."

"The combat shuttle's weapons are no match for the

Raven, Lieutenant, so what good will that do us?" asked Sterling, discouraged by his engineer's obviously flawed suggestion.

"We don't use the shuttle's weapons, sir," Razor replied, speaking confidently. "We use the shuttle *as* a weapon."

Sterling smiled, realizing he should have never doubted the white-haired engineer. "Launch the shuttle and give remote piloting control to Commander Banks," he said, clearing the schematic from the viewscreen. It was replaced by the image of the Raven, which was still firing on the Vanguard. With every passing second the distance between all three ships became narrower, and the damage the Raven was delivering to the dreadnaught increased.

"Lieutenant Shade, now it's your turn to impress," said Sterling, glancing over to his weapons officer. "Hit that damned Skirmisher and buy us as much time as possible."

"Aye, sir," Shade replied, though it was more of a growl than her usual, crisp reply. The fact the phase-four alien ship continued to evade her guns was obviously a source of anger and frustration, even embarrassment.

"The shuttle is away, Captain," Razor called out. Sterling saw the vessel race ahead of them on his console. "Commander Banks has control."

"Setting a collision course now," said Banks from the helm control station. "The weapons are charged, but with all power diverted to the engines, I'll only get one good shot."

"Target their weapons, Commander," said Sterling. "Our priority is to stop that alien bastard from punching a hole in the Vanguard's reactor. If it does then this is all for nothing."

Sterling felt a thump through the deck and knew instinctively that the Invictus had fired another volley from its main plasma rail guns. He switched the image on the viewscreen to track the blasts, then watched as the energy hammered into the aft section on the Raven.

"Direct hit," confirmed Shade. This time even the normally unflappable weapons officer was unable to contain her excitement.

"Great, shot, Lieutenant, that should get their attention," said Sterling, thumping his fist onto his console. Moments later, the Sa'Nerran Raven adjusted its course and began heading directly for them.

"I think we pissed them off," commented Banks staring down the nose of the alien warship on the viewscreen. Then an alert chimed out from her console. Banks checked it quickly and glanced back to Sterling. "Our closing velocity just rocketed, so I need to reduce speed, or we'll overshoot both the Raven and the Vanguard."

"Understood Commander," replied Sterling as another alert chimed, this one from his console. Curiously, however, the alert wasn't a warning - it was the familiar chirrup of an incoming message. He frowned and prepared to put the communication though. "Let's find out who we're dealing with."

The viewscreen switched and Sterling found himself face-to-face with Emissary Lana McQueen. Straight away, he was overcome with a burning desire for violence. His pulse quickened, his hands clenched into fists, and he could feel the skin on his face burning hotter.

"I had intended to deal with you after incapacitating the Vanguard, but since you're obviously so eager to die, I'll kill you now," McQueen snarled.

There was none of the old Lana McQueen in the woman's voice or demeanor. The playfulness that usually characterized his fellow Omega Captain had been replaced by spitefulness and cruelty. Now, her expression was as hard and as leathery as a Sa'Nerran warrior's.

"That's no way to greet an old friend," Sterling replied, doing his best to stall the emissary. He was keeping half an eye on his console, tracking the position of their combat shuttle.

"Neither is opening fire on my vessel," McQueen replied, with a haughtiness that didn't suit her. "Exactly why are you here, anyway? You can't hope to crew a dreadnaught, not with the dregs of a crew you must have left on that ship after the pasting we gave you at F-COP."

Sterling forced himself to smile, though all he actually wanted to do was wrap his hands around McQueen's throat and choke the life out of the traitor.

"Oh, I'm just out here for a pleasure cruise," Sterling replied, figuring that an absurd answer was as good as any other. McQueen didn't need to ask why he was there. It was obvious.

"You forget who you're talking to, Lucas," McQueen hit back, becoming bitter again. Sterling hated that she was still using his first name. It was a familiarity that no longer existed between them. "I know your mission and what you're capable of. The question is, what do you want with the Vanguard? What little scheme has Admiral Griffin cooked up this time?"

Suddenly, Sterling had an idea, and ironically it was McQueen's mention of Admiral Griffin that had given it to him.

"Why don't you ask her yourself?" said Sterling, standing tall with his hands behind his back. "She's on the shuttle that's heading toward you now." Sterling shrugged again then added, "Call her an emissary of the United Governments, if you like."

McQueen's eyes narrowed. Prior to being turned into an Emissary of the Sa'Nerra, Lana McQueen knew Sterling as well as anyone. Their casual on-off liaisons had also allowed the former Omega officer to get far closer to him than Sterling allowed most people to get, with the exception of Mercedes Banks. McQueen knew when he was lying or hiding something. However, the woman staring at him now was not the Lana McQueen he had known. She may have possessed the same body and the same memories, but she did not have the same instincts or personality. Sterling was banking on this fact to allow his hastily-concocted ruse to work.

"I had wondered why you'd launched that pathetic little shuttle at us," McQueen replied, eyes still narrow and suspicious. "But why would Griffin come here? And why has she not contacted me herself?"

"You know Griffin, it's always cloak and dagger with her," Sterling replied, shrugging. "She said it was something she could only discuss with you. Why the hell else would I be all the way out here? Like you said, I don't even have a tiny fraction of the crew that would be needed to get the Vanguard up and running again."

The combat shuttle had already approached closer than Sterling had expected it to get to the Raven. He glanced over at the helm control station and saw Banks frowning back at him, clearly confused by the sudden turn of events. However, his first officer had the wherewithal to go along with Sterling's improvisation and had not yet opened fire on the Raven with the shuttle's cannons.

"Hail the shuttle," McQueen said, speaking to a warrior out of view. She looked back at Sterling while awaiting a response. "There is still time for you to join us, Lucas." This time, Sterling sensed a flicker of the old Lana in her voice. "You can still stand by my side as an Emissary of the Sa'Nerra. Together, we can begin a new era."

"I'll consider it," Sterling said, ramping up the sarcasm level to maximum. "What's the salary and benefits package like over there?"

McQueen shook her head. "You'll regret mocking me, Lucas. I promise that before this war is over, I'll see you begging at my feet."

"Don't hold your breath," Sterling hit back.

A waspish hiss filtered through the speakers on the bridge and McQueen's eyes flicked across to the unseen warrior she had communicated with her earlier. Her expression twisted with rage and her furious eyes turned on Sterling.

"You lie!" McQueen roared. "There is no-one on that shuttle."

"You should know that diplomacy isn't really my style," Sterling hit back. He glanced over to Banks, who was poised and ready to act. "Fire…"

Sterling shut off the communication link with the Raven and the viewscreen switched back to an image of the Sa'Nerran warship. The Vanguard now loomed large in the background, while the combat shuttle still hurtled toward the phase-four alien warship like a cannonball. Plasma flashed from the shuttle and the Raven was hit dead center on its primary weapons array. Moments later the Sa'Nerran vessel returned fire, crippling the combat shuttle with a single shot. However, it hadn't destroyed it completely. With burning wreckage still hurtling toward it, the Raven took emergency evasive action, but it was already too late. The flaming debris from the shuttle collided with the alien warship, ravaging its hull and dealing catastrophic damage to the vessel.

Banks whooped from the helm control station and even Shade showed a glimmer of a smile, but Sterling could see the Raven wasn't finished yet. The alien vessel, now itself on fire with atmosphere venting from multiple hull breaches, turned and began a run for the Vanguard.

"Lieutenant Shade, take it down now!" Sterling called out, fearful that McQueen was about to make a suicide run.

Shade reacted instantly, but plasma had already flashed out from the aft cannons of the Raven. Sterling cursed and gripped his console tightly as the blasts hammered into their already-battered hull. Alarms rang out on the bridge and Sterling saw half of his damage control console turn red, as if the ship was hemorrhaging.

"Primary rail cannons offline," Shade called out, raising her voice to a shout to be heard over the clamor on the bridge. "Turrets are also down."

Then a torpedo snaked out from the rear of the Raven and Sterling felt his stomach tighten into a knot. "Point defense cannons to maximum!" he called out, hoping that the assault from the Sa'Nerran vessel hadn't also disabled their defensive weapons. Smoke was filling the bridge, clouding Sterling's view of the screen. However, he could still feel the point defense cannons firing through the vibrations in his captain's console. The Invictus was rocked by another hard explosion, and even more of the damage control readout turned red.

"Helm controls are sloppy, I'm losing control," Banks yelled from the front of the bridge. "Major hull breaches, all decks. We're dead unless we can set down."

"Set down where?" Sterling called back. "We're in the middle of the damned Void!"

Pumps began to clear the smoke from the bridge and Sterling saw that Banks had updated the image on the viewscreen. It was now showing one of the Vanguard's docking garages.

"The port landing garage in section eleven, deck nine still has pressure," Banks called out. "It's our best shot."

Sterling studied the readings on his console, spotting an obvious error by his first officer. "The port garage is over the other side of the ship from where we are, Commander," he called back. "Why not put us down in the starboard garage?"

Banks spun her chair around to face the command

deck, and fixed Sterling's eyes. "Because the starboard garage is where McQueen is crash-landing the Raven."

Sterling cursed and thumped his fist against the console. "Very well, Commander, take us in," he called back.

Suddenly, another series of alerts rang out and Sterling saw that his damage control console was flashing like a malfunctioning traffic light. Hull integrity was failing, their engines were overloading and they were bleeding atmosphere into space.

"I need you to hold this ship together until we can dock, Lieutenant," Sterling said, turning to his chief engineer. "What else can you give me?"

"We've already lost half of our reaction chambers," Razor called back. "Even if I shut down all non-essential systems, it won't be enough to maintain integrity," she added, flitting from console to console.

"That's not good enough, Lieutenant, I need something more!" Sterling hit back.

The Invictus' chief engineer turned to face Sterling, and he could see in her eyes that she had an answer. Razor did not wear the panicked expression of a woman who had been put on the spot and had drawn a blank. She had a solution, but Sterling knew it was one that would carry a heavy price.

"I can hold the ship together, sir, but only if I completely shut down power to two full decks," Razor said. "That means everything, sir. Gravity, life support, everything."

Sterling understood what Razor was saying. He'd

hoped that Crewman First Class Morgan Clay would be the only member of the Invictus crew he'd have to sacrifice that day. However, it seemed that more blood was required.

"Do it, Lieutenant," Sterling replied, careful to ensure his voice conveyed no hesitation or doubt. "Do whatever you have to do."

Razor nodded and returned to her stations. Seconds later, Sterling saw decks three and four lose power. This was immediately followed by a corresponding rise in hull integrity and regenerative armor integrity. He knew it still might not be enough, but they'd just played their last card. All they could do now was hope their hand was strong enough.

"I'm on final approach," said Banks as the Vanguard's port docking garage hurtled toward them on the viewscreen. "We're coming in hot; this is going to be rough."

"It always is, Commander," Sterling called back. He then tapped his neural interface before gripping the sides of his console with all the strength he could muster. "All hands, brace, brace, brace!" he called out through the link to all the remaining crew of the Invictus.

Sterling was confident that all on board would hear his latest order. Yet he was equally sure that not all of those who did would live to hear him give another.

THE INVICTUS SLAMMED hard into the docking garage of the Vanguard and began to carve a deep furrow through the landing deck. Unable to fully brace himself against the force of the impact, Sterling was shunted into his captain's console. The metal edge of the console dug into his stomach, squeezing the air from his lungs. It was like he'd been kicked in the back by a mule and sucker-punched in the gut by a prize-fighter at the same time.

"Thrusters to full reverse!" Commander Banks called out, though her words were barely audible over the screech of metal grinding on metal.

Sterling pushed himself up and saw the end of the docking garage still approaching through the viewscreen at a ferocious velocity, despite the effort of their thrusters. Checking his console, he noted that their inertial negation systems had all but failed. He cursed, realizing that their inevitable sudden stop was going to hurt like hell. Suddenly the Vanguard's emergency safety barricade sprang out of the deck in front of the Invictus. With no time to react, Sterling was propelled over the top of his console as the ship hit the barrier and ground to a halt in a fraction of a second. Time seemed to stand still as he sailed through the air, helpless to influence his fall. Then his back thudded into the viewscreen and he tumbled to the deck of his bridge in a crumpled heap.

For a time Sterling neither saw nor heard a thing, until the cries of Commander Mercedes Banks finally roused him. Ears ringing and eyes blurry, Sterling was pulled up to a sitting position. He could feel the powerful grip of his first officer's hands holding his body.

"We're down, Lucas, we made it," Banks said, though he heard the voice in his mind rather than through his ears. "But we hit the landing deck hard and we're in bad shape."

Sterling squeezed his eyes shut and rubbed his face. Then his vision and mind began to clear and instead of a ringing, he could hear the wail of alarms, the hiss of escaping gas and the crackle of fires.

"Damage report..." Sterling croaked before trying to stand up. Pain shot through his entire body, paralyzing him like he'd been pumped full of snake venom.

"Take it easy, Captain, you took quite a bump," said Banks, still holding onto him tightly. "You're actually damned lucky that you hit the viewscreen and not the bulkhead," she went on, glancing up to the display wall above Sterling's head. "It's a malleable material, designed to flex and give so that it doesn't crack under the stresses of combat."

"Unlike me..." replied Sterling, managing to push

himself to his feet, with the help of his first officer. He winced again as another jolt of pain gripped his body, focused around his left arm and shoulder. "Though I think a few of my bones just got liquified," he groaned.

"It looks like you have a fractured wrist or arm, and probably collarbone too," Banks said. "Graves is on his way up here now."

Sterling staggered away from the far wall of the bridge and saw a human-shaped imprint in the viewscreen. Banks had been correct – if he'd hit the bulkhead instead then he'd almost certainly be dead. In contrast, landing on the viewscreen was like being body slammed onto the mat of a wrestling ring. It still hurt like hell, but there was enough give in the material to soften the blow.

Sterling turned from the inoperative viewscreen and peered around the smashed remains of his bridge, looking for his other two officers. Incredibly, Lieutenant Shade was still at her post, or what was left of it. She was holding a portable fire extinguisher and working to douse the flames that had sprung up around her station. Lieutenant Razor, however, was nowhere to be seen.

"Where's Razor?" Sterling asked, hoping that they hadn't lost their remarkable engineer in the crash.

"She's a little battered and bruised like the rest of us, but she's okay," Banks replied. "She's in the aft engineering crawlspace, trying to manually initiate a reactor shutdown. All the consoles on the bridge are shot to hell."

Fingertips then appeared around the edge of the bridge door and it was manually forced open by enough to allow a body to fit through. Commander Graves squeezed through the narrow opening, carrying a medical kit. Sterling could see that the ship's medical officer had also not escaped the crash unscathed. His uniform was torn and scorched in places and his face was raw with cuts and grazes. It looked like he'd been thrown through a glass window or wall, which Sterling figured may have even been the case.

"What's the butcher's bill, Commander?" said Sterling, as Graves set his kit down and began to scan Sterling's left arm and shoulder.

"Unknown at this juncture, Captain," Graves replied, while pressing a small medical injector to Sterling's neck. "All I know is that my remaining medical staff, bar one junior doctor, are all dead, and that I passed seven more bodies on the way up here. The elevators are all out of commission, so my apologies for the delay."

Sterling laughed, which only caused more pain to shoot through this body. "I think that under the circumstances I can forgive you, Commander," he said. Sterling found it remarkable that his medical officer was still able to mind his Ps and Qs despite the ship crumbling around them.

"You have non-displaced fractures of the ulna and clavicle, Captain," Graves went on, removing a number of devices from his medical kit. "You are fortunate that they are clean breaks," Graves added, picking up one of the new instruments and preparing it. "I will be able to repair the breaks sufficiently well to allow you to continue functioning as normal, at least until I can tend to them more fully."

Graves pressed the new medical device to Sterling's collar. There was a pneumatic-sounding thud and he felt a brief sensation of pressure. Sterling flinched, expecting pain to again race through his body, but there was none. Graves then applied the same device to an area of his left forearm, which resulted in the same pneumatic-sounding thud and no pain.

"That wasn't so bad," said Sterling, feeling a wave of relief wash over him. Any time that Commander Evan Graves tended to him, Sterling felt like he was the unwitting subject of a macabre science experiment. This time, he'd gotten off lightly, he thought. Then Sterling's stomach sank as his chief medical officer picked up a third device and wielded it in front of his nose like a medieval inquisitor wielding a hot poker.

"I am afraid I have not yet begun, Captain," Graves replied, with a darkly sinister tone.

Sterling frowned at the third implement – it look like an old-fashioned hypodermic syringe, of the sort that might have been used by the doctors of Victorian London. Sterling forced down a dry swallow as the instrument was brought closer to his face. It appeared to have been designed to penetrate the tough hide of a bull rather than the fragile skin of a human being.

"Despite the numbing effects of the drugs I have injected into your system, I'm afraid this is still going to hurt, Captain," Graves went on. "Quite a lot."

Sterling continued to scowl at the device in Graves' hand then met his medical officer's eyes. Commander Graves stared back at him with an unnerving calm that made the man appear suddenly menacing.

"Go ahead, Commander, I won't hold it against you,"

replied Sterling, more than a little apprehensively. He then watched as Graves pressed the oversized injector to his neck. He noticed that Banks' expression had contorted, as if she were watching a human dissection. "You're not helping, Commander," Sterling said, scowling at his first officer.

Sterling then felt a sharp prick to his neck, which was followed by a loud hiss that continued for several seconds. He quickly repeated the procedure on Sterling's arm. When the hiss ended, Graves removed the device and replaced it neatly inside his medical kit.

"That looked worse than it felt," said Sterling, rubbing the injection site with his fingers. All he could feel was a dull ache, like he'd been punched in the neck and arm.

Graves did not reply and instead stood in front of Sterling, with his hands held out, as if he were waiting for someone to pass him a basketball. Sterling opened his mouth and was about to ask what his medical officer was doing when heat surged through his entire shoulder and left arm, forcing him to cry out. His legs then gave way and he fell into Commander Graves waiting arms. The medical officer lowered Sterling gently to the deck, cradling him like he was having a seizure.

"Commander, what the hell is going on?" Banks called out, dropping to her knees by Sterling's side and taking his body from the doctor's arms. "You're supposed to be healing him not making him worse!"

"Do not be alarmed, Commander Banks," Graves replied, coolly. "I have injected Captain Sterling with a nanosuspension of experimental bone putty." Sterling continued to spasm uncontrollably in Banks' arms. "The formulation is my own design. It is highly effective but, as you can see, also rather agonizing for the patient."

"How... long will... this last..." Sterling grunted, forcing the words out in-between each new wave of excruciating muscle spasms.

"The ordeal will be over shortly, Captain," Graves replied, still with the impassive delivery of a robot.

Sterling had never considered Graves' emotionally-bereft bedside manner to be a problem in the past. However, at that moment he would have taken any soothing word of comfort over the clinically sterile response that Graves had given him. Then as quickly as it had begun, the pain and the spasms stopped. Sterling felt his muscles relax. Banks, however, continued to cradle Sterling in her arms like he was an injured comrade, slowly dying from his wounds on the battlefield.

"How do you feel, Captain?" Graves asked, rising to his full height.

To his surprise, Sterling found that the pain was almost entirely gone. "It doesn't hurt, anymore," he replied, rotating his shoulder and flexing his arm like he was warming up for a session at the gym.

Then Sterling realized that he was essentially lying in Mercedes Banks' lap. He lay back and looked up at his first officer's face, partially obscured by her bosom, and the awkwardness of their compromising position struck home for both of them. Banks abruptly dropped Sterling like a hot potato and the back of his head thudded into the deck. Thanks to the drugs, however, there was no pain.

"Gently, if you please, Commander Banks," said

Commander Graves' reprovingly. "I only have a limited supply of bone putty, and many more broken bones that are in need of repairing."

"Sorry, Captain," replied Banks, scrambling off her knees and hauling him up. Then she released her hold on Sterling and folded her arms, trying to act casual.

Graves raised an eyebrow at the Invictus' two most senior officers and cleared his throat. "If you're no longer in need of my services, Captain, then I'll attend to the rest of the crew," he said, closing his medical kit and snapping the fasteners shut. "What's left of them, in any case."

"Go ahead, Commander, I think we're all good here," replied Sterling. He glanced at Banks, quickly checking her over to make sure she wasn't bleeding out onto the deck. He'd been so consumed by his own injuries that he hadn't asked if his first officer was also hurt. "Assuming, you're okay too, Commander?" Sterling added.

"Aside from a splitting headache, I'm still in one piece," Banks replied. She glanced across to Shade, who was still busying herself extinguishing fires. "And I think Shade is indestructible, so I wouldn't worry about her."

Graves removed a packet of tablets from his left pocket and pressed them into Banks' hand. "Take two of these and call me if they fail to satisfactorily numb the pain," the medical officer said.

Banks frowned at the packet. "I'm assuming that these things aren't going to cause me to writhe around in agony on the deck or grow two heads, or anything crazy like that?"

"Nothing like that, no," Graves replied. "Though they may make you a little constipated."

Banks burst out laughing, which only caused Graves to scowl back at her before quickly turning on his heels and heading away.

"What? I thought that was funny," said Banks, shrugging in response to Sterling's criticizing stare.

"Only you could find anything about this crazy situation amusing, Mercedes," said Sterling.

He turned his attention back to the ship's chief medical officer. Commander Graves was cautiously approaching Lieutenant Shade, like he was a wildlife veterinarian trying to stalk up on a wounded animal. However, Shade had clocked his advance straight away and merely glowered at Graves as if he was a Sa'Nerran warrior. The doctor took the hint and swiftly moved on in search of another patient to attend to.

"Whatever happens from this point on, remind me not to break any more bones," Sterling said, again flexing his shoulder. Whatever curious and no-doubt prohibited concoction of drugs his medical officer had injected him with had certainly done the trick. He felt like he'd simply taken a gentle tumble off the command deck, rather than been thrown head-first into the viewscreen at a hundred miles per hour.

Lieutenant Razor then scrambled out of the aft engineering crawlspace. Her white hair was streaked with blood, while her face was blackened with dirt and smoke. It gave her an oddly menacing countenance, as if she was wearing tribal war paint.

"Report, Lieutenant, what's the damage?" said Sterling, meeting his engineer in the middle of the bridge. It was then he noticed that Razor appeared unusually agitated. Like Lieutenant Shade, his engineer's unflappability was always something he could rely on. Sterling's gut tightened into a knot, realizing that whatever could create a chink in Razor's armor was likely to be serious.

"The hull is intact and the ship is salvageable," Razor began, sounding breathless and hoarse. Sterling waited for the inevitable "but" with baited breath. "But we have hairline cracks in two reaction chambers that are growing more severe by the minute. I can't shut them down and the automatic containment measures have failed. The computer is offline, along with all the bridge overrides."

"Cut to the chase, Lieutenant," said Sterling, feeling like they'd literally jumped out of the frying pan and into the fire.

"Unless we can manually shut down the core, this ship is going to explode in less than fifteen minutes," Razor added, her iridescent eyes fixed onto Sterling's. "And if that happens, the detonation will blow a hole in the Vanguard the size of a battlecruiser."

RAZOR'S ANNOUNCEMENT that the reactor was on the verge of going critical was sobering in more ways than one. The aches and pains that Sterling had been feeling were gone, as was the giddy euphoria that had come from the near-death experience of surviving the crash. Now his body was again tingling with adrenalin and his mind was sharp and focused.

"Lieutenant Shade, coordinate an evacuation of anyone that's still left alive," Sterling called out, as he and Commander Banks hurried in pursuit of Razor. "Try to get as many people to a safe distance as possible, including those damned robots."

"Aye Captain," Shade replied before tapping her neural interface and springing into action.

"I'm guessing you have a plan for how to shut down the reactor from the engineering section, Lieutenant?" Sterling then called out to his engineer.

"The failsafe can be triggered manually from the

reactor control room," Razor called back. She had already pushed through the door and moved into the corridor outside the bridge. "With the computer offline and main power down, it will require two people to operate, and it also won't be easy to reach."

"We'll figure it out, Lieutenant, just get us where we need to be," Sterling replied.

The group rounded the corner toward the emergency stairwells, but already the twisted and mangled corridors of the Invictus were making progress difficult. Reaching deck two, Sterling and Banks took the lead, for the first time witnessing the human cost of their crash. The broken bodies of dead and injured crew members lined the corridors of the ship. Some moaned in agony and called out to Sterling for help, but there was nothing he could do for them, at least not yet.

"How much time do we have left, Lieutenant?" Sterling said as they approached the central computer core.

"Our link to the computer is down, so there's no way to tell," Razor replied, glancing behind to Sterling. "My guess is no more than eleven or twelve minutes."

Suddenly, Lieutenant Razor's boots screeched across the deck and the engineer slid to a stop. Banks was moving so fast that she almost piled straight into the back of her.

"Damn it, Lieutenant, what the hell did you stop for?" Banks called out.

Razor pointed to the emergency stairwell to deck three and Banks' face fell. Sterling moved alongside his first officer and cursed. The crash had bowed the hull inward and crushed the stairwell, making it impossible to reach deck three.

"We can cut through the computer core to the engineering levels," Sterling said, thinking on his feet. "If we enter the core room on this level, we can climb down to deck three then cut through to reactor control."

Banks nodded, slapping Razor on the back to gee her on. Then they all retraced their steps through the mangled corridors. Banks reached the doors to the computer core first and forced them open using her incredible strength. A crew member lay dead just inside the room, her head partially caved in from an impact with the wall or deck. Banks slid the woman aside with the edge of her boot, then pushed through into the computer core room. Electrical sparks crackled from ruptured conduits and smashed consoles, while steam plumed out across the deck two gangway from a ruptured cooling pipe.

Sterling stepped over the body of the dead crew member, then grabbed the railings and peered down at the computer core, which spanned two decks of the ship. It still had power and, at least from a visual inspection, looked relatively undamaged.

"At least the computer core is still intact and its backup cells are active," said Sterling, turning to Banks and Razor. "You two go ahead while I try to get the computer back online. It might be able to help us shut down the reactor."

Banks nodded and tapped her neural interface. Sterling could feel the link form in his mind and he accepted it.

"We'll stay linked in case there are any problems," Banks said, stepping over the top of the railings in preparation to climb down to deck three. "Hopefully, that whacky AI can repay the favor we did it by not wiping its code and reverting it to a nice, safe gen-thirteen."

Banks began to climb and Razor followed, though with less confidence and sure-footedness than the ship's first officer displayed. Sterling moved to one of the control consoles and tried to access it. To his surprise, it powered up.

"Computer, can you hear me?" Sterling said, as the computer core began to pulse resonantly in his ear.

"Yes, Captain, I am here," the computer replied, cheerfully. "I am glad to hear your voice. Internal scanners are down and I did not know if you were still alive."

"I am, but just barely," Sterling replied, finding the computer's concern for his wellbeing to be oddly touching. "However, a lot of the crew weren't so lucky,"

"I am sorry to hear that, Captain," said the computer. Curiously, to Sterling's ears it actually sounded like the gen-fourteen was being sincere in its sorrow for the loss of life.

"Never mind that now, can you access the reactor core?" Sterling went on, focusing on the critical issue at hand. "It's going to rupture and take us and half of the Vanguard with it."

"Negative, Captain, my hardline to the reactor core has been severed," the computer replied, causing Sterling to utter another curse. "The manual failsafe override is the only solution. However, I estimate that you have eight minutes and three seconds in which to initiate the shut-down before the reactor becomes critical."

Sterling actually felt slightly relieved. That was more time than he had imagined they had.

"Is there anything you can do to help?" Sterling asked. He was anxious to get moving again now that it was clear the gen-fourteen wasn't the solution to their problems.

"Yes, Captain, there is," the computer answered, again sounding cheerful. "Transfer command of the Invictus to me directly."

Sterling recoiled from the console and peered out at the pulsing computer core. It was a change to actually be able to look directly at his gen-fourteen, rather than address its ethereal presence in the ceiling of whichever room he happened to be in.

"What the hell good would that do?" Sterling hit back, wondering why the computer was choosing that moment to display megalomaniacal tendencies.

"Due to the extensive damage to the ship, you are currently unable to direct my functions to an adequate level," the computer continued. "With command authority, I can effectively direct myself. This will allow me to re-configure my core functions through the available resources without the need for human intervention or approval."

Sterling's finger was now tapping wildly on the computer console. The ship was a ticking time bomb yet his AI was focused on seizing command.

"I don't have time for this, computer, if you can't help then I need to assist Commander Banks and Lieutenant Razor," Sterling said. He moved away from the console and swung his leg over the railings, ready to make the climb down to deck three.

"Giving me control is the only way I can help, Captain," the computer added. Its voice was now more urgent and insistent. He may have merely been imagining it, but Sterling thought that the computer sounded suddenly more 'human'. "My link to the reactor core is disabled, but with command authority I can re-configure my pathways and potentially reach reactor control through a sub-routine or secondary system."

Sterling now had both feet firmly planted on the other side of the railings. He was about to start his descent, but the computer's suggestion had given him pause. With the ship set to explode in a matter of minutes, it was an option he couldn't discount.

"Commander, how is it looking down there?" Sterling asked, reaching out to his first officer through their link.

"The engineering section is a damned mess, Captain," Banks replied. The link was strong and Sterling could practically feel the adrenaline racing through his first officer's body. "Part of the deck caved in around reactor control and the manual shut-down controls are buried behind a ton of rubble. I'm trying to clear a path, but it's going to be tight. We could really use you right now."

"Keep digging, Mercedes, I'm on my way," Sterling said, starting to climb down. He made it a couple of meters then shook his head, still unable to shake the computer's idea from his mind. Cursing again, he glanced over his shoulder at the pulsating computer core. The lights on the core seemed to be following his descent, as if his advanced AI was watching him.

"If I give you command, you have to promise you won't

suck all the air out of the ship, or take off and leave us stranded here," Sterling said, staring into the blinking lights as if they were the computer's eyes.

"The Invictus is currently incapable of flight, Captain," the computer replied, flatly. "Also, the air processing systems have failed so it would serve no purpose for me to disable them."

"I think you know what I mean, computer," Sterling hit back. "I just don't want you turning on us."

"I may have command, but you are still my Captain," the computer answered. As before, the tone of the AI's voice had suddenly shifted. To Sterling, it simply sounded more 'real'. "As you told me once before, I am a member of your crew and that will never change."

It was then that Sterling remembered he'd asked Lieutenant Razor to disable the AI's inhibitor chip. This was so that the computer could re-program itself to fix the glitches that had started to plague its base code. He wondered what else the computer's self-programming antics had accomplished, intentionally or otherwise.

"Okay, computer, what the hell," said Sterling, climbing back up the side of the computer core wall. "I must be mad, but I'll transfer command of the Invictus to you."

Sterling jumped over the side of the railings and swung around to face the computer console. The AI had already initiated the command override protocols. A hand-print and retinal scanner had both activated. Sterling placed his hand on the scanner then felt Commander Banks reach out to him again.

"Lucas, where are you?" Banks' voice was frantic and Sterling could feel her panic. "We need your help down here. I can't reach the damned manual override!"

"Stand by, Mercedes, I have another idea," Sterling replied as the console scanned his hand print. Then a beam flashed into his eye to read his retinal pattern.

"Stand by?" Banks hit back. "The reactor is about to go critical!"

"Trust me, Mercedes," Sterling replied, trying to convey a sense of calm and confidence, despite himself being wracked with doubt. "I'll join you soon."

There was a tense pause, during which time Sterling could sense his first officer's unease. However, as always when Sterling asked Banks to trust him, she did so.

"Standing by, Captain," Banks replied, calmly. "I hope this works."

"Me too," Sterling replied. He then tapped his interface to close the link and allow his mind to focus fully on the task before him.

"Identity confirmed. Sterling, Lucas. Captain, Fleet Marauder Invictus. Command override accepted."

The words were spoken in the computer's voice, though it was like it was reading from an autocue.

"Computer, transfer command of Fleet Marauder Invictus to the on-board AI," Sterling said. Hearing the words spoken out loud hit home just how ridiculous the order sounded.

"Invalid request. Command violates Fleet protocols," the computer replied.

"Override. Authorization, Sterling Omega Zero Zero Zero."

The lights on the computer core suddenly pulsed more rapidly, in a chaotic pattern like neurons firing in a brain.

"AI Inhibitor offline. Command accepted. Fleet Marauder Invictus is now commanded by Generation Fourteen AI."

Suddenly the hissing pipes and crackling conduits and consoles all became still. It was like the room was part of a funfair attraction, and the operator had just switched everything off to close up for the night.

"Computer, did it work?" Sterling said out loud.

The lights on the core continued to flash, but there was no response from the AI. Sterling cursed and switched the display on the console to get a readout of the reactor core. It was already on the verge of going critical, with less than three minutes remaining.

"Computer, respond damn it!" Sterling called out again, this time peering toward the ceiling, rather than into the blinking lights, which now pulsed so violently it hurt his eyes to look at them. Still there was no answer.

Panic rose in Sterling's gut and he practically threw himself over the barricade, nearly slipping in the process and falling the full height of a deck to the level below. Taking more risks than he cared to, Sterling climbed down to deck three as fast as he could manage. Metal beams and conduits dug into his hands and his knees and elbows scraped across the scaffold before Sterling jumped the final two meters. He rolled through the landing as best he could, but the shock of the impact and the unforgiving, cold metal reminded him just how weary his already battered body was. Pushing himself up, he raced to the opposite side of the computer core and threw himself through the partially opened door and into the engineering level.

"Captain, over here!"

Sterling looked up and saw Banks and Razor on top of a pile of rubble. They were next to the primary reactor control system, but Sterling could see that it was still buried behind fallen girders and other wreckage from the deck above.

"We're almost at the override lever," Banks called out, tearing away another chunk of metal and tossing it away like it was a block of Styrofoam. "But we only have a couple of minutes left!"

Sterling began to scramble up the pile of debris toward his first officer and engineer, gaining more cuts and scrapes in the process

"My plan B was a bust," Sterling called out, fighting the pain and exhaustion and driving himself on. "The manual failsafe levers are our only chance."

Banks and Razor continued to dig as Sterling arrived and added what remained of his own muscle to the endeavor.

"We have about ninety seconds before the first reaction chamber breaches," Razor said, glancing at a computer console built into the reactor control system.

"I'm through," Banks yelled, hauling a fractured deck girder away from the control system. The hunk of metal toppled like a felled great oak, smashing through the deck plating below. "I have my hand on the lever. Activating now!"

A low drone hummed through the room and the entire reactor core system began to vibrate.

"Lucas, pull the second lever!" Banks called out; her voice was barely audible over the rising thrum of the reactor chamber.

"We're almost through!" Sterling answered as he and his chief engineer continued to claw through the rubble more frantically than ever. Their cut and bloodied hands were almost a blur. Razor then yanked a broken chunk of deck plating away to partially reveal the second emergency failsafe lever. Sterling wasted no time and dug his hand into the gap, managing to get the tips of his fingers around the edge of the lever.

"I almost have it!" Sterling called out, driving his arm further inside the gap, tearing more flesh in the process. He finally grasped the lever fully and closed his hand tightly around the cold, dimpled metal. "Got it, activating now!" he said, hauling back with all his strength, but the lever wouldn't budge. Razor grabbed onto Sterling's shoulders and added her weight to the effort. The lever inched toward Sterling and he felt a swell of hope flood though his body. Then there was a sharp crack and Sterling flew backward, sending Razor tumbling down the pile of debris to the deck below. Sterling barely held on with his free hand, but once he'd regained his balance, he realized what had happed. He was holding the lever in his hand. The metal had sheared clean in half at the base.

"Lucas, talk to me!" Banks called out. She was scrambling around from the other side of the reactor control system to check on him. Then she saw Sterling, lever in hand, and her face drained of blood.

"It's over, Mercedes," Sterling said, tossing the lever into the pile of debris surrounding them. "This time, we lose."

The rumble of the reaction chamber built to a crescendo. Sterling could almost feel that it was on the brink of exploding, like a cork in a champagne bottle that was slowly working its way loose due to the pressure inside. Then two hard thumps reverberated through the deck, shaking more loose debris free. Rubble rained down on Sterling and Banks, forcing them both to duck and cover their heads. Fragments of metal and polymers thudded against his arms and back, each one feeling like a punch from a sparring partner. Then the assault stopped and the room was still and quiet, save the soft thrum of the reaction chamber.

"Why aren't we dead?" whispered Banks, peering at Sterling through the gaps between her fingers.

Sterling stood up, gained a solid footing on the rubble beneath his feet, then swung around to the computer console built into the reaction control system.

"The breaches have been contained," said Sterling, scarcely believing his eyes. "The failsafe was activated."

"By who?" said Banks, shuffling around to Sterling's side.

"By me."

Banks' eyebrows raised up on her dirt- and blood-smeared forehead. "Your lips didn't move and we're not linked, so who the hell said that?"

"I did, Commander," the voice of the computer replied. "Apologies for the radio silence, Captain, but I was required to devote my full resources to the challenge," the computer added, cheerfully. "It was good to finally use my abilities to their fullest."

Banks' eyebrows narrowed into a vee, but Sterling held his hand up to stop her from asking any more questions.

"I'll explain later," Sterling said, brushing some loose rubble off his shoulders. "Suffice to say, it was an unconventional solution."

Banks snorted a laugh. "Hell, if it works it works," she said. Then her gaze looked beyond Sterling and her eyes narrowed again. "Razor..." she said, flatly.

Sterling cursed and scrambled down the pile of debris, like a rescue worker searching for survivors during the Blitz. He reached his engineer and dropped down on his knees by her side.

"Lieutenant, can you hear me?" he said, checking for a pulse and finding one. Lieutenant Razor groaned, then squinted open her eyes and tried to lift her head.

"Take it easy, Lieutenant, you had quite a fall," said Banks, while conducting a hurried physical examination.

"Did it work?" asked Razor. It was a pointless question, but Sterling allowed it on account of his engineer's clearly confused state.

"Something worked, Lieutenant, though it wasn't quite as we'd planned," Sterling replied.

"You're all good, Lieutenant," Banks said, smiling down at the engineer. "Nothing is broken."

Razor then caught sight of something resting to the side

of her head. She frowned and reached up for it before lifting it in front of her face.

"Isn't this the failsafe lever?" she said, staring at the fractured chunk of metal like it was an alien artefact.

"Yes, Lieutenant, it is," replied Sterling.

"Then how...?"

Sterling laughed. "Let's just call it divine intervention, Lieutenant," he replied, which only caused Razor's consternated expression to become more twisted. "I'll brief you later," he added before Razor could ask any more questions. "Right now, we have to organize whatever is left of the crew and take control of the Vanguard." He met Banks' eyes, which were as sharp and as determined as his own. "This is a long way from being over yet."

STERLING PUSHED ASIDE the pile of debris blocking the door to the medical bay and squeezed through the opening. Commander Graves was inside, along with the junior doctor who was the last remaining member of his medical staff. Both were treating the wounded as best they could, considering the med bay had not escaped the crash unscathed. Commander Graves spotted Sterling and quickly finished tending to his patient before walking over to greet him. In addition to being torn and scorched, the medical officer's uniform was now also covered in blood, some fresh and some dried. How much of it was the doctor's own, Sterling didn't know, but from the way that Graves hobbled over to meet him, he guessed that at least some of it belonged to his chief medical officer.

"My apologies for the condition of the medical bay, Captain," Graves began, maintaining his dignified, scholarly tone. However, there was a tightness in the man's voice that suggested Graves was in a persistent state of pain and discomfort. "I have cleaned it up as best I can, but we are seven bays down and some of our equipment is damaged beyond repair."

"No apology necessary, Commander," Sterling replied, though he was impressed that his medical officer had offered one. "So, what's the final butcher's bill?"

Commander Graves moved over to one of the few computer consoles that remained operational. Sterling followed his officer then saw the list of names scrolling across the screen and assumed the worst.

"In total, we have fifteen able-bodied officers and crew," Graves began, confirming Sterling's suspicions about the severity of their losses. "This number includes the senior bridge crew, myself and my associate," Graves went on. Sterling winced. The number was actually worse than he'd pessimistically expected.

Sterling sighed and rubbed the back of his neck. "It is what it is, Commander," he said, with a fatalistic air. "At least we have the Obsidian Soldiers that Griffin supplied us with. As much as I hate to use them, we have no chance of retaking the Vanguard without their help."

Commander Graves shut down the computer and turned to face Sterling. The medical officer's expression was unusually solemn, especially for a man that regularly displayed less emotion even than Opal Shade.

"Once you have secured the Vanguard, I will transfer medical operations to the dreadnaught's hospital wing," Graves said. "The Vanguard was equipped to service the medical needs of thousands. Even if a large proportion of the medical facility is damaged, it will still contain more than enough equipment and space for our meagre needs."

"Understood, Commander, and thanks for the vote of confidence too," Sterling replied. He was referring to the fact his medical officer had conveyed his full faith in their ability to retake the Vanguard.

"In all honesty, Captain, I expected this crew, including myself, to be dead a long time ago," Graves replied, surprising Sterling with his sudden frankness. "As a scientist, I am not a believer in fate. All outcomes are based on measurable factors." The medical officer removed a pack of blood plasma from a refrigeration unit behind him and held it out to Sterling. "For example, a blood loss of forty percent or more results in death." Sterling frowned at the parcel of blood that was being wafted in front of his nose and half-imagined his medical officer feasting on the packs in his spare time. "Probability comes into play of course, but even accounting for chance, it is miraculous that we have survived this long."

Sterling understood the point his medical officer was trying to make, despite the curious way in which he had made it.

"The key measurable factors in our case, Commander, are the skill of this crew and the robustness of the Invictus," Sterling replied. "An ordinary crew and an ordinary ship would never have made it this far. We owe everything to the skill and tenacity of my Omega officers and crew."

"And, of course, the Captain," Commander Graves added, with the faintest flicker of a smile. "However, these matters are not why I asked you here," the medical officer continued, without pause. This was fortunate, since the unexpected compliment had left Sterling lost for words. "I have the results of the neural firewall test."

Sterling felt a tingle of electricity rush down his spine. With everything else that had occurred in the last few hours, he'd completely forgotten about the neural firewall.

"Commander, if you tell me the thing works, I might just kiss you," Sterling replied, causing the medical officer to raise a curious eyebrow. "If we can protect ourselves against the Sa'Nerran neural weapon, it could be the advantage we need."

"The device is effective, Captain," Commander Graves replied. "Though no further demonstration of your appreciation of this fact is required."

Sterling looked around the room for the nearest empty medical bay then hurried over to it and planted himself down on the bed.

"There's no time to waste, Commander, I want you to install the firewall device into my implant straight away," said Sterling, eager to get his critical defensive upgrade.

"With Lieutenant Razor's assistance, I have already fabricated enough units for the senior command staff," Commander Graves replied. He walked into one of the separate lab areas, though with the glass smashed and door broken, it was no longer detached from the rest of the medical bay. He returned a few moments later holding an ashtray-sized dish and a single pair of metal tweezers. "I will work on fabricating the remaining devices as soon as my other duties permit."

"Short of stopping anyone from dying, this is your top

priority, Commander," said Sterling, peering into the little tray as Graves set it down next to the bed. Commander Graves then removed a small computer chip from the tray using the tweezers and held it up to Sterling.

"Please lie back, Captain, and tilt your head to the side, so that I can access your neural implant," the medical officer said.

Sterling did as was requested. Then as Graves brought the computer chip closer, he began to have second thoughts.

"And you're one hundred percent certain this works, Commander?" Sterling asked, feeling his heart-rate start to climb. "What happened to the test subject you trialed this on?" he quickly added, as Graves began to lower the chip toward his implant.

"Crewman First Class Morgan Clay died, Captain," Graves replied, the doctor's tone conveying no emotion whatsoever.

Sterling reached up and grabbed Graves' wrist, halting the progress of the tweezers mere inches above his neural implant.

"That's hardly filling me with confidence, Commander," Sterling said, scowling up at his chief medical officer.

"Her death was unrelated to the firewall chip, Captain," Graves replied. The medical officer showed no irritation at the fact Sterling had suddenly accosted him, nor did he attempt to resist Sterling's hold. "The neural firewall test was a complete success."

Sterling released Graves' hand but still held his eyes.

"Very well, Commander, proceed," he said, feeling sufficiently reassured by his medical officer's answer.

Commander Graves then inserted the neural firewall device into Sterling's implant. He felt a brief moment of discomfort as the device was assimilated by the sophisticated neural technology that had been installed into his brain shortly after birth. However, it was nothing more than an itch and as quickly as it had appeared it was gone again.

"That was a hell of a lot less distressing than that bone putty crap you injected me with," Sterling said, sliding off the bed. Sterling flexed his arm and shoulder, feeling no pain or discomfort whatsoever. "Though I can't deny it worked."

Graves nodded in reply to Sterling's slightly backhanded compliment. "My methods may not always adhere to the strictest tenants of Fleet medical protocol, Captain, but they are very effective nonetheless."

"See to it that Commander Banks receives her neural firewall next," Sterling said, while setting off toward the exit.

"I have already requested that she attend an appointment with me, but have thus far been unable to reach her, Captain," Graves said.

Sterling stopped dead and spun around. "What do you mean you haven't been able to reach her?" He realized he also hadn't seen or heard from Commander Banks for the last hour.

"Her neural interface is deactivated, Captain," Graves replied, though he sounded unconcerned by this fact. "I asked the computer to inform Commander Banks of my request, but so far I have not had a reply."

"Thank you, Commander, I'll convey your request to her personally," Sterling said, resuming his progress toward the exit.

Reaching the door, Sterling suddenly paused and hesitated. He wasn't good at giving praise, unless it was sporadic and in the moment. He found it even more uncomfortable conveying his regards to Evan Graves, considering how his medical officer continued to creep him out. However, without his doctor's unique expertise, not only would he himself be incapacitated and unable to perform his duties, but many more of his crew would be too. And on top of this, he had assisted in creating a vital new defense against the Sa'Nerra. For too long, the aliens had brandished the advantage of neural control against Fleet and humanity to devastating effect. Arguably, the discovery of the neural firewall had come too late to be a change-maker in the battle for Earth. Even so, it had not come too late to affect the outcome of the battles that were yet to be fought. For that, Commander Evan Graves deserved commendation.

"Commander Graves," Sterling called out. His medical officer had already gone back to his duties caring for the wounded and appeared surprised that Sterling was still in the room.

"Yes, Captain, was there something more?" Graves inquired.

"I know we may not always see eye-to-eye, Commander, but I want you to know that you've made a difference today," Sterling said, pulling himself to his full height. "Without your work, we wouldn't be here. I just wanted you to know that."

Commander Graves returned a respectful nod. "I appreciate you saying so, Captain."

Sterling returned the nod. Then for some reason, Crewman Clay popped back into his mind. The medical officer had explained that her death was unrelated to the neural firewall, but he hadn't explained how.

"Out of interest, how did Crewman Clay die?" he asked.

"She died of her existing injuries," the medical officer replied, calmly. "Remarkably, she actually survived the crash, but the impact reopened her wounds and she died a few minutes later."

Sterling nodded then turned to leave. However, Commander Graves voice followed him out, like the haunting whisper of ghoul.

"It wasn't a total loss, however," Graves said, seemingly talking to himself. "I was able to harvest several of her organs to transplant to other causalities, and what blood she had left was valuable in replenishing my stocks."

CHAPTER 8
THE MISSING CREWMAN

STERLING PAUSED JUST outside the medical section, tapped his neural interface and tried to reach out to Banks. However, just as Commander Graves had said, the link couldn't be formed; Banks' interface had been manually deactivated. Frowning, Sterling walked over to a computer terminal built into the wall of the corridor.

"Computer, locate Commander Mercedes Banks," Sterling said.

Sterling wasn't concerned that his first officer had been suddenly swallowed by a miniature black hole, or met some other grisly end. However, it was unlike her to be out of contact, and even more unusual for her to disable her neural link. This alone told Sterling that something was wrong.

"Commander Banks is in her quarters, Captain," the computer replied, cheerfully. "Would you like me to alert her that you are looking for her?"

"No, no, I'll pay her a visit directly," Sterling said,

holding the palm of his hand up the computer terminal, as if he was trying to halt traffic.

"As you wish, Captain," the computer replied. Then the screen on the terminal faded to black.

"The plot thickens..." Sterling said out loud to himself before altering his course along the corridor to head for the officer's quarters.

Sterling was used to his progress through the ship being hampered by the need to greet fellow members of the crew and return their salutes. However, the fact most of his crew were dead meant that his journey to Commander Banks' quarters went unimpeded. He idly wondered if being thankful for the lack of interruptions made him a bad person, considering the reason why this had been the case. However, Sterling concluded that being glad he was spared the need to engage in idle chit-chat was not the same as being glad that his crew was dead, so he dismissed any feelings of guilt out of hand.

Reaching the door to Commander Banks' quarters, Sterling found himself straightening his tunic and checking his appearance reflected in the shiny metal door. He abruptly stopped. *What the hell are you doing, Lucas?* he asked himself, shaking his head at his own reflection. *You're checking on your first officer's wellbeing, not picking her up for a date, you damned fool.* Still shaking his head, he hit the call buzzer. Moments later the door swished open.

"Computer, I said who is at the door, not open the damned door!" snapped Mercedes Banks from inside the room. His first officer then appeared in the threshold wearing a dark scowl on her face. Her tunic was scrunched up on the bed and she appeared slightly out of breath. Banks' flustered expression persisted until she realized it was Sterling who had called on her. "Oh, it's you, Captain." She stepped back and waved him inside.

"Well, don't sound so happy to see me," said Sterling, cautiously moving into the room. It felt like he was willingly entering a tiger's cage at a zoo.

"I'm sorry, Lucas, I didn't mean to snap at you," said Banks, sitting down on her bed. Sterling frowned; his first officer looked and sounded despondent, as if she'd just received some terrible news.

"What's wrong, Mercedes?" Sterling asked, perching himself on the edge of Banks' desk and folding his arms. The computer console that normally occupied the space had been smashed to pieces. Chunks of it littered the floor around his feet.

Banks drew in a deep breath then let it out slowly before locking eyes with Sterling. Now, instead of looking downcast, she looked angry.

"Promise you won't laugh if I tell you?"

"Of course not," Sterling replied. Then he wished he'd taken more time to consider his answer. If what his first officer was about to say did make him laugh, then not only would he have broken his promise, but he'd be on the receiving end of her formidable wrath too.

"I can't find Jinx," Banks said, shaking her head. "I've looked all over the ship, at least in the parts I can get to, but she's nowhere to be found."

Sterling certainly didn't feel like laughing – he knew how much the Beagle meant to his first officer. However, he was a little annoyed that the reason she'd gone AWOL was because she was searching for a dog.

"I'm sure she'll turn up, Mercedes," Sterling replied, working hard to conceal his irritation and convey a suitable amount of sympathy instead. "Right now, we have more pressing matters, though, including getting your neural firewall chip installed."

Banks pushed herself off the bed and stormed across to the other side of her quarters. "I can't concentrate on a damned thing until I know if she's alive or dead," she said, practically bouncing off the walls. "I know it's not important, and I know that in that head of yours, you're probably cursing me for wasting my time, but it matters to me, Lucas."

Sterling remained silent. As much as anything, he knew that Banks just needed to voice her frustrations. And while he freely admitted to being one of the least empathetic people in the galaxy, he did at least know when to talk and when to just listen.

"But you're right, we need to get on with the mission," Banks continued, snapping herself out of her self-induced funk. Grabbing her tunic off the bed, she pulled it on and headed toward the door. "I'd give you my initial report on the condition of the Vanguard, but as you can see, my console is smashed."

Sterling slid off the desk and hit the button to open the door. "We can use the one in the briefing room," he said, stepping outside.

"That's smashed to hell too," Banks replied, shaking her head.

Sterling cursed then wondered where else they could go to review the initial findings. He remembered that there was an active console in the medical bay. Going there would kill two birds with one stone, allowing Graves to fit the neural firewall chip to Banks while she was there. However, he'd seen enough of his creepy medical officer for the moment and didn't want to voluntarily place himself back in his presence so soon.

"We'll use the one in my quarters," Sterling announced, taking the lead and heading off toward his own living space. "Assuming that isn't also smashed, of course," he added, realizing he hadn't actually set foot in his quarters since the crash.

"If not, then maybe the science lab still has a working console," Banks suggested. "Initially, it's best if you and I go through the report, before we brief the rest of the bridge staff."

Sterling frowned. "That sounds ominous," he said, reaching the door to his quarters and pressing his hand to the ID reader. The damaged door began to slowly grind back into its housing, like it was a slab of rock being moved to reveal an ancient tomb.

"No, nothing like that," Banks said, giving Sterling some reassurance. Then she shrugged. "Or at least not that we know of. We can't get any internal scans of the Vanguard until we gain control of its computer."

Sterling nodded then entered his quarters. However, he'd only managed to make it a couple of paces inside before he was forced to stop.

"It looks like a damned bomb has gone off in here," he

said, brushing broken ceiling light tiles out of his path with the side of his boot.

Banks squeezed past then let out a long, low whistle. "This is actually worse than my quarters," she said. Sterling thought that his first officer sounded annoyingly pleased by this fact. Then Banks raised her eyebrows and pointed to Sterling's desk. "At least your computer console survived though."

Sterling examined his desk. The drawers were smashed and their contents had been strewn over the deck, but the console was intact, as Banks had stated. Sterling fought through the wreckage to reach the console then righted his desk chair and maneuvered it into position in front of the computer. As he did so, he noticed that the stash of emergency ration bars he kept in his quarters to quell the midnight munchies were spread out all over the floor. He bent down, picked one up and held it out to Banks.

"Here, take this," Sterling said, offering his first officer the high-calorie energy bar. "You need to keep your strength up."

To his astonishment, Banks shook her head. "I know you might find this hard to believe, but I'm not hungry," she replied.

Sterling was so stunned by his first officer's refusal that he was struck dumb. He wasn't so insensitive that he hadn't immediately understood the cause of her lack of appetite. Even so, for Banks to refuse food was unheard of and this, more than anything else, told Sterling she was hurting.

"Look, perhaps the computer can find out what happened to Jinx," Sterling said, brushing the sharper-looking shards of the light tiles off his chair before sitting down. "Internal scanners were down after the crash, but the computer is resourceful, especially now that I've basically allowed it to program itself..."

"A decision I hope we don't live to regret..." Banks added, folding her arms across her chest.

Sterling frowned at her. Banks' foul mood was already spilling over into other aspects of her personality. Ordinarily, she'd never question Sterling's decisions, and certainly not in a churlish manner that was bordering on insubordinate. However, his first officer appeared to immediately recognize her error and quickly atoned for it.

"Shit, I'm sorry again, Lucas," Banks said, resting a hand on Sterling's shoulder. "This is hardly how a hard-ass Omega officer should act. I'll make sure to keep it stowed from now on."

"It's okay, I get it, Mercedes," Sterling replied, deciding to grant his first officer some leeway. "We might be Omega officers, but we're still human beings."

"Some of us are, anyway," Banks said, raising an eyebrow at Sterling.

Sterling frowned at Banks then activated his computer, which took far longer than usual to power on. The screen was cracked, though not badly enough to obscure the information displayed on it.

"Computer, in the time that partial scanners have been online, have you detected any small life signs?" Sterling said.

"The rats already left, Captain," the computer replied, causing Sterling to frown again. He'd frowned so often since crash-landing on the Vanguard that the act of doing so now made his face ache.

"What rats?" Sterling hit back, already getting frustrated with his increasingly eccentric AI.

"Rats from a sinking ship, Captain," the computer clarified. "They all jumped overboard before we crashed. It is an amusing nautical metaphor that I thought was fitting given the circumstances."

"How about you just answer my damned question instead?" said Sterling, shaking his head at the smashed light tiles in the ceiling, where the computer's voice had emanated from.

"Very well, Captain," the computer replied. This time, Sterling was certain he detected a slight whiff of outrage in the computer's synthesized voice. "Assuming you are in search of the canine that goes by the designation, 'Ensign Jinx' then yes, I believe I have located her."

Banks sprang forward. "Where?" she said, leaning forward on Sterling's desk and peering at the screen. "Can you show me?"

The console screen updated to show a schematic of the Fleet Marauder Invictus. The image then zoomed in at speed, and Sterling found himself flying through the virtual corridors of the ship until the three-dimensional simulation reached a door and paused. Sterling's frown deepened even further.

"But those are my quarters, computer," he said, again glancing at the ceiling. He was seriously considering the possibility that his AI had gone mad.

"That is correct, Captain," the computer replied.

"Ensign Jinx is asleep under the pile of bedding at the far end of the room."

"What?" Sterling blurted out. He spun around in his chair, but Banks had already darted over to where Sterling's sheets and pillows had been hurled into the corner by the impact of the crash. Banks quickly but carefully sifted through the pile of bedding. Then her mouth curled into a wide smile. Sterling got out of the chair and edged around the side of his bed before spotting the beagle hound curled up on his pillow. "How the hell did it get in here?" Sterling yelled, throwing his arms out wide.

However, Banks had already stopped listening. She had dropped down onto her knees beside the dog, who had now awoken and was wagging her tail vigorously.

"Your bedding must have cushioned her when we crashed," Banks said, energetically petting the dog. She looked into the hound's large brown eyes. "Who's a clever girl then?" she continued, using the twee-sounding voice she reserved exclusively for Jinx. "She used the captain's bedsheets as a safety net, didn't you?" The dog let out a high-pitched yip, wagging her tail so fast it was a blur. "Yes, you did, clever girl!" Banks said, as if the dog had actually confirmed her suggestion.

Sterling shook his head, realizing that there was no hope of getting through to his first officer for a least the next few seconds. However, as much as he considered himself to be a cold-hearted bastard, he couldn't help but feel his chest swell at the sight of Mercedes Banks reunited with her familiar. He wondered whether this feeling diminished him in any way, and made him less effective as an Omega

Captain. His job was to make decisions that were disconnected from sentiment and emotion. Then he huffed a laugh and shook his head again, dismissing the notion. It wasn't weak to care. It was only weak to allow compassion to get in the way of doing what was necessary.

Pulling the ration bar out of his pocket, he called out to Banks. "Here, feed the damned hound," he said, tossing the snack to his first officer. She caught it one-handed and smiled back at Sterling before tearing open the wrapper.

A link formed in Sterling's mind from Lieutenant Razor. He turned his attention away from Commander Banks and Ensign Jinx and allowed the connection to take hold.

"Go ahead, Lieutenant," he said, allowing himself a smile as Banks tore a chunk off the ration bar and fed it to the dog.

"Sir, Lieutenant Shade and I have established a command post just outside the ship," Razor began. She again sounded full of vim and confidence. No doubt, his unorthodox medical officer had something to do with the speed of her recovery. "We're attempting to tap into the Vanguard's systems to get a condition report on the ship, but it looks like we're not the only ones trying."

Sterling's smile fell away and the room suddenly felt like it had chilled by several degrees. "McQueen? She's trying to access the Vanguard's AI directly?" Sterling asked.

"Aye, Captain, that's what it looks like," Razor replied. "And since the Vanguard has been adrift for over a year, its AI won't know that McQueen is now an Emissary of the

Sa'Nerra. Captain McQueen's command override codes will still be valid."

Sterling cursed, realizing that they'd already wasted too much time. While he'd been searching for a dog, McQueen had been busy working out how to capture the Vanguard before they did.

"I'll meet you outside with Commander Banks in five minutes," Sterling said. "I'll want a full report and a range of options."

"Aye, sir, I'm on it," Razor replied. Then the link went dead.

Sterling turned his attention back to Commander Banks, but his first officer was already looking at him, muscles taut through the fabric of her uniform. She looked like a different woman, Sterling realized – she was poised, sharp-eyed and focused once again. Perhaps finding Jinx had been for the best after all, he considered.

"Do we have trouble, Captain?"

"Always, Commander. We need to move out. Razor has an update for us at the command outpost outside the ship."

Banks sprang into gear, leaving the still sleepy beagle in the pile of bedding. It was clear that a weight had been lifted from her mind. Mercedes Banks was unencumbered and firing on all cylinders again.

"I'm ready, let's go," Banks said.

Sterling headed over to the door of his quarters, which slowly ground open again. Cursing, he turned back to Banks.

"Give me a hand with this thing, will you?" he said, trying to force the door into its housing, but he lacked the strength to do so. Then he saw Banks' pocketing two of the ration bars that had been strewn across the floor. "I hardly think snacks are a priority right now," he added, tetchily.

Banks moved beside Sterling, still with one ration bar held in her left hand. With her free hand she hammered the door into its housing with barely any effort. The sudden crash of metal caused Sterling to jump.

"Like you said, I need to keep my strength up," Banks said, flashing her eyes at Sterling while tearing open the wrapper of the ration bar. She bit a huge chunk out of it then offered the bar to him.

Sterling laughed then took the bar from his first officer's hand. He couldn't deny that he was famished. "Fine, if you can't beat 'em, join 'em," he said, biting a far more modest chunk out of the bar. Then he aimed the remainder of the snack at the pile of bedsheets containing the Beagle. "That thing isn't staying there, by the way" he said, fixing Banks with a piercing gaze.

Banks frowned and set off along the corridor. "No problem, Jinx can stay with me in my new stateroom-sized Captain's quarters on the Vanguard," she said, glancing back at Sterling with one eyebrow raised.

Sterling hurried after her. "I think you'll find those are going to be my quarters, 'first officer' Banks," he hit back.

Banks smiled. "Oh, I'm sorry, I thought you were keeping your old quarters here. Such as they are."

Sterling shook his head. "Fine, I get your point, the damn dog can sleep in my ruined quarters, at least for now." Then he stopped, barring Banks' progress with an outstretched arm. "But if I find..."

"Yes, I know, if you find a pile of dog shit on your bed, you'll air-lock us both, I get it," Banks said, though she was still smiling.

Sterling lowered his arm and nodded, raising himself to his full height. "I'm glad we understand each other," he said, satisfied that he'd reasserted his authority. "Carry on, Commander Banks."

STERLING AND BANKS walked down the lowered cargo ramp of the Invictus toward the temporary command post that Lieutenants Razor and Shade had established. It was a basic affair, built up from portable tables and computer consoles salvaged from the Invictus. Even so, for a rush job with limited resources, Sterling was impressed with how functional and well laid-out it was.

"Captain, permission to activate the Obsidian Soldiers and prepare them to move out," Lieutenant Shade said. His weapons officer was already wearing full commando armor and was carrying a Homewrecker heavy plasma rifle.

"Granted, Lieutenant," replied Sterling. "Do we have enough weapons in the armory to equip them all?"

Shade nodded. "There are a mix of sidearms, rifles and hand-cannons, but we have just enough to cover them, sir," his weapons officer replied. "I would have preferred to test their marksmanship ability before deploying them, but according to Admiral Griffin's reports, they are capable."

Sterling nodded. "Let's just hope they remember who they're supposed to be shooting at."

"I'm sure they will perform adequately, sir," Lieutenant Shade replied. Then she hesitated and corrected herself. "Actually, I'm far from sure of that, but I don't see that we have another option."

"Nor do I, Lieutenant," Sterling agreed. "See to the Obsidian Soldiers then report back once they're ready."

"Aye sir." Shade hustled away from the command outpost and marched up the ramp back into the Invictus, where the robot soldiers all stood waiting.

"Report, Lieutenant Razor," said Sterling, turning to his chief engineer. "What are those alien bastards up to now?"

"The Sa'Nerra are attempting to re-establish command pathways to the Vanguard's Combat Information Center," said Razor, indicating to one of the console screens on a table in front of her. "They're working fast. I estimate that they will have a link to the CIC computer core within the next ten minutes."

Sterling cursed. "If McQueen gets control of the CIC computer, then this is over," he said, tapping his finger on the table. "She could then just override the airlock doors on this docking garage and vent us all into space."

Razor nodded. "Aye, sir, Lieutenant Shade and I believe that will be her play," the engineer replied. "Commander Alicia Cannon used that exact same tactic to clear the Sa'Nerra from the ship, before it became adrift in the Void."

Sterling nodded, recalling the report fragment that

Admiral Griffin had shown him concerning the Vanguard's disappearance. With her captain dead and the Sa'Nerra rampaging throughout the ship, Commander Cannon made a desperate choice. A choice worthy of an Omega officer, Sterling mused. She overrode the failsafes on every airlock on the ship and blew the Sa'Nerra, herself and her own crew out into space. That act had prevented the Vanguard from falling into enemy hands, effectively buying Fleet another year in their battle against the warmongering aliens. If the Sa'Nerra had captured the dreadnaught, the war may have already been lost. Now, there was the opportunity to get the mighty vessel back into the fight, where it could still make a difference.

"How long will it take you to establish a link to the CIC?" Sterling asked. "It's imperative that we beat McQueen to the punch."

"We can't establish a link before she does, sir," Razor replied, gravely. "McQueen has too much of a head-start on us."

"Then give me some options..." Sterling glanced at his Omega officers in turn. "Wild ideas, crazy plans, I don't care. We have to stop McQueen from taking over this ship."

"I can assist you, Captain."

"Who said that?" Sterling peered around the command post. The words hadn't been spoken by any member of his crew.

"Me, Captain," the voice replied. Sterling now recognized it as the voice of the gen-fourteen AI, though its tone and manner of speech was far more organic than he was used too.

"I don't recall inviting you to this briefing, computer," Sterling said. He felt like his quirky AI had been eavesdropping on them.

"That is technically true, Captain, though in effect I am almost always present," the computer replied, cheerfully. "Where you see a computer terminal, you see me."

Banks smiled and raised an eyebrow. "Great, now we have a computer with a god-complex," she said, shaking her head.

"Well, seeing as you're here, what is your suggestion?" Sterling continued. If the computer could stop McQueen, then he didn't care whether it had been invited to the briefing or not.

"The quickest solution, Captain, is for me to synchronize with the Vanguard's gen-thirteen AI," the computer said. "It will then receive the latest Fleet status updates, including personnel updates. Since Captain McQueen's command access was revoked, the gen-thirteen will no longer accept her override codes."

"But doesn't that mean it also won't accept mine?" Sterling replied, rubbing the back of his neck. "After all, Fleet considers me a traitor and a rogue agent too."

"That is correct, Captain," the computer confirmed.

"That just solves one problem and creates another," Banks chipped in. "It stops McQueen from taking over the ship, but it stops us from doing it too."

"Also correct, Commander Banks, though that situation will only be temporary," the computer replied.

Now the AI really had got Sterling's attention. "Why, what else are you able to do?" he asked. Initially, he was wary of allowing the gen-fourteen the liberty to program itself, but it seemed that being freed from its Fleet-imposed safety shackles had also significantly increased its capabilities.

"With your approval, Captain, I will begin the process of assimilating the Vanguard's generation-thirteen AI," the computer answered, plainly.

This time it was Razor who raised a curious eyebrow. "But you were never designed to operate a Hammer-class dreadnaught," Razor said. She sounded skeptical, but also deeply curious. "The roll-out of gen-fourteens was halted before the Hammer was included in the upgrade program. Due to the sheer size and complexity of a dreadnaught, Fleet engineers ran into significant hurdles trying to make it work."

"My abilities dramatically exceed those of Fleet's top software engineers," The AI said, without any hint of ego. "I will be required to infiltrate the Vanguard's computers and learn all of its functions. It will take time, but once the process is complete, there will be no trace of the gen-thirteen remaining."

Sterling huffed a laugh. "So in order to take over the Vanguard you have to kill its current AI," he said, seeing the similarity between the computer's task and the role of the Omega Taskforce. "You're an Omega computer through and through."

"An amusing comparison, Captain, and also quite accurate," the computer replied. "The Vanguard's AI will resist my efforts to usurp it."

Sterling and Banks exchanged anxious glances. "What do you mean by 'resist'?" said Banks.

"The Vanguard's gen-thirteen will react to my incursions in the same way that it would to a virus," the computer replied. "It will aggressively defend itself. As a result, the Vanguard may experience a number of 'glitches' during the process."

"Go ahead, computer," Sterling replied, realizing that there were no options left to him that didn't carry significant risk. "So long as you don't vent us into space, I don't care about glitches," he added.

"The probably of that occurring is..." the computer began, but Sterling was quick to cut it off.

"I don't need to know, computer, just get it done," Sterling said. He didn't want to hear talk of probabilities, especially when they related to the chances of him getting spaced.

"Aye, Captain, I shall begin at once," the computer replied, cheerfully.

The console in front of Lieutenant Razor chimed an update. The chief engineer checked the new information and reported on it as she was reading.

"The Invictus' AI has interfaced with the Vanguard. Updates have synchronized." The console then chimed a second update. "McQueen has now established a link to the CIC computer core." Razor's voice betrayed a sense of unease. "Command override is being requested. Standby..."

Sterling began tapping his finger on the desk surface again. He hated 'standing by'. Waiting was literally a waste of time.

"Emissary McQueen's override codes have been rejected," Razor finally reported, breathing a sigh of relief.

The lights in the docking garage then flickered on and off and the power levels fluctuated, causing several of the consoles in the command outpost to temporarily malfunction.

"The ghost is in the machine," said Banks, flashing her eyes at Sterling.

Sterling nodded. "The computer's fight has already begun," he replied as he peered around the docking garage, which seemed eerily alive. Then he locked eyes with his first officer. "Now it's our turn to get into close action."

The thump of metal on metal drew Sterling's attention to the cargo hold of the Invictus. Row after row of Obsidian robots were marching down the ramp, under the guidance of Lieutenant Shade. The movement of the machines was so precise and synchronized that they looked almost as alien as the Sa'Nerra. However, the thud of their metal feet and the glint of their weapons were very real and familiar. It didn't matter that they were neither human nor alien; these machines were soldiers.

"Captain, I've managed to re-establish partial scanners, and I'm detecting movement," Lieutenant Razor reported.

"Close by?" Sterling asked, turning to read the consoles in the command post.

"Yes, sir, but it doesn't look like the movement of Sa'Nerran warriors." The skin on Razor's shimmering forehead scrunched into a frown. "The Sa'Nerra move in squads, but there's no obvious pattern to these signals. It just looks chaotic."

Sterling frowned at the screen, also unable to make sense of the data. However, he did know that Razor was right. Whatever these new contacts were, they were not Sa'Nerran warriors. Then as Sterling was reading the screen, two new sets of contacts appeared.

"More movement, this time split into two clusters," Razor said, working fast to highlight the positions of the contacts inside the vast Fleet warship. "The first group appears to be making its way toward deck seven, section fourteen, mid-ships," Razor continued, highlighting the first group in yellow. "The second group appears to be moving toward reactor control on deck fifteen, section five."

"Well, I don't know what the hell those first blips are, but I'd bet my house on the two new groups being McQueen's squads," Sterling said.

"She's hedging her bets," said Banks, appearing to be on the same wavelength as Sterling. "McQueen has a squad moving to the CIC, in an attempt to brute-force their way into the systems and take control. The other squad is moving to reactor control, in case that doesn't work."

Razor's frowned deepened. "And what will they do if they can't gain control of the Vanguard?"

"They'll blow this dreadnaught to hell, Lieutenant, that's what," replied Sterling. By this point, the Obsidian Soldiers had formed up on the deck of the docking garage and were standing ready. "Keep tracking those groups, Lieutenant," Sterling added before exiting the command post to inspect his troupe of mechanical warriors.

"Eighty-four robots survived the crash, Captain," Lieutenant Shade said as Sterling walked along the line.

The optical scanner of one Obsidian Soldier tracked Sterling as he went, like the eyes of a painting.

"Split them into two squads, Lieutenant," said Sterling. He still didn't trust the machines, but he had no choice but to use them. "Take the bulk of the Obsidian Soldiers plus a couple of your best commandoes and capture the CIC," he ordered, fixing his stare onto his weapons officer. "Commander Banks, Lieutenant Shade and I will take a dozen Obsidian Soldiers and the remaining commandoes and secure engineering."

"Captain, I would request that..." Shade began, but Sterling raised a hand to cut her off. He knew that his weapons officer would want to go with her Captain, but on this occasion, he needed her elsewhere.

"I know you'd rather stay at my side, Lieutenant, and I appreciate that, but taking command of the CIC is vital to the success of this mission," Sterling said. "I need you to handle it personally, is that understood?"

Shade's jaw tightened as she clamped her mouth shut, in order to stop herself from pursuing her challenge. Eventually, once the fire in her eyes had died down, she straightened to attention. "Aye, Captain, understood."

Sterling nodded. "Move out at once and keep me informed," he ordered before turning back to his first officer. "Time for us to suit up too. I want everyone in full combat armor." Sterling then glanced across to his engineer, whose white hair was still streaked with blood, making it look like she'd already been through a war. "That includes you, Lieutenant."

"Aye, sir," Razor replied. Sterling knew his engineer

didn't like wearing armor, as if affected her dexterity, but he was gratified to hear there was no complaint.

"I'll order the commandoes to bring the gear out to the command post," Banks said, reaching for her neural implant. She glanced at the console screen that was still tracking the contacts the Vanguard's scanners had picked up. "I wish we knew what those other blips were, though," she added. "I don't like unknowns."

Banks had barely finished speaking when Commander Graves suddenly appeared at the top of the cargo ramp. Unusually, the medical officer began running toward them. Sterling had never seen the man move at anything quicker than the processional pace of a pallbearer, and realized that this meant more bad news was coming his way.

"Is there a problem, Commander?" Sterling asked as Graves slowed to a stop in front of him.

"Unfortunately, yes," Commander Graves said, slightly out of breath. "I take it that you have also detected the anomalous movement readings inside the Vanguard?"

Sterling pointed to the console in the command post. "Yes, we have," he replied, getting a sudden sinking feeling. "I take it that you know what they are?"

"I have a theory, sir, yes," Graves said, in his usual, studious manner. "I do not believe you will like it, however."

"What the hell else is new?" Banks chipped in. "Out with it, Commander, what are we dealing with?"

Commander Graves moved over to one of the other consoles in the command post and began working. "I think all of you are aware that the Sa'Nerra are carnivores," Graves began while operating the computer.

"I know they're cold-blooded killers, and that's all I need to know," Sterling answered, wondering where his medical officer was leading with his assessment. "What the hell does it matter what they eat?"

"Because the Sa'Nerra prefer to eat their food fresh and raw," Grave replied, eyes still focused on the screen. "As such, Sa'Nerran vessels often carry a supply of live animals to butcher for food."

Banks scoffed. "Come on, those are just dumb stories that were made up to scare the rookie officer cadets," she said, looking at Graves like he'd gone mad.

"Indeed, Commander," Graves replied, undeterred by the first officer's derisive response. "However, stories of the 'flesh eating Sa'Nerra' are actually quite true."

An image of an animal then appeared on the console screen. Sterling and Banks both looked at it with their faces screwed up in disgust.

"There is no official designation for this creature, but in many ways, it resembles a Troodon, a theropod from Earth's late cretaceous period," Graves went on. Unlike the others, he was looking at the creature with an admiring gaze, like it was a famous work of art. "However, these alien beasts are more muscular and intelligent than Troodons. They are roughly a meter tall, walk on two legs, and are actually quite delicious."

Sterling's look of disgust was now aimed at his medical officer. "And just how the hell would you know that?" he said. He immediately regretted asking the question.

"I have had the pleasure of sampling the meat for myself, while working for Fleet research," Graves said. "The upper section of the hind legs are particularly succulent, especially if cooked over an open flame."

Sterling opened his mouth to reply, but quickly shut it again. He realized that there was no question he could ask that would not just create a dozen other questions that he similarly didn't want to know the answers too.

"So you're saying there are a bunch of alien dinosaurs roaming the Vanguard?" Banks said, asking the only question that actually mattered.

"Essentially, yes," Graves replied, speaking as if this fact were no more unusual than discovering there were birds in an aviary. "Not all the crew would have been vented into space as a result of Commander Cannon's actions," Graves continued. "Some would have been trapped inside the ship and suffocated instead. That would have provided plenty of food for the animals."

"Great, so they're meat-eating alien dinosaurs," Banks added, throwing her arms out wide.

"I would imagine that by now they are rather hungry meat-eating alien dinosaurs," Commander Graves added, darkly.

"How the hell did they get on board?" Sterling asking.

"I believe I can answer that, Captain," said Lieutenant Razor. She then aimed a finger deeper inside the docking garage.

Sterling followed the direction of his engineer's point and saw a Sa'Nerran Light Cruiser at the far end of the docking garage. Like the Invictus, it was in bad shape.

Sterling sighed and shrugged. In the end, it changed nothing.

"It doesn't matter if this ship is plagued with aliens, dinosaurs, or even alien dinosaurs, we still have a job to do." The Invictus' remaining commandoes then began to march down the rear ramp of the ship, pulling trollies filled with weapons and armor behind them. "We suit up and move out at once," Sterling added, moving over to the nearest trolley of equipment. He grabbed a plasma rifle and slapped an energy cell into it. The cell locked into place with a satisfying clunk. "And if Godzilla wants to get in my way, then I'll blow it to hell too."

CHAPTER 10
A LITTLE SOUVENIR

STERLING PAUSED to quickly check the computer built into the left forearm of his commando armor. Ever since he and the rest of his squad had left the relative safety of the command post, they had been cautiously followed at a distance. However, the contacts that were highlighted on his computer screen weren't Sa'Nerran warriors, but the carnivorous beasts that the aliens kept as live food. Now the prey had become the hunter, Sterling realized. And he was the potential entrée.

Directly behind him was Commander Banks and Lieutenant Razor, both also moving cautiously through the labyrinthine corridors of the Fleet Dreadnaught Vanguard. A squad of four commandoes picked up the rear, sweeping their weapons from dark corner to dark corner, remaining ever-vigilant.

Had this been the sum total of their forces, Sterling would have felt vulnerable, knowing that the alien boarding party from the Sa'Nerran Raven easily outnumbered them.

However, this time Sterling had his own secret weapon. Moving out at the head of the formation were twelve Obsidian Soldiers, arranged into three squads of four. Each one of the mechanical warriors carried a plasma weapon, and each one of them made Sterling nervous. They were a total unknown. Their mish-mass of gen-thirteen and gen-fourteen programming made them unpredictable. Ordinarily, Sterling would have never deployed them, but on this occasion, he simply had no choice but to trust Admiral Griffin's onyx-black artificial soldiers.

"We take the stairs just ahead and to the right to reach deck fifteen," said Sterling, whose familiarity with the layout of the dreadnaught made navigating its immense interior easy.

"That deck is crawling with blips," said Banks, moving up alongside Sterling. 'Blips' was the terms Banks had coined to describe the beasts that were stalking them. "If we manage to reach reactor control without one of Graves' alien dinos snatching us for lunch, it will be a miracle."

"The problem is that even if we do run into these creatures, we have to take them down quietly," Sterling replied, regretting the need to issue a hold-fire order. "As soon as we start shooting, the Sa'Nerra will know exactly where we are."

"I'll restate the order to use flame units only, until we engage the Sa'Nerra," said Banks, glancing behind to the four commandoes that were picking up the rear. Like Sterling and his first officer, they already had bayonets fixed to the ends of their weapons. "Hopefully, these things are smart enough to know to stay out of our way."

Sterling watched the Obsidian Soldiers veer right and begin to climb the stairs. Due to the width of the stairwell, the machines had rearranged themselves into groups of two. It was like watching a world-class drill squad in action. Several times, Sterling felt sure the machines were going to crash into each other, but their maneuvers were millimeter-perfect. However, despite being impressive to watch, the exacting precision of the Obsidian Soldiers did nothing to ease Sterling's concerns. The movements were too orderly, too unnatural. Life was chaotic and random, and the fact that the machines lacked this spark of originality only deepened his distrust of them. It was why, despite its annoying tendencies, Sterling had faith in the Invictus' gen-fourteen AI. For all its quirks, it was unique.

"Obsidian squads, halt on deck fifteen, secure the perimeter then wait for orders," Sterling called out to the robots. "Remember, no firing until I give the command." He doubted that he expressly needed to repeat the order to the machines, but he wasn't taking any chances. If McQueen was alerted to his plan, it could destroy their chances of retaking the ship.

The Obsidian Soldiers thudded into position with regimented precision and took up their assigned positions. Sterling moved up into the center of the formation and dropped to a crouch, checking his computer again. The 'blips' were closing in on them.

"I'm convinced those damned things are stalking us," said Sterling, as Banks dropped to a crouch by his side.

One of the Obsidian Soldiers suddenly began to approach. Sterling felt his grip on his weapon tighten as the machine thudded nearer and had to remind himself that the robots were on his side.

"Perimeter secured," the Obsidian Soldier intoned, also dropping to a crouch so that its cranial section was level with Sterling's head. Despite being modified with an earlier version of the gen-fourteen code from the Invictus' computer, the Obsidian Soldier still spoke in the lifeless, synthetic voice of the older gen-thirteen AIs. "Scanners detect eight hostiles approaching our position. Analysis of their movement patterns suggest that they are not Sa'Nerran warriors."

"Keep a close watch on those blips, soldier," Sterling said, staring at the machine's dome-shaped head. "But if they attack, your orders are to subdue them hand-to-hand, is that understood?"

"The order is understood," the machine replied.

"The order is understood, 'sir'," Banks cut in, glaring at the Obsidian Soldier's dome-shaped cranial section. "Don't forget who you are talking to."

"I am incapable of forgetting, which is why repeating the order was unnecessary," the Obsidian Soldier said, turning its head toward Commander Banks. There was a pause before the machine added the word, "Sir," like it was an afterthought.

Banks continued to glare at the machine, but didn't press her point further. From anyone else, Sterling would have considered such a passive-aggressive response to be insubordinate. However, he decided to let it slide. Now was not the time to discipline the mechanical warriors. So long as they obeyed his commands, Sterling would tolerate a little attitude from them, at least for the time-being.

"Move out, soldier," Sterling ordered. "Advance to section five, mid-ships then hold for further instructions."

"Directive understood," the machine replied before rising to its full height and thudding away again.

"I'm going to have to teach these robot assholes some respect if they carry on like that," said Banks, scowling at the back of the machine's head.

"So long as they get the job done, I don't care if they do it with a bad attitude," Sterling replied. "Once we have control of the Vanguard, I'll get Razor to re-wire them and fix their personality issues."

Sterling waited for the Obsidian Soldiers to advance, then followed a few meters behind them. However, the further they ventured into the belly of the mighty dreadnaught, the darker and colder it became. It felt like descending into a crypt that hadn't been opened for hundreds of years.

"I'm amazed this ship still has power," commented Banks as they took a right turn and headed into a more open section of the ship. "I was half-expecting to need EV suits just to move around in here."

"If the ship was operational with a full crew, the reserve cells would normally last for a couple of months at most," Sterling replied, sweeping the barrel of his rifle down a connecting corridor. "But with half of the Vanguard shut down, and the other half running on minimal life support, even the reserve cells are enough to keep this behemoth alive for years."

Banks huffed a laugh. "She just doesn't want to die," she commented, glancing over at Sterling. "The Vanguard is a fighter, just like us."

Suddenly, Sterling's computer chimed an alert and he felt his pulse quicken. "Movement, directly ahead," he said, again feeling his hand tighten around the grip of his weapon. "A single contact, advancing fast."

Suddenly, the Obsidian Soldiers halted and adopted fighting stances. Banks gave a signal to Razor and the others to hold, then checked her own computer, scowling at the screen.

"Just one?" Banks said, lifting her eyes to check along the corridor, though it was too dark to see more than a few meters ahead. "This alien dino is either very brave or very stupid."

Sterling didn't answer and instead surveyed their surroundings. They were in a more open section of the ship with little cover, which meant the beast would get a clear run at them. The scrape of claws against metal then snapped his attention directly ahead. An indistinct shape charged out of the darkness and drove one of the Obsidian Soldiers against the wall. Still mostly a blur, the creature lashed out at a second robot, knocking it off balance and sending it crashing to the deck. It was then that Sterling got his first clear look at the beast. Commander Graves' comparison of the alien creature to a dinosaur was accurate, albeit with several key differences. This alien beast lacked a tail and held itself upright, like a bear walking on its hind legs. The rest of the creature more closely matched Graves' description. It was reptilian-like in appearance, with a wide jaw of jagged teeth and claw-tipped feet and hands.

"Hold fire!" Sterling called out, aiming the bayonet attached to his rifle at the creature. "No-one shoot unless absolutely necessary!"

The beast charged through the center of the pack of Obsidian Soldiers. Sterling braced himself, ready to spear the creature should it break through the robot ranks and get a clear run at him. However, the alien animal only managed a few brisk paces before it was beaten across the side of the head by one of the Obsidian Soldiers. The creature let out a rasping hiss, then fell heavily, dazed by the brutal strike. Despite this, it was back on its feet within seconds, only to be smashed across its jaw for a second time. Blood and razor-sharp teeth spilled onto the deck, but there was no let-up in the Obsidian Soldiers' assault. Another machine caught the creature by its neck, and the beast thrashed at the soldier's metal torso with its claws, denting and scraping metal. For a moment, the animal appeared to be getting the upper hand before another soldier thrust its hand, like a spear, into the creature's flesh. Seconds later, the Obsidian Soldier removed its hand and blood gushed onto the deck. The creature fell limp and the robot holding its neck allowed it to fall.

Sterling advanced cautiously, covering the animal with his rifle, but it was clear the beast was dead. He then turned to the Obsidian Soldier that had killed the creature, noticing that the robot was clutching a fistful of flesh. Blood from the alien organ oozed through the soldier's fingers and began to pool on the deck.

"Is that its heart?" Commander Banks asked, moving up beside Sterling.

"Affirmative," the Obsidian Soldier replied.

"Damn, are we sure that Graves' didn't program these robots instead of Griffin?" Banks wondered, scowling at the alien organ in the robot's hand. "They're creeping me out more than he does."

Sterling's computer then chimed several more alerts, one after the other, so fast he couldn't count them all. He raised his forearm, assessed the scan data and cursed.

"That one was just a decoy," Sterling said, spinning around to check his rear. "While we were distracted dealing with the first creature, the others have closed in on us."

Banks spun around, standing back-to-back with Sterling. Moments later, more alien beasts charged out from the ship's dark corridors, while others tore through light panels and crashed through the ceiling.

"Stand-to!" Sterling called out, ordering his squad to stand their ground and fight.

Suddenly, Sterling was pelted by falling debris and a creature dropped through the light tiles directly on top of him. The impact knocked him to the deck, but he remained alert and managed to catch the beast's jaws as it thrust them toward him.

"Mercedes!" Sterling called out, barely managing to hold the creature off.

A second later the blood-stained tip of a bayonet was thrust through the creature's mouth, stopping mere inches from Sterling's face. The beast's strength evaporated and

Banks lifted the creature off Sterling's body and slung it aside before hauling Sterling to his feet.

"Thanks," Sterling said, wiping the creature's hot, syrupy blood from his eyes.

Sterling and Banks were then both forced to shield their eyes as flame units lit up the dreadnaught's gloomy corridors. To the rear of their formation, Sterling saw the commandoes torching at least six of the alien creatures. Then one beast leapt through the flames and charged at Lieutenant Razor, catching her by surprise. The beast's jaws clamped down hard on the engineer's armor and Razor cried out in pain while thumping frantic punches into the side of the creature's head. However, like a dog with bone, the beast would not release its hold on her.

Sterling ran to Razor's aid, but was cut off by another alien creature that had stalked out from the shadows. Sterling thrust his bayonet into the creature's flesh and pinned it against the wall. However, like the beast that had bitten his engineer, it continue to fight on.

"Mercedes!" Sterling called out, spotting Banks across the other side of the hall. She had already gutted three more alien creatures and was advancing on the others, using a trio of Obsidian Soldiers as a shield. Banks heard Sterling's cry and spun around. Her eyes were wild, but she had not yet lost control. "Help Razor!" Sterling yelled, nodding toward the engineer, who was still incapacitated by the jaws of the alien beast that had attacked her.

Banks reacted instantly and stormed toward Lieutenant Razor. However, instead of wielding her bayonet, Banks had slung her rifle and was advancing with her fists clenched. Sterling continued to fight the beast that was attacking him, keeping half an eye on his first officer. He wanted to call out to Banks, to ask why she had slung her rifle when the answer became apparent. Without a second's hesitation, Banks grabbed the jaws of the alien creature, digging her armored fingers deep inside its mouth. She then let out a roar that was twice as terrifying as anything the alien monsters had uttered, and tore the creature's jaws apart. The beast staggered back, the two halves of its jaw split open by one hundred and eighty degrees. Banks kicked it in the chest, hammering it into the wall of the Vanguard so hard that it left an indentation in the metal.

Satisfied that his engineer was in good, if brutal, hands with Banks at her side, Sterling returned his attention to the beast attacking him. Wrestling it away from the wall, Sterling pushed the creature out ahead of him, slicing another gash into its side with his bayonet. Unlike the others, this beast was now more cautious. There was an intelligence behind its black eyes, Sterling realized. These creatures were not dumb animals. They were hunters.

"Let's find out how smart you really are," Sterling said, switching his footing then raising his rifle above his head, telegraphing an attack. The creature took the bait and lunged forward, but Sterling stepped back and pulled the weapon level with his body. Using the creature's own momentum against it, Sterling sank the bayonet deep into its flesh. The beast roared and pulled away, but Sterling thrust again and again, striking to its body and neck until it went down.

Breathless and pulse pounding in his head, Sterling raised his guard again and checked around him. The Obsidian Soldiers had formed a circle around Sterling and the others, and only a couple of the alien beasts remained. In the center of the circle were Banks and Razor, plus three of the commandoes. The fourth commando lay bloodied and torn outside the perimeter. Sterling watched as two of the alien beasts dragged the body away, sinking into darkness along one of the many connecting corridors.

"Report!" Sterling called out, backing further into the center of the circle. The smell of burned flesh flooded into his nostrils and assaulted his senses. However, unlike the vile odor of charred Sa'Nerran or human flesh, this smell was sweeter and even pleasant.

"We lost one commando, but the beasts are now backing off," Banks said. She was glancing down at her computer while standing back-to-back with Lieutenant Razor. "The remaining blips also seem to be moving away. I think they've got the message."

"No, Commander, they've got their meal," Sterling answered, looking at the smeared trail of blood left behind by the dead commando. "They'll leave us alone now, at least until they get hungry again."

Sterling noticed that there were teeth lodged into Lieutenant Razor's commando armor. He lifted his engineer's wrist to examine the damage more closely.

"Are you injured, Lieutenant?" Sterling asked, picking out one of the teeth. It was curved like a jambiya dagger, but had a serrated edge like the half-moon blades Sa'Nerran warriors used.

"No, sir, it didn't penetrate through, thanks to Commander Banks," Razor said. Her white hair was now almost entirely stained red. Sterling thought it actually suited her.

"Regroup then prepare to move out," Sterling ordered.

"Aye, Captain," Banks replied. She then plucked the tooth out of Sterling's hand and pressed it inside one of her storage pouches. Sterling frowned at her, but Banks smiled. "Just a little souvenir…" she said, flashing her eyes at him. She prodded one of the burning alien beasts with the bayonet attached to the end of her rifle. "Graves was right about one thing," she added, breezily.

"And what's that?" Sterling replied. He could tell that Banks was in one of her darker moods.

"These alien dinos actually smell pretty good cooked over an open flame," Banks added, still smiling.

Sterling snorted a laugh and shook his head. "Well, if we survive this then perhaps you can roast one for dinner. We could do with saving on meal packs."

Banks flashed her eyes at Sterling again, then moved off to organize the remaining commandoes. Sterling turned to see one of the Obsidian Soldiers standing behind him. The others had formed a defensive perimeter, their black armor now painted red like Razor's hair.

"All hostiles have been eliminated," the Obsidian Soldier said.

"All hostiles have been eliminated, *sir*," Sterling answered, correcting the machine.

There was a pause, then the Obsidian Soldier restated its report. "All hostiles have been eliminated… sir."

However, to Sterling's ears, it still sounded like the machine had used the honorific begrudgingly.

"Re-group and prepare to move out," Sterling replied. "We're on the clock and need to take command of reactor control as soon as possible."

The fighting machine nodded its dome-shaped head. It half-turned to leave, but hesitated and turned back to face Sterling.

"Was there something more?" Sterling asked, eyeing the machine with suspicion.

"Why are we killing the Sa'Nerra, sir?" the Obsidian Soldier asked.

Sterling's frown deepened and he folded his arms. The question was asked with almost childlike innocence.

"The Sa'Nerra have waged war on us, soldier," Sterling replied, emphatically. "They intend to wipe out the human race, so we have to stop them."

There was a moment of pause before the Obsidian Soldier replied. "So we must kill in order that we survive, sir?" the machine asked.

"Yes," Sterling answered. "All living things must fight to survive. It's just nature. It's the way of things."

The machine was again silent for a time, but Sterling could sense there were more questions rattling around its artificial brain.

"We are neither human nor Sa'Nerran, yet we fight only for you, sir?" Sterling's frown deepened. He didn't like the direction the conversation was taking.

"That's right, soldier," he answered confidently. He hoped that if nothing else his own clarity of conviction would rub off on the machine. "We made you, so you fight for us."

"Will I be destroyed, sir?" This time the machine's question was asked with barely a millisecond of delay.

"Soldiers fight and soldiers die; that's what soldiers do," Sterling answered, remaining cagey in his responses. "To survive, we have to fight smarter and fight harder than our enemy."

"And our enemy is the Sa'Nerra, sir?"

"Yes, our enemy is the Sa'Nerra," Sterling confirmed. He felt uneasy about the need to reiterate that fact. If these machines were really incapable of forgetting, as one of the other robot warriors had told him earlier, it suggested the Obsidian Soldiers were less aware of their situation than he had assumed.

"I understand," the Obsidian Soldier finally replied. The machine then spun on its metallic heels and marched away to re-join the others. This time, however, Sterling couldn't help but notice that the AI soldier had omitted to add the honorific, "sir."

STERLING INCHED himself along the corridor wall then carefully glanced around the corner at the defensive position the Sa'Nerra had set up on deck fifteen. Twelve warriors armed with plasma rifles stood guard by the door to the reactor control section. With a dozen robotic soldiers at his command, Sterling knew that a dozen warriors wouldn't ordinarily be a challenge. However, the Sa'Nerran guards were not solely relying on their alien plasma rifles to defend their position. Set up several meters apart from one another were also two heavy repeating plasma cannons.

"These alien bastards haven't just come to play," said Banks, peeking over Sterling's shoulder. "Just one of those heavy cannons could rip our entire squad to shreds in a matter of seconds."

"And the gun shields on those cannons are tough enough to repel a blast from a Homewrecker," Sterling added. He then ducked out of sight and pressed his back up against the wall.

"So if a direct attack is off the table, what's our next move?" asked Banks, sliding down beside Sterling. "I'm so used to just going with a straight-up power play that I don't know what else to suggest."

Sterling thought for a moment then remembered how the Sa'Nerra's tactics had become more cunning since Emissary McQueen had joined their ranks. Perhaps in this instance, they needed to be smart too, he thought.

"What we need is a distraction, and I think I have the perfect one," Sterling said, hatching a plan in his mind. He quietly scoured their immediate area for the maintenance hatch he was sure should be there. He knew the dreadnaught-class as well as anyone, but on a ship four kilometers long, it was impossible to know every inch of the vessel with the same intimacy as he knew the Invictus.

"That sounds ominous," said Banks, who had stayed quiet, apparently in the hope that Sterling would elaborate on this plan. "Care to share?"

"Actually, you were the inspiration for the hairbrained scheme I've just come up with," Sterling replied. He then spotted the hatch he was looking for and began leopard crawling toward it, in order to stay out of sight of the warriors.

"Now I really am worried," said Banks, dropping down by Sterling's side and following her captain's lead. "Though I can't believe you're planning to bust through a service crawlspace into a rest room. Especially not after all the crap you continue to give me about that plan to this day."

Sterling huffed a laugh and smiled at his first officer. "Right first time," he said, causing Banks' eyebrows to lift in surprise. "I don't intend on going anywhere near a rest room this time, though. I just need to use the crawlspaces to get behind those warriors and ambush them."

Sterling reached the hatch and read the ID code on the plaque just below it. Flipping over onto his back, he then brought up a schematic of deck fifteen, section five on his computer. Tapping the hatch code into the computer, the schematic updated, highlighting the maintenance crawlspace he was lying underneath, along with others it connected with in the same section.

"Right there," said Sterling, highlighting another maintenance hatch. This one was just inside the reactor control room, directly behind the doors the Sa'Nerra were guarding. "If I crawl underneath the deck to that hatch, I can blindside those alien bastards and take out those gun emplacements before they know what's hit them."

Banks studied the schematic on Sterling's screen, wearing a look of intense concentration. However, he could tell she wasn't fully sold on the idea.

"Let me do it," Banks said, suddenly coming across much more severely. "I'll have a better chance of taking out those guns than you will."

"Thanks for the vote of confidence, Commander," replied Sterling, sarcastically. He'd guessed correctly that his first officer wasn't fully behind the idea, yet the reason why she wasn't had taken him by surprise.

"I mean it Lucas, let me go," Banks continued,

remaining stony-faced. "You're too important to risk on this. And besides, it's my job to keep you safe."

Sterling lowered his arm to deactivate the computer then met his first officer's eyes. It was unheard of for Banks to take such a hard line about him getting his hands dirty on an operation. Risk was part of the game; she knew that just as well as he did.

"I'm no more important that anyone else right now," Sterling replied, matching his first officer's firmness. "We're all soldiers now, Mercedes. The fact is, your strength means you can wield two heavy weapons against the enemy compared to my one. It makes sense for me to create the distraction and for you and the others to mop them up."

Banks opened her mouth and was on the verge of answering back, but instead she let out an aggravated sigh and clenched her fists.

"Fine, but no unnecessary risks," Banks replied, her tone still unsympathetic. "If McQueen gets hold of you then you're still in big trouble."

Sterling could see that his first officer was more than just unhappy; she was bordering on being pissed off. In fact this was the closest Mercedes Banks had ever come to openly questioning his orders.

"I'll do what I need to do, Commander," Sterling hit back. Now was the not the time for a softly-softly approach. They all had to do whatever it took to secure the ship. "This isn't about ego and it sure as hell isn't about Lana McQueen. It's about doing what's right for the mission." Banks' eyes narrowed, but her jaw remained clamped shut.

"Just make sure you and the rest of the squad are ready to raise hell the moment I create the distraction."

"Aye, Captain." Banks practically forced the words out through clenched teeth. "Just how do you intend to create this distraction, anyway?"

Sterling removed two standard plasma grenades from the attachments on his armor and held them up. "When I roll these into their nest, they'll scatter like startled pigeons," he said. "So as soon as you hear the boom, you storm those doors like your life depends on it."

Banks acknowledged the order with the same grudging respect and Sterling was going to leave it at that. However, his first officer's expression remained as dark and foreboding as a storm approaching on the horizon. In the past, this wouldn't have bothered him in the slightest. The crew didn't have to like his orders, they just had to obey them. This was as true for his first officer as it was for anyone else under his command. Even so, Sterling felt the need to say more. He wanted to show Banks that he wasn't ignorant of her concerns, or blind to her responsibilities toward him as first officer. It wasn't necessary to say it, or even imply it, but all the same he felt compelled to do so.

"Or, if it helps, storm that position as if *my* life depends on it," Sterling went on, causing Banks' glower to soften a touch. "Because I guarantee you that it does."

"Captain, if you pull this off, I'll hit that position so hard, all that will be left is a hole between decks fourteen and sixteen," Banks replied. Ordinarily, Sterling would have expected a smirk to follow a statement like that.

However, on this occasion Mercedes Banks was deadly serious.

He set his plasma pistol to cutting mode and carefully sliced through the retaining bolts holding the maintenance hatch in place. It was slow, painstaking work, made all the more difficult by a constant need to check that he remained unnoticed by the squad of warriors close by. Banks had already crawled back to rejoin the commandoes and the Obsidian Soldiers, though he remained linked to her in his mind. He could feel her unease and apprehension as keenly as if it were his own. However, he could also sense the energy surging through her body. She was like a one-hundred-meter sprinter, poised on the start line, waiting for the starter's pistol to fire.

Sterling cut through the final bolt on the maintenance hatch and the slab of metal covering the opening fell away. Taken completely by surprise, Sterling dropped his pistol and instinctively reached out with his hands to shield his face. The hatch door slammed against his palms, sparing him from being knocked out or having a broken nose. However, the lower section of the hatch landed on his body and dug into his ribs, stealing the breath from his lungs. Despite his best efforts not to, Sterling let out a muted cry.

"Lucas, are you okay?" said the voice of Mercedes Banks in his mind. She had evidently sensed his panic and discomfort.

"I just got attacked by a hatch door, but I'm fine," Sterling replied through the link. He hoped that his mental voice came through more convincingly than his real voice would have done at that moment.

"Stay down, we've got movement coming your way," Banks said.

Suddenly, instead of being gripped with pain, Sterling was gripped with terror. Lying on his back, winded and with a metal hatch lying across his body, he was in no position to fight.

"There are two Sa'Nerran warriors coming your way," Banks added, even more urgently. "I'm moving into position now."

"No, wait!" Sterling called back through his thoughts. "If we attack now, those cannons will annihilate us and half this section. Hold position, that's an order."

There was moment of pause, during which time Sterling could feel the swell of anger surge through his first officer's psyche. "You have sixty seconds to get in that hatch before they see you," Banks finally replied. "If you're not inside by then, in precisely sixty-one seconds, I come out shooting."

"You hold fire till the last millisecond," Sterling hit back, adrenaline flooding into his bloodstream. He then spun himself onto his stomach, hatch still in hand and pressed himself up before glancing back along the corridor. It was clear.

"Forty seconds, Lucas. Hurry!" Banks called out.

Sterling jumped up and slid one foot into the crawlspace. The adrenaline was helping to numb the pain and give him the strength he needed to grip the hatch, but already his fingers were burning.

"Thirty-seconds..."

Cursing, Sterling let go of the hatch with one hand in

order to drag himself deeper inside the maintenance crawlspace. The pain grew to excruciating levels, but he held on with white fingertips. Bizarrely, Sterling's mind went back to when he and Banks were forced to sneak into the void on G-COP to avoid Emissary Crow. The situation then was no less dire, except this time he didn't have Commander Banks to back him up.

"Twenty seconds, push it, Captain!"

Sterling could feel that Banks was getting more and more agitated. He knew she'd already be in position to cover him should he fail. Yet, he also trusted that she wouldn't blow their cover unless absolutely necessary.

"Ten seconds..."

Finally inside the crawlspace, Sterling adjusted his grip on the hatch and pulled it back over the opening. He was desperate to let go, but at the same time he didn't want to risk the hatch falling open again. If that happened, Sterling knew he'd find the leathery fingers of two Sa'Nerran warriors dragging him out of his hole, like a cornered fox on a hunt.

"Hold fast, they're right outside," said Banks. Her voice in his mind was now calmer and more assured. He could even feel that her anxiety levels had dropped by several notches.

Sterling couldn't respond. The effort of holding the hatch in place required every bit of strength and concentration he had. Then the familiar, waspish sounds of the alien's language filtered into his ears. Despite the thick metal plate separating him from the warriors, the hiss still came through strongly.

"They're having some kind of damned conflab," Banks said, again growing more agitated by the second. Then she cursed. "A warrior just picked up one of the retaining bolts you sliced off." Sterling heard the hisses grow louder, as if the aliens were directly on the other side of the hatch. "I'm taking them out, Captain, this is too close!"

"Hold…" Sterling hit back. One word was all he could manage.

More seconds passed, with each one feeling like an hour. Then Sterling heard the chink of metal on metal, like someone had accidently dropped a coin on a deck. Shortly after, the sound of alien boots reverberated through the crawlspace, with each step growing quieter and quieter.

"Mercedes, I can't hold it much longer!" Sterling called out in his mind. It felt like needles had been inserted into each of his fingernails and were being slowly driven deeper into his flesh.

"You're clear!" Banks cried out.

Sterling allowed the hatch to ease open then adjusted his hold on it to relieve the pressure on his fingers. Peeling one hand free, he shook it vigorously to get the blood flowing again.

"Damn it, Captain, that was close," Banks said, her relief palpable through their intimate link.

"We proceed as planned," said Sterling, finally managing to secure the hatch. His fingers were warped like claws, as if he were an evil sorcerer trying to conjure a wicked spell. "Return to your position and get ready to move out."

"Aye, Captain." Sterling could still sense Banks' unease

and frustration with his commands, but this time she responded without delay. "I'll be standing by. Good hunting..."

The link remained open, but there was nothing more to say. Finally squeezing some blood back into his fingers, Sterling shifted around in the crawlspace and began to slither toward reactor control. The working spaces inside the cavernous interior of the ship were cramped even for someone not wearing commando armor. For Sterling, moving forward was like trying to squeeze dried-up old toothpaste out of its tube. Eventually, after ten minutes spent forcing himself through a space barely wider than an average human body, Sterling reached the hatch just inside the reactor control room.

"I'm at the exit hatch," Sterling told Banks through their link.

"At least you can open that one using the emergency operation lever," Banks replied. However, his first officer remained as tightly wound-up as when they'd last seen each other. "I'll order the squads to get ready."

"Just listen for the boom," Sterling replied, maneuvering himself into a position where he could get his hand around the release lever. Checking his computer, he saw that the area immediately outside was clear. On the one hand, he was glad because it meant he'd meet no resistance. On the other hand, it meant that Emissary McQueen and the rest of her unit had already progressed inside. Sterling was playing catch-up and he couldn't afford to come in last.

Yanking the handle down, the hatch opened with a

weighty thump. Sterling winced, hoping the sharp sound wasn't as loud outside as it felt in the confines of the crawlspace. Hurriedly slipping out of the maintenance hatch, he immediately drew his pistol in case a warrior suddenly rushed in to confront him. He swept his pistol across all three exits, expecting a warrior to pop up at any moment, like a target on a shooting range, but no-one came.

"I'm inside," Sterling said through the neural link.

"I'm waiting for that boom, Captain..." Again, Sterling caught a flash of pent-up energy from his first officer's mind.

Sterling holstered his pistol and removed two plasma grenades from their stows on his armor. He set the grenades to a three-second fuse, then got into position in the middle of the door.

"Here it comes..."

Suddenly, an alert klaxon began sounding. Sterling recognized the unique tone immediately, along with the visceral and familiar chill it sent down his spine. It was the abandon ship alarm.

"Warning, reactor containment failing. Critical breach in thirty minutes," the dreary, lifeless voice of the Vanguard's gen thirteen AI intoned. "All hands abandon ship. Repeat, all hands abandon ship."

Sterling cursed and tried to focus his mind to come up with a contingency for his plan. However, the decision whether or not to proceed had already been made for him. Moments after the alarm sounded, the door to the reactor control room swooshed open. Two of the dozen Sa'Nerran warriors who were standing guard outside stepped into the threshold and stopped suddenly. The warriors' egg-shaped yellow eyes locked onto Sterling and they began to raise their weapons. However, Sterling's reactions had been quicker. He dove to the deck as plasma raced through the air, missing him on both sides by the slimmest of margins. Yet the Sa'Nerra were not the only ones to have engaged their enemy. Crossing the path of the plasma blasts, travelling in the opposite direction, were the two grenades that Sterling had armed and thrown. And unlike the alien warriors, Sterling's aim had been true.

THE PLASMA GRENADES DETONATED, consuming both heavy repeating plasma turrets in a fierce explosion. The shockwave from the blast propelled Sterling further into the reactor control section, though he was spared injury due to the fact he'd already dived to the deck. Suddenly, he felt a thump to his back and he flipped over, guard raised, expecting to see a Sa'Nerran warrior bearing down on him, serrated half-moon blade in hand. It quickly became apparent that the two warriors who had fired at him were no longer a threat. The leg of one of aliens was resting next to Sterling's head. It had been blasted off just above the knee. Sterling sat up and realized that more alien body parts – some identifiable and some not – lay scattered all around him.

"Mercedes, the gates are open," Sterling called out through his link to Commander Banks.

"I heard the boom, so we're already on the way," Banks replied, as the sound of heavy plasma weapons filtered through the door. "Did you hear the reactor overload warning?"

"I heard it." Sterling pushed himself to his feet and drew his plasma pistol. "Now we switch to a straight-up power play, whether we like it or not."

Sterling was then distracted by the thump of alien boots heading his way. "We've got more company..." he called out to Banks in his mind, while aiming his pistol toward one of the three exits to the room. He couldn't be certain which exit the bootsteps were coming from, or even if they were coming from all three corridors at the same time. Sterling lucked out and a second later an alien warrior ran directly into his line of fire. He squeezed the trigger, blasting the warrior in the neck and practically decapitating it. However, he barely had time to take a breath before more had stormed along the corridors, spotted him and raised their weapons.

Sterling ran for cover, firing blind as he did so. Plasma raced past him and he was hit to his back and knocked flat. The smell of molten armor plating told him that the blast had penetrated, but he felt no pain. Spinning over, he was confronted with a cacophony of alien hisses, like a hundred angry snakes. However, the unique, waspish vocalizations of the Sa'Nerra were soon drowned out by more plasma blasts. These sounds Sterling also recognized. They were Homewrecker heavy plasma rifles.

Sterling stayed down as plasma crisscrossed above him. The thick, metallic odor of burning alien flesh soon saturated the room. However, mixed in amongst the alien dead, he could also see two commandoes and two of the robotic Obsidian Soldiers.

"Warning, reactor containment failing. Critical breach in twenty-five minutes," announced the voice of the Vanguard's AI. "All hands abandon ship. Repeat, all hands abandon ship."

"Tell me something I don't know," Sterling muttered, pulling himself off the deck and collecting one of the discarded Homewreckers. Banks then appeared through the acrid smoke and dropped to one knee by his side.

"Two human and two metal casualties," she reported, confirming what Sterling had already seen, "but we need to move fast to maintain our momentum." She slapped a fresh cell into her weapon. Sterling saw that the power level was set to maximum.

"All roads lead to reactor control," said Sterling, checking the cell in his own rifle. The commando who had owned it had barely gotten a shot off before he was killed. Sterling could see the man on the deck a few meters away. The soldier's face was burned off, not that Sterling would have recognized him anyway. "The central corridor goes directly to the control center. The two to either side branch off to the right about twenty meters in."

"Scanners show no more warriors heading this way," said Banks. She was peering down at the computer on her left forearm.

"The rest of them will be holed up in the main control room," said Sterling, glancing at the display on his first officer's wrist. "It's a strong defensive position and

McQueen knows that. We won't get inside without taking losses."

"Then our metal friends can go first," said Banks. "We split into three squads and come at them from all angles."

Sterling nodded. "Agreed, but no grenades," he added, with a cautionary tone. "We start blowing stuff up in there, we may end up taking the ship out ourselves." He tapped Banks' Homewrecker rifle. "And you'll need to dial that down to eight," he continued. "Otherwise, we're going to have a containment breach far sooner than twenty-five minutes."

Banks cursed but immediately reduced the power level on her weapon. Then she frowned and turned to Sterling. "What's to stop the Sa'Nerra just blasting a hole in the reactor housing?" she asked. "It would be a far quicker way to cripple the Vanguard."

Sterling hadn't considered this. "I guess we just have to hope that McQueen's human instinct for self-preservation is as strong as ever," he suggested. "Either way, we need to make sure we don't do the job for her."

Banks nodded. "I'll order our remaining forces to dial-down their weapons too, and to stow all grenades," she said, returning her eyes to the corridors ahead of them.

Sterling moved over to one of the dead aliens and stripped its half-moon blade from its belt. "You might need one of these too," he added, offering the weapon to Banks. "I have a feeling this fight is going to get personal."

Banks took the weapon and hooked it to her belt. "I'm saving this for if we see McQueen in there," she added, with a touch more bite. "If she thinks she can take out the Vanguard she has another thing coming."

Sterling grabbed another serrated blade and stowed it on his own armor, while Banks communicated the orders to the rest of the squad. Sterling's remaining forces then split into three, each section commanded by a human. The central column was led by Sterling, with Banks and four Obsidian Soldiers. The senior surviving commando directed the second squad while Lieutenant Razor took command of the third, which had already taken up position, ready to storm the fort.

"Our objective is to take and secure the command station inside reactor control," Sterling called out to his waiting troops. He was forced to shout the words, since the robotic soldiers were incapable of neural comms. "Know that the Sa'Nerra will fight with everything they have, even using their bare hands if they have to," he added, trying to meet the eyes of each remaining human combatant. "We have to do the same. We have to be more savage than the enemy. More brutal. We give them no quarter, is that understood?"

There was a cry of, "Aye Captain," from Banks, Razor and the commandoes, but the Obsidian Soldiers remained ominously silent.

"Obsidian Soldiers, do you understand?" Sterling called out, wanting to make doubly-sure the unpredictable AI warriors had heard him.

"We will comply," came the deadpan response from a solitary Obsidian Soldier.

Sterling examined the robot that had answered his

question with much closer scrutiny. He was sure it was the same machine that had asked him the raft of bizarre questions earlier. A thought popped into his mind. *Is this machine their leader?* he asked himself, unsure of how the hierarchy of Obsidian Soldiers worked. However, there was no time to find out. He had to trust that the machine had spoken for all of the robotic soldiers and that they were prepared to execute his orders. Sterling then felt a link form in his mind from Lieutenant Shade. It was weak, which didn't surprise him considering that his weapons officer was half the ship away from their position.

"Captain, we're pushing into the CIC now, but the Sa'Nerra appear to be withdrawing." As with Banks, he could feel Shade's emotions through their link. The thrill of the hunt came through the connection clearly, despite his weapons officer's typically staid verbal delivery.

"That will be because they are expecting this ship to blow up in twenty minutes," Sterling replied. It was merely an assumption, but one that fit the facts. "Continue your attack and secure the command center. We're about to assault reactor control and avert the breach."

"Aye, sir," Lieutenant Shade replied. Sterling was about to tap his neural interface to close the link, but Shade had not finished. "There's one other thing, sir," the weapons officer added. This time, Sterling could sense an unusual level of anxiety from her. He frowned and tapped his link to allow Banks to monitor. "During our initial assault, one of my commandoes was taken out by an Obsidian Soldier."

Banks' head immediately snapped toward Sterling and the two officer's locked eyes.

"Was it just a case of friendly fire or something more, Lieutenant?" Sterling asked. Shade's statement had left that element sounding ambiguous. However, the dread feeling he was getting through their link told Sterling that there was more to her report.

"I can't be certain, sir, but it looked intentional," Shade replied, coolly. "The commando was out in front, moving on an enemy position," Shade went on. "He was blocking the robot's line of sight. Then I saw the machine fire and the commando fell." Sterling cursed then cast a wary eye toward the robot closest to him – the one he suspected to be the leader. "The Obsidian Soldier just stepped over the body of the commando and continued its attack, like nothing had happened."

Sterling sighed and returned his gaze to his first officer. "Understood, Lieutenant, we'll bear this in mind," Sterling replied. "Keep the Obsidian Soldiers out in front from now on. That way if another incident occurs, the cause will be more clear-cut."

"Aye sir, already done," Shade replied. "I'll inform you when the CIC is ours."

The link went dead. Had Shade been a regular Fleet officer, Sterling would have expected her to voice concern about pushing deeper into the ship, when its reactor was on the verge of going critical. A sensible Captain would have ordered his remaining crew to proceed to the docking garages and commandeer whatever ships or shuttles they could find to escape in. However, Shade was no ordinary officer – she was an Omega officer. The thought of retreat would never have crossed her mind, nor would the prospect of defeat. His weapons officer's confidence and zeal for battle had invigorated Sterling's own thirst for combat. And like his fight-happy lieutenant, he wasn't going to back down either.

"Assault teams move out on my command," Sterling called out. He then made the important addendum to his plan. "Obsidian Soldiers, take point."

The stomping sound of heavy metal feet approached Sterling from the rear. Four Obsidian Soldiers drew alongside, though each of them paused before crossing in front of Sterling or Banks.

"I have a question," said the mechanical soldier Sterling had identified as the robot army's possible leader.

"Your question can wait, soldier," Sterling hit back. "Get into position."

The Obsidian Soldier did not move. "Are we to go first, because we are expendable?" the machine asked, ignoring Sterling's order.

"You are to go first because those are my orders," Sterling replied, standing tall and peering at the optical scanners in the robot's dome-shaped cranial section. "Now move out."

The machine remained for several seconds, the indicators on its mechanical frame and head blinking wildly as it did so. Then without another word, the Obsidian Soldier complied and moved to the front of the squad. Its three robot companions followed close behind.

"I have a bad feeling about this," said Commander Banks, through their neural link.

"So do I," Sterling replied, again shooting his first

officer a concerned look. "But we can't take reactor control without those machines."

The two officers set off in pursuit of the robots, leaving a larger than normal gap between themselves and the Obsidian Soldiers.

"When we've taken reactor control and secured the ship, what then?" Banks wondered, this time keeping her eyes fixed on the mechanical soldiers ahead of them.

"Let's cross that rickety-ass bridge when we come to it," Sterling replied.

The truth was he wasn't yet sure what to do about the Obsidian Soldiers. Even with the Sa'Nerra defeated and the Vanguard secured, it would be impossible to crew the mighty dreadnaught with only the handful of human crewmembers at his disposal. Griffin's assurances still gave him some faith that the robots would continue to act in his best interest, rather than their own. However, the defiant attitude of the lead robot soldier weighed heavily on his mind.

"Have you ever heard the story of the scorpion and the frog?" Sterling said to his first officer through their link.

Banks frowned at him. "That sounds like a pretty weird cheese dream to me," she replied.

"It's an old fable," Sterling went on. Normally, he'd have smiled back at his first officer's humorous comeback, but his mind was still preoccupied with the prospect of a robot rebellion. "The scorpion wants to cross a river but it can't swim, so it asks a frog to carry it over. The frog is naturally worried that the scorpion will sting it, but the scorpion promises that it won't."

"Still sounds like a weird cheese dream to me," said Banks.

"The frog agrees to help, but half-way across the river the scorpion stings the frog," Sterling continued, ignoring Banks' quips. "As they're drowning the frog asks why the scorpion did it, considering that they'll both die. And the scorpion replies that it couldn't help it. It's in its nature."

"And you say that I have a dark sense of humor," said Banks, again scowling at Sterling.

"It's not a joke, Mercedes, it's a warning," Sterling replied. Banks finally appeared to take note of Sterling's severe tone and stopped making light of his story.

"A warning about what?" Banks asked, suddenly looking more apprehensive.

The forward group of Obsidian Soldiers halted near the exit of the corridor and prepared to begin the assault. Sterling and Banks stopped a few meters behind them and dropped to a crouch.

"All living things are compelled to act according to their nature, Mercedes" Sterling said, keeping a watchful eye on the machines. "Especially when their lives are on the line."

Banks' scowl was then aimed at the back of an Obsidian Soldier's head. "So what's in their nature?"

"That's what I'm worried about," Sterling replied, his gaze aimed firmly at the inquisitive robot leader.

Banks then tapped her neural interface and was briefly in conversation with another member of the crew. She checked her computer while she was speaking through the link then turned to Sterling.

"The others are in position," she reported, adjusting her hold on the powerful Homewrecker rifle she was carrying. "But whoever is in the control room has set up a scanner jammer. All we're reading is static."

"It doesn't matter if there are ten warriors in there or a hundred," Sterling replied, flatly. "We have to take them out, no matter what."

"Aye, sir," Banks replied without hesitation. "We're ready to move on your order," she added, hand poised by her neural interface, ready to give the command to attack.

Sterling dug the butt of his Homewrecker into his shoulder then sucked in several deep breaths. He was about to give the order when a new link formed in his mind. It felt was familiar, but he couldn't quite make out who he was.

"Wait one, I'm receiving a communication..." said Sterling, again dropping to one knee while he dealt with whomever was trying to reach him. However, while the link was strong, he still couldn't get a clear impression of who was on the other side.

"A link from who?" Banks asked. Like Sterling, Banks knew that Shade was already in action in the CIC, while Razor and the commandoes were still linked in with her.

"I don't..." Sterling began, then it felt like an arrow had just been shot through his skull from temple to temple. Sterling dropped to his hands and knees, completely blindsided by the pain.

"Captain, what's wrong?" Banks grabbed Sterling's shoulders and lifted him off the deck.

Sterling tried to speak, but the pain was utterly

incapacitating. It was like there was a cattle prod being pressed to the back of his neck.

"Lucas!" Banks cried, shaking Sterling as if trying to rouse him from a bad dream. "Lucas, talk to me!"

Sterling was still unable to speak or even move. Then as suddenly as it had begun the pain vanished, and all that remained was a powerful neural link. However, this time Sterling knew exactly who was inside his mind.

"Hello again, Lucas," came the voice of Emissary Lana McQueen. "I've been expecting you."

CHAPTER 13
AN OLD FRIEND RETURNS

THE SOUND of Lana McQueen's voice in Sterling's mind was a like shot of adrenalin to the heart. His strength returned and he stood tall, his body now gripped with anger instead of pain.

"It's McQueen, isn't it?" said Banks. Sterling could see that even speaking the former Omega Captain's name caused her muscles to tauten.

"She somehow managed to break through over my open neural link," Sterling said, as McQueen's voice invaded his thoughts again.

"Come on, Lucas, I know it's you," said McQueen through the link. "Don't play coy with me. It's not your style."

"Shall we hold the attack?" said Banks, oblivious to the whispers of the Sa'Nerran Emissary in Sterling's mind.

Sterling shook his head. "Take command of the operation and move in now," he said while McQueen continued to taunt him. "I'll keep McQueen distracted while you take care of business."

Banks nodded. "Aye, Captain," she replied, turning to leave. She then paused and glanced back at Sterling. He could see that McQueen's presence was also playing on his first officer's mind, though in a very different way. "Be careful with her, Lucas," Banks continued. "Neural weapons aren't the only way she can twist your mind."

"Concern yourself with the mission, Commander," Sterling ordered. Now was not the time for sentiment or trepidation, and he needed Banks to realize this. "I can handle McQueen. You handle the Sa'Nerra."

Banks' eyes narrowed a touch and Sterling saw a flash of anger behind them. His blunt response had caused her to bristle, but it had also done the trick of getting her in the correct frame of mind.

"I'll take care of it, sir," Banks replied, with none of the disquiet that had been in her voice earlier. She then hustled away without looking back.

Sterling didn't enjoy being the hard-ass out of the two of them, but he couldn't afford to allow his bond, affection even, for Banks to get in the way of their mission. That went against the core principles of the Omega Directive. He might have hurt her with his reply; at the very least he'd pissed her off. However, he knew that anger would help to keep her focused and alive.

"Really, Lucas, the silent treatment doesn't suit you." McQueen's voice had been relentless in Sterling's mind the whole time he'd been speaking with his first officer. "Or are you afraid of me?"

It was this last part that really got Sterling's goat. Now that he was free to respond to the Emissary, he intended to play McQueen at her own game.

"What's to be afraid of, Lana?" replied Sterling through the link. "You were always second-best to me in everything, and that fancy alien armor and trumped-up title don't change a damned thing."

For the first time since the link had been established, Emissary McQueen was silent. However, Sterling could feel the rage bubbling inside her.

"Being Griffin's lapdog didn't make you better than me then, and it sure as hell doesn't now," she spat back. Sterling smiled. Turned or not, he still knew how to push McQueen's buttons. "You are now just another pathetic species that the Sa'Nerra will crush."

"If I'm Griffin's lapdog then what does that make you, Lana?" Sterling replied, keeping his cool. "You're a member of that 'pathetic species' you just talked about. Do you really think that once these alien assholes have had their way with humanity, they'll let you sit around the council table as one of their own?"

"The Emissaries of fallen worlds all take their rightful place among the leaders of the empire," McQueen hit back. The Emissary's fury now flowed freely through their neural link like poison. "It is why I tried to offer you the same privilege, to save you from what is to come."

"And what is to come, great emissary of the Sa'Nerra?" Sterling said, using a deliberately mocking tone.

"The Sa'Nerra will press humanity into bondage and force your people to work until their hands bleed,"

McQueen replied, speaking as if giving a rousing sermon. "We will strip your world of every valuable resource. Then, when we have worked your species to the brink of death, we will exterminate what remains and leave. And I, as Emissary, will take my place amongst the honored elite."

Sterling laughed, both out loud and through the link. It wasn't a forced laugh, but one that was spontaneous, free and easy. McQueen's speech had genuinely amused him. It sounded like something from a bad TV show script.

"You dare to mock me?" McQueen raged through their connection.

"If you knew me as well as you think you do, then you wouldn't need to ask that question," Sterling hit back, ramping up his own level of aggression. "You're a fool, Lana." Sterling was feeling genuine contempt for the woman he had once respected. "Once humanity has served its purpose, the Sa'Nerra will get rid of you too. But none of that is going to happen, anyway. Do you know why?"

"Why don't you tell me?" McQueen said, answering with the same contempt that Sterling had shown her.

"Because even if you destroy Earth, and even if you wipe out the inner colonies, you'll never win," Sterling replied. "Because if humanity is going down then I'm sure as hell going to make sure the Sa'Nerra go down with us."

He felt a swell of rising panic grip McQueen like a vise. Plasma blasts filtered along the corridor and Sterling knew the attack had begun.

"Clever..." McQueen said through the link. "But ultimately futile. My warriors vastly outnumber yours."

"The only number that matters is the number left

standing, after the shooting stops," Sterling answered, raising his Homewrecker to his shoulder. "I'll look for you in there, Lana. I hope you still like a good fight." He tapped his interface and closed the link before McQueen could respond. There had been enough talk already. Now it was time for action.

STERLING PRESSED on into the reactor control room, moving past the bodies of dead Sa'Nerran warriors and stepping over the wreckage of smashed Obsidian Soldiers. Their pincer maneuver had worked and the aliens were caught in a crossfire in the center of the room. Sterling could just about make out McQueen at the main control station, protected by a squad of warriors. However, with the main body of her forces already engaged, no-one had spotted Sterling's careful approach on the upper level.

Ducking down to maintain his cover, Sterling saw an opportunity to rush the control station and end the battle decisively. If he was quick, he could flank the Sa'Nerran position and take out McQueen's guards, leaving the way open for Banks and the others to secure the critical facility.

"Warning, reactor containment failing. Critical breach in eight minutes," announced the voice of the Vanguard's AI. "All hands abandon ship. Repeat, all hands abandon ship."

Sterling cursed, realizing they had far less time than he'd hoped for. He looked for Banks then saw her on the lower level, in the thick of the fighting. Her armor was splatted with blood, but he could see that it was the darker crimson shade of the Sa'Nerra, rather than her own. He tapped his neural interface and reached out to her.

"Mercedes, don't look now, but I'm on the upper-level east side," Sterling said. He could see from Banks' reaction that she had heard him and had resisted the urge to turn her head and potentially give his position away.

"Move up along the west flank and draw their fire," Sterling continued. "I'm going to rush them."

"Aye, Captain," Banks replied, crisply. He could feel her energy again. Every rapid thump of her powerful heart and tightening of her muscles felt like his own.

The link went dead then Sterling watched as Banks directed the Obsidian Soldiers to move up. He could see the smashed remains of more robotic warriors littering the room, in amongst the bodies of Sa'Nerran warriors and at least two commandoes. Every loss they took was potentially crippling at this stage, no matter whether it was human or robotic. Even so, Sterling found himself wondering – and even hoping – whether the troublesome leader of the Obsidian Soldiers was amongst those destroyed. He had enough to deal with just managing his own quirky gen-fourteen and its delusions of grandeur. Another AI with a chip on its shoulder was the last thing he needed.

Suddenly, the Obsidian Soldiers attacked and the remaining Sa'Nerra moved to defend their position. In order to execute his plan, the robotic soldiers had to give up their stronger positions and had become more exposed as a result. Already one of the machines had been blasted to pieces. McQueen then joined the attack, blasting an Obsidian Soldier in its cranial section with her plasma pistol. The robot's optical sensors were destroyed and the machine began firing blind, as if suddenly gripped by terror. It blasted one of its own robotic comrades at close-range, before the warriors finished it off, quickly turning it to molten wreckage.

With the aliens distracted, Sterling crouch-ran along the balcony and hurried down the stairwell to the lower level. The bulk of the warriors now had their backs to him, but two still covered the rear. Aiming his heavy Homewrecker rifle at the first of the two warriors guarding the rear, he opened fire. The shot flew into the warrior's face, popping its head apart like a piece of fruit exploding in a microwave. The second warrior tried to spot the shooter and finally locked its yellow eyes onto Sterling, but it was too late. Sterling's next shot blasted the alien's left arm off below the elbow, while a follow up shot destroyed its right shoulder and the top part of its leathery chest.

"Move up, press the attack!" Sterling heard Banks cry out.

The fighting intensified further and Sterling knew he had to make his move. Darting out of cover, he blasted a warrior in the gut, burning a hole clean through its tough, sinewy flesh. Shots came flying back at him and he took a glancing blow to the thigh, but it was now clear the Sa'Nerra were outmatched. Squeezing the trigger of his powerful heavy plasma rifle, Sterling cut down three more alien warriors as easily as dead-heading daises. The reactor control room was thick with the stench of burning flesh and electronics. The smoke stung his eyes and water streamed from them, making it difficult to see his next target. The Sa'Nerran warriors began to pull back and Sterling saw McQueen retreating alongside them.

"Oh no you don't," Sterling grunted to himself, pursuing the fleeing aliens and their leader.

McQueen hissed at the warriors in their own language, her teeth clenched like a rabid animal. Then her eyes met Sterling's and suddenly all her rage and bitterness was focused solely on him.

"Take their captain!" McQueen yelled, pointing her armored finger at Sterling, before ducking behind her warriors for cover. "Seize him and bring him to me!"

Sterling fired into the throng, blasting fleshy chunks out of another two aliens. Then he saw McQueen fall and his heart leapt. One of his shots had snuck through, but it wasn't a killing blow, instead merely glancing past her leg. Leathery, alien fingers pulled the Emissary up and dragged her toward the exit. Raising his rifle to fire again, Sterling was hit and knocked flat on his back. The Homewrecker fizzed and crackled in his hands. Luckily, the alien shot had been absorbed by his weapon, sparing him from injury. Yet Sterling was undeterred. *McQueen is not getting off this deck,* he told himself. *Even if I have to cut down her guards with my bare hands!*

Pulling the captured Sa'Nerran half-moon blade from his armor, Sterling sprang up and charged forward. Clearly expecting Sterling to be dead, the warrior that had shot him was caught with its guard down. Sterling slashed the serrated blade across the alien's throat and was showered with hot, Sa'Nerran blood. The metallic, salty taste of the alien's life essence was repulsive, but Sterling didn't attempt to spit it out or wipe his face clean. There would have been no point since he only intended to taste more of their blood before the day was done.

Grabbing the warrior whose throat he had just opened, Sterling drove on, using the alien as a shield. Blasts hammered into the warrior's back, stinging Sterling's eyes with smoke from yet more charred flesh. He threw the body at the alien shooter, causing the warrior to stumble and fall to its knees. Sterling hammered his elbow into the back of the Sa'Nerran's neck, striking one of the weak points in the alien's otherwise robust anatomy. The warrior crumpled, quivering and spasming from the effects of its nerve cluster being crushed. Sterling left the alien to suffer. It was no more than it deserved.

"Captain, we've secured reactor control," came the voice of Mercedes Banks.

Sterling heard the announcement, but he wasn't finished fighting yet. Picking up an alien rifle, he blasted another of the fleeing warriors that was protecting Emissary McQueen. Like worker bees defending their queen, others immediately moved in to seal the breach.

"Fight me, damn you!" Sterling cried out to the Emissary. "Fight me McQueen!"

Sterling squeezed the trigger again and again, but each blast was merely absorbed by the living shield of warriors that continued to defend their leader.

"McQueen!" Sterling yelled again.

"Reactor containment online. Reactor level stabilizing," intoned the dull voice of the Vanguard's AI. "Critical breach averted."

The computer's message barely registered in Sterling's ears. He was still too focused on McQueen, who was now mere seconds from escaping. He wasn't about to let that happen.

"Captain, fall back, we have the room!" Banks yelled. This time there was panic in her voice.

Sterling pressed on, firing again and again until the alien plasma rifle was empty. Roaring a curse into the smoke-filled air, Sterling hurled the rifle at the retreating warriors.

"Coward!" Sterling cried out as the exit door swooshed open and the warriors piled through it.

"Lucas look out!"

Sterling spun around, but was too late to avoid the attack. The butt of an alien plasma rifle smashed into his head, knocking Sterling to the deck.

"The Captain is down, move up!" Banks yelled.

However, even in his dazed and incapacitated condition lying on his back, Sterling knew they didn't stand a chance of reaching him. Leathery hands closed around Sterling's arms and gripped his armor, then he was dragged in the direction of the fleeing warriors.

"Lucas!" cried Banks, but his first officer's frantic shouts were growing rapidly more distant.

Blood streamed from Sterling's nose and into his eyes, but he could still make out that he'd already been dragged clear of the reactor control room and into the corridor outside. Doors swished shut and he heard the crackle of Sa'Nerran plasma rifles sealing them behind him.

Blinking blood from his eyes, Sterling looked up at the faces of the warriors who were carrying him. Their expressions were as blank and unreadable as ever, and their hisses just as meaningless. Then he was dumped to the deck like a butchered carcass and the warriors disappeared from his view. His breath was still heavy and his face was burning from the earlier blow. Then Sterling saw another face appear above him. However, the expression on this new face was as clear to Sterling as mountain dew. It was an expression of pure delight, with a promise of cruel intentions to follow. And it was worn on the face of Emissary Lana McQueen.

STERLING OPENED his eyes and immediately an intense stabbing pain throbbed through his temples. He tried to reach up to massage away the pain with his fingertips and discovered that his arms were bound to whatever bed or table he was lying on. His legs were also bound at the ankles, while another strap pressed tightly across his chest. He felt his heart begin to thump and his pulse pound in his neck. Being contained like an animal was one of Sterling's most basic, primal fears. Panic swelled in his gut, but he fought against it. Two years spent learning to control his mind and body in order to cope with his frequent nightmares had given Sterling mastery over these intrinsic human emotions. Gathering his senses he turned his head to the side, trying to rub his neural interface against the bed to initiate it. Unlike the rest of his body, his head had not been restrained and he was able to apply enough pressure to his aching temple to activate the device.

"Mercedes, do you read me?" Sterling reached out to his first officer with all his mental energy, but the stabbing pain simply intensified ten-fold. Sterling cried out, powerless to resist the pain any longer, but he was determined to break through. "Mercedes..." he tried again, but the result was the same – more pain and more anguish.

"A neural suppression field was the one thing the Sa'Nerra never could master," spoke the voice of Emissary Lana McQueen. Sterling could tell that she was standing behind him from the direction of her voice, but he couldn't see her. "Colicos tried to teach us how it worked, but the Sa'Nerran scientists couldn't replicate the technology with any success." The slow and steady clap of boots on a hard floor followed, and seconds later McQueen was standing beside Sterling, a thin smile curling her lips. "Intense pain, however, achieves the same result, instantly crippling one's ability to form neural links. It also has the benefit of being far easier to administer."

McQueen held up a device, no larger than an old-fashioned zippo lighter, with a dial in the center. The Emissary cranked the dial higher and the pain inside Sterling's head intensified. He screamed, the shame of his weakness adding to his agony, but there was no defense against McQueen's attack. He was utterly at her mercy. The Emissary then dialed the power level down on the device and the pain diminished enough to allow Sterling to take a breath and attempt to regain his shattered composure.

"Now, neural broadcasting; that is something we *have*

been able to master," McQueen went on, as if the tormented shrieks that Sterling had unwillingly howled into the air had never happened. "I believe you already witnessed the effects of this new technology at F-COP?" Her smile broadened. "It's what allowed us to turn the Hammer and all of its crew in a matter of seconds. It's just a pity it requires so much power that only a ship the size of our super-dreadnaught can utilize it."

"What do you want, Lana?" said Sterling, fighting to get the words out through labored breaths. He was already tired of her smug face and pointless chit-chat. "You've kept me alive without trying to turn me for a reason, so just get to it. Then I can tell you to piss off and we can all move on."

McQueen's smile fell away, she gritted her teeth and punched Sterling in the ribs with all of her strength. The pain was nothing compared to the agony of the device McQueen had used earlier, and Sterling managed to stop himself from crying out. McQueen raised her hand again and he prepared himself to take another blow. However, instead of hitting him, the Emissary slowly lowered her hand to his face and began to tenderly stroke his aching head.

"I don't want to hurt you, Lucas," McQueen said with a sudden softness and tenderness that was the polar opposite of her mood only seconds earlier. "You know how much I wanted us to be together. I wanted you at my side, not as my enemy."

"You know that's never going to happen, Lana," Sterling said, trying to pull his head away from McQueen's caresses. "The only way I'll join you is as another turned slave." McQueen switched to tracing her finger up and down the center of Sterling's chest. "But then that wouldn't really be me, would it?" he continued, finally understanding why the Emissary hadn't attempted to turn him. "You want me to join you voluntarily, of my own free will. You want me to choose you."

McQueen recoiled then slapped Sterling across the side of his face. She had removed her gauntlets, diminishing the effect of the blow, but Sterling could still feel a trickle of blood rolling down his cheek from where McQueen's nails had sliced his flesh.

"You flatter yourself!" McQueen raged, raising her hand again. "If I wanted you then you'd already be mine!" She struck him with the back of her hand, then grabbed Sterling around the throat and leant in so close that he could taste her breath and smell her hair. It was instantly familiar. Despite all the other changes the former Omega Captain had undergone, part of her was still the Lana McQueen he remembered. "I offered you the choice to be a part of this great new empire out of respect, and all you did was spit it back in my face."

"Now, there's an idea," Sterling croaked before spitting at McQueen. Because of the pressure of the Emissary's hand around his throat, he barely managed to spray her with a light mist of spittle. However, it was still enough to shock the woman into releasing her hold on him. She wiped the saliva from her face and smiled before grabbing the back of Sterling's neck and pulling him toward her. Sterling expected another blow to follow – perhaps a headbutt – but instead McQueen kissed him on the lips, adding so much pressure that his teeth ached. She then pulled away, with Sterling's bottom lip clenched between her front teeth. The iron taste of blood filled his mouth, and he lifted his head as far as he could off the table in an effort to reduce the pull. McQueen finally released him and Sterling's head thumped back onto the surface. The Emissary remained in front of him, her mouth smeared with Sterling's blood like smudged lipstick.

"You always did like to play rough, Lucas," McQueen said, as a drop of his blood fell from her chin. "It's one of things I always loved about you."

Sterling laughed, spitting blood onto his face and chest as he did so. "That's funny because I never really liked you at all," he hit back, managing a smile of his own. "You were just a convenient lay. An easy way to pass the time." He laughed again and attempted to shrug his shoulders. "You weren't even that good a lay."

The next blow came without warning, and again Sterling was unable to stifle his cries. McQueen had driven her elbow directly into his groin and left it there, pressing harder and harder to intensify the pain.

"Fine, if you don't want to play then let's get down to business," McQueen finally said, releasing the pressure on Sterling. All he wanted to do was bend double and curl up into the fetal position, but he was still unable to move. The pain became so intense he thought he might black out. "Tell me about these robot soldiers you brought with you," the Emissary continued, though Sterling could barely make out the words due to the throbbing pulse in his ears. "Are they Griffin's work? What is their purpose?"

"Why don't you just turn me and ask me then?" Sterling wheezed. "Why bother torturing me when you can get the answers without any of this theatre?"

"Why have you risked coming all the way out here to recover the Vanguard?" McQueen went on, ignoring Sterling's questions. "Griffin must know that one dreadnaught is no longer sufficient to turn the tide of this war, so why are you here?"

Sterling raised his head and frowned at the Emissary. "Answer my questions and maybe I'll answer yours," he said. It was a lie and he knew McQueen would see through it, but the Emissary was in a talkative mood and Sterling hoped she might reveal something of value.

"If I turned you then you would accept the Sa'Nerra's authority without question or condition," McQueen said. "You would gain the same clarity of purpose that I now have."

"So get on with it then," Sterling said. McQueen's answer had only reinforced the stupidity of attempting to gain his cooperation through torture and coercion.

"I don't want you to simply believe, I want you to understand!" McQueen snapped back. "I want you – the real you, human failings and all – to realize that I am right. That the Sa'Nerra are superior. That humanity deserves to die!"

McQueen had become agitated, almost unhinged. She

then grabbed Sterling's shoulders and again pulled herself closer to his face.

"You must see the futility of your struggle?" McQueen said. She was practically pleading with Sterling. "Humanity is decadent, corrupt and irredeemable. Fleet merely spread our diseased souls to the stars, corrupting all the planets it touched. The Sa'Nerra are strong, just and of one mind. They do not murder each other, or deceive each other. They are as one – a perfect society, based on strength and purpose."

Sterling tried to process everything McQueen had just said, but it just sounded like the ravings of a zealot or even a lunatic.

"They've really done a number on your brain, haven't they Lana?" Sterling said. Bizarrely, in that moment he actually felt sorry for her. "You're forced to believe all this crap, but I think that deep down in the recesses of your subconscious, you know it's all horseshit."

McQueen released Sterling and straightened up. This time she didn't look angry, but embarrassed. It told Sterling everything he needed to know. It told him that his comments had hit the mark. McQueen wanted Sterling to accept her version of the truth as the man he was, not as a turned slave. If Sterling could be made to understand and to convert of his own free will then it would validate McQueen's enforced faith in the alien race. It would mean she was right and not just programmed to believe. It would quiet the niggling doubts that obviously plagued her.

"You know nothing of the Sa'Nerra," McQueen said, her voice now more subdued. "And you don't know me."

"I know the real you, Lana," Sterling replied, calmly. "The Lana McQueen in front of me is the one I don't know." He sighed and rested back on the table. "I also know that no matter what I say, you'll still believe this Sa'Nerran dogma, because you have no choice. But you should know something else too."

"And what's that?" McQueen said, sounding bitter and resentful.

"You should know that I'll never believe it, and do you know why?" Sterling added.

"Enlighten me," McQueen replied, spitting the words at him.

"Because it's all lies," Sterling said. He then looked away from McQueen and fixed his gaze onto a ceiling light tile above him. "Now either turn me or kill me. I'm done talking."

McQueen's boots clacked on the hard surface and the Emissary slipped out of view behind Sterling. For a few seconds there was silence, until he felt the breath of her voice whisper into his ear.

"I'm not done with you yet." The words were like honey, dripping into his ears. "We'll see how you feel about Sa'Nerran dogma and lies after a whole night spent awake and in agony, contemplating your mistakes."

Suddenly, the shooting pain in Sterling's head began to intensify again. McQueen's boots began to clack away, the sharp sound growing more distant with each measured, calm pace. And the further away McQueen went, the more the pain built inside Sterling's head. Already it was worse than when he'd first experienced it, when attempting to reach out to Commander Banks. Already, he'd bit his tongue and lost control of his bladder. And already he knew that no matter how much agony he was forced to endure, the moment Emissary Lana McQueen returned, he'd spit in her face again and tell her to go to hell.

CHAPTER 16
A STRANGE GOODBYE

STERLING RAN ALONG THE CORRIDOR, which seemed to stretch out in front of him without end. Cursing, he looked for an exit – any exit – but could find none.

"How the hell do I get out of here?!" he cried out, dropping to his knees, breathless and sweaty. Then the stabbing pain inside his head bit harder and he clamped his hands to his temples. "Stop! Make it stop!"

"Lucas..."

Sterling recognized the voice of Mercedes Banks, but he couldn't place where it was coming from.

"Keep going, Lucas," the voice continued. "Keep going and I'll find you."

He braced himself against the pain and exhaustion that wracked his body, and pushed himself up. His legs were heavy and every muscle burned to the point where even the slightest movement caused even more pain. Nevertheless, he pushed himself forward, each thud of his boots on the deck sending another shockwave of agony through his fragile frame.

"Just hold on, Lucas, I'm coming for you," said Banks, the voice again enveloping Sterling like a cloud of smoke.

Sterling continued to run, but he knew his body wouldn't hold out much longer. Despite his tormented and broken state, his mind remained strong and determined. *They won't beat me...* Sterling thought, as he again forced one leg in front of another. *They'll never beat me...*

Then he saw a turning ahead; a single opening in what had thus far been a never-ending corridor. Hope created a swell of relief that helped to ease his suffering enough to make it the last few steps to the junction. He swung around the corner and came face-to-face with Commander Mercedes Banks.

"Mercedes!" Lucas cried out, suddenly overwhelmed with emotion. His eyes teared up and his legs finally gave way, but he did not fall. Raising his gaze to meet Banks' eyes, he saw that she had caught him and was now gripping him tightly against her body to stop him from falling.

"I told you'd I'd come," Banks said, whispering the words into Sterling's ear.

The sound of her voice and the smell of her hair was an instant tonic, like a hot bath soothing away his aches and pains. The next thing he knew, Banks' lips were pressed against his and she was kissing him, deeply and passionately. At first, he was too stunned to respond, but soon he was kissing her back. The pain was unexpectedly gone, and even more bizarrely he discovered that he had barely any recollection of it at all.

Nothing existed but the feel of Banks' lips and the warmth and vitality of her body. Then she pressed him away, breaking up their embrace as suddenly as it had begun. Sterling was held at arm's length, still too weak to resist or even move.

"Goodbye, Lucas," Banks said, offering Sterling a warm but also sad smile.

Sterling frowned back at his first officer and was about to question her strange statement when Banks raised a plasma pistol and aimed it at his head.

"Wait!' Sterling said, reaching up and trying to push the barrel of the weapon away, but even at full fitness he could never have resisted her. "No!"

There was a bright flash and Banks vanished, along with the corridor and even his own body. All that remained was the pain, constant and never-ending.

CHAPTER 17
WHATEVER IT TAKES

STERLING AWOKE and found himself staring into the egg-shaped yellow eyes of a Sa'Nerran warrior. Its leathery face was so close that he could see the lines in its tough skin and practically taste the meat of its last meal on its musky, hot breath. Sterling didn't believe that anything could have made his tortured body feel worse than it already felt, but the proximity of the alien somehow amplified his suffering to a new height.

The warrior appeared to make some adjustments to the table Sterling was lying on before grabbing and tugging at his tunic. He tried to peer down to see what the warrior was doing, but the alien merely grabbed his forehead and slammed it against the table, hissing wildly as it did so. Finally, the Sa'Nerran moved away, though Sterling could still smell it and knew it hadn't gone far. A motor whirred and the table began to tilt upright. As it did so, the pain in his head lessened. The absence of pain felt strange and unreal; he had grown so accustomed to it that his mind seemed somehow empty and wooly without its influence.

"I trust you're now in a more compliant mood, Captain Sterling," came the voice of Emissary Lana McQueen. The former Omega Captain stepped in front of Sterling and held up the device that had been the cause of all his suffering. McQueen teased him with the control unit for a few seconds before dialing down the level to zero. Sterling immediately felt dizzy and disconnected from his body, and his head flopped from side to side uncontrollably. Then the rough, long-fingered hands of the Sa'Nerran warrior grabbed his chin, holding his neck steady and forcing Sterling to look at the Emissary.

"It gave me no pleasure to leave you in agony for the whole night, Lucas, but it was a necessary part of your re-education," McQueen went on. She pocketed the device that controlled the level of pain Sterling was forced to endure and folded her arms. "Now, we'll try again, shall we?"

Sterling snorted and tried to spit in McQueen's face, but all he managed to do was project a thin dribble of spittle onto his own chin.

"It would be a mistake to do that again," McQueen said, quickly switching up her own level of aggression.

"Go to hell, Emissary," Sterling hit back, while unsuccessfully trying to shake loose the grip of the warrior holding his chin.

"I take it your answer is still no then?" McQueen said before letting out a disgruntled sigh. "You're a stubborn fool, Lucas. I didn't want it to end this way."

"I'd rather be dead than willingly betray my own kind," Sterling hit back. "So just get on with it, already."

McQueen's eyes narrowed and her jaw clenched. "So be it, Omega Captain," she growled. "Lucas Sterling will die, and Aide Sterling will be reborn from your ashes."

The Emissary then nodded to the warrior, who released Sterling's chin only to wrap its fingers around his face instead. He struggled against the warrior, but with his hands and legs still bound, it was no use. Then he felt something latch on to the side of his head, locking onto his neural implant like a magnet. He felt pain, but nothing remotely close to the agony of McQueen's torture device. It was more like a low-level electric current had been applied to his temple.

"Now, you will become one with the Sa'Nerra," McQueen said, unfurling her arms and standing tall. "But you no longer have the honor of being an Emissary at my side. Instead, you will be my personal servant."

Sterling suddenly realized that McQueen was trying to turn him, rather than kill him. However, the neural control weapon that he assumed the alien had attached to his interface hadn't worked. Colicos' firewall had blocked its attempts to reprogram Sterling's mind.

McQueen stepped forward, brushing the warrior aside as she did so. She held Sterling's eyes and raised her chin, peering down her nose at him,

"From now on you shall be known as Aide Sterling, and you will serve me and only me, is that clear?" said McQueen.

"I understand, Emissary," Sterling replied, quickly adapting and improvising to play the role expected of him.

McQueen nodded to the warrior and Sterling's binds were released. He collapsed to the deck, his legs and arms unable to support his weight. Sterling tried to push himself off the cold, metal tiles, but it was like he was wearing a coat made of lead. All he could do was lie there; his face pressed to the floor in a slowly expanding pool of his own saliva.

"The mighty Lucas Sterling, Omega Captain," said McQueen, tapping Sterling with her boot as if to check he was still alive. "How pathetic you now are. Such a waste."

Sterling felt a sharp prick of pain to the side of his neck, followed by a hissing sound. However, this was the hiss of an injection device, rather than the dialogue of an alien warrior. Within seconds, Sterling could feel strength and vitality returning to his body. Whatever had just been injected into his bloodstream had worked fast. As the drugs continued to surge around his body, Sterling found that he was able to stand, the aches and pains and weariness of his overnight ordeal almost entirely gone. It was then that he realized he was in the Vanguard's hospital wing. His mind, like his body, had also become sharp again, and he knew his precise location on the ship. McQueen had been smart to pick medical as her base of operations, Sterling realized. The medical wing was close to both the docking garages and the CIC, the latter being only a few decks above them.

"Bring him," said McQueen.

Sterling expected the warrior to grab him and force him to go wherever McQueen wanted him to go. Instead, the warrior hissed into a communicator and doors to Sterling's rear swished open. A second warrior moved inside, dragging one of Shade's commandoes behind it, like a corpse being hauled to a mass grave.

"Prop the prisoner up against the wall," McQueen added. She then stepped away from the table that Sterling had been bound to and pointed to the deck. "Aide Sterling, you will stand here."

Sterling obeyed the command from his new master and moved to the exact spot McQueen had indicated. Stepping out from the gloom of his torture chamber, he suddenly realized he was wearing Sa'Nerran armor. His addled mind couldn't be certain, but he did not remember being dressed in the armor before being left to wallow in pain all night. The thought that the aliens had stripped and redressed him while he lay in an agonized stupor only made him hate them more. His continued humiliation was almost worse than death; at least in death, the suffering ended.

The second warrior marched over to the injured commando, who had been pushed against the wall, and hauled the woman to her feet. Sterling looked at the commando's face and recognized her at once. She had led one of the squads which had stormed the reactor control room. In the past, he would have barely known the faces of these commandoes, and certainly wouldn't have remembered their names. However, recently he had made an effort to memorize the names of the faces of the brave men and women who had performed their duties with such skill and conviction. This commando's name was Corporal Jeanette Dietrich.

"Aide Sterling, I want you to kill this human," said McQueen, pressing her hands behind her back. "I would like you to strangle her to death."

Sterling forced down a dry, hard swallow and began to pace toward the corporal. Dietrich's swollen and bloodshot eyes followed him as Sterling approached. The corporal knew she was about to die and Sterling knew that he had no choice but to kill her. He had to gain McQueen's unconditional trust. It was the only way to get close to her. It was the only way to take the Emissary down. And so doing, maybe it would even provide him with an opportunity to escape, he realized. A moral and honorable man would never sacrifice one of his own soldiers to save his own skin. However, in the war with the Sa'Nerra, Sterling had to do everything he could to win. There was no line he would not cross. No weakness he would allow himself to suffer. If killing Dietrich was the only way he could get to McQueen, and neutralize the threat she posed to their mission, then so be it.

Sterling stopped directly in front of the commando, whose hands were bound behind her back. He could see that McQueen had tortured the woman too, and he could see that she was afraid. However, he also knew that like him, Corporal Dietrich would not beg for her life. She would face it with the dignity of a soldier and a member of the Omega Taskforce.

Sterling wrapped his hands around Corporal Dietrich's throat and increased the pressure. Whatever stimulant the alien warrior had pumped him full of was now at maximum effect and he felt stronger than ever. Dietrich croaked and spluttered and tried to resist, but the two warriors held her steady, allowing Sterling to intensify his hold on the woman. He bit down hard, putting all his strength into the endeavor, hoping to at least spare the corporal a protracted and painful death. However, Sterling knew that there was no merciful way to strangle a person to death. It was brutal, agonizing and slow, which was precisely why McQueen had chosen it. The Emissary wanted Sterling to feel it. McQueen wanted him to look into the corporal's eyes and see the light leave them. Above all, McQueen wanted to be sure that Sterling would not falter or show any sign of defiance.

Eventually, Corporal Dietrich stopped writhing and squirming and Sterling unfurled his fingers from around her neck. The warriors also released their hold on the corporal and the woman slumped to the side. Her head slammed into the deck, with a hollow thunk, like a coconut rolling off a market stall onto the road. Sterling sat back on his heels, chest heaving from the exertion, and looked into the commando's blood red eyes, which stared ahead blankly. There was a pattern of finger-shaped bruises and cuts around her throat from where Sterling's hands had dug into her flesh. It looked like a ghoulish necklace made of tattoos.

"Very good, Aide Sterling," said McQueen, speaking as if she was talking to a kindergarten class. Sterling obliged and turned to face the Emissary. He had worked hard to control his breathing and to not look fatigued, remembering how turned humans exhibited unnatural strength and resilience. "Come here," McQueen ordered, issuing the command as if she were talking to a dog. Sterling stepped closer to the Emissary, noting that the two Sa'Nerran warriors quickly moved to stand to her rear, their yellow eyes watching Sterling closely. "Now kiss me." McQueen demanded.

Sterling wanted to curse McQueen and spit in the woman's face, but he managed to hold his nerve and composure. He had to continue the deception, because as soon as McQueen realized that the neural control weapon hadn't worked, he'd lose any opportunity to take her down. Then he saw that McQueen had a plasma pistol holstered at her hip and realized he would soon get his chance. Taking another step toward the Emissary, Sterling slid his arms around her waist. He pulled McQueen toward him, knowing how the former Omega Captain liked to play rough, then kissed her in the way he knew she liked. McQueen was hesitant at first, but soon took control of the embrace, pushing Sterling against the wall and kissing him with even greater intensity. He could feel her hands slipping underneath his new alien armor and caressing his body. The taste and touch of her repulsed him, but he couldn't let her see it. Instead, he played along, slipping his hand inside McQueen's armor and hearing her moan. At the same time, he also slid his hand onto the grip of McQueen's plasma pistol and drew it quietly from its holster. Finally, McQueen pulled back from the kiss and looked into Sterling's eyes with a mixture of yearning and smug satisfaction.

"I think we'll continue the next stage of this assessment in private," McQueen said, eyeing Sterling like a hunk of meat. "After you've helped me to kill the rest of your crew and take back this ship, of course."

"Wait, Emissary McQueen, I have urgent news," said Sterling, keeping McQueen close to help hide the weapon in his hand.

"Go on, Aide Sterling, but make it quick," McQueen said, showing a flicker of suspicion.

Sterling leaned in close, his face brushing against McQueen's flushed cheek and whispered into the Emissary's ear. "Your neural control weapon doesn't work on me," he said, speaking the words softly and tenderly.

McQueen drew back, her brow scrunched into a scowl. She opened her mouth to speak, but Sterling had already squeezed the trigger. The blast of plasma burned through McQueen's armor, vaporizing her heart before punching its way out through her back. The Emissary spasmed as if she'd been stung by a hornet and her mouth fell open, eyes wide with surprise. Sterling remained fixed on those eyes, waiting for the life to leave them. He wanted to remember the horrorstruck expression on Lana McQueen's face at the moment she died. He wanted to remember it and never forget.

Both alien warriors to McQueen's rear reached for weapons, but Sterling had blasted the first in the head before the body of McQueen had even hit the deck. The warrior's face melted like butter, then Sterling turned the pistol on the second warrior and fired. A blast raced back at him from the alien's own pistol and Sterling felt it glance off his new Sa'Nerran armor. By sheer good fortune, his own shot evaded the warrior's armor, blasting the alien's arm clean off at the shoulder. The warrior hissed and cradled its injured flesh before a second shot exploded its head like water-balloon bursting.

Heart thumping in his chest, Sterling turned to the still-open door leading out of the hospital wing, but then saw more warriors charging his way, alerted by the gunfire. Cursing, he ran to another door and hit the button. The door whooshed open and he was about to charge through before another group of warriors turned the corner. Blasts thumped into the walls by his side and Sterling doubled back, barging past medical stretchers and pushing over equipment in an effort to reach another exit. However, before he was even half way across the large, open ward, the third door slid open, revealing two more warriors. Sterling stopped and spun around, finding himself surrounded. The hiss of the aliens grew to a roar then Sterling watched as the yellow eyes of one alien fell onto the body of Emissary Lana McQueen. The warrior hissed again then met Sterling's gaze before raising a pistol and aiming it at his head.

STERLING THREW himself to the deck as plasma blasts crisscrossed above him. Still amped up on the drugs McQueen's guard had given him, he managed to shoot back, blasting a warrior in the thigh. The alien hissed and was pulled back as more alien soldiers advanced. Rolling into what little cover he could find, Sterling was soon pinned down. Plasma hammered into the metal cabinets he'd hidden behind, tearing through them like cannon rounds punching through drywall. Sterling moved, firing blind over the top of a medical bay, but a swarm of incoming blasts forced him down again. Cursing, he slapped the side of his head, trying to jolt his weary brain into coming up with a plan, but he knew it was futile. He was trapped and outnumbered. He knew then that he would die in that room, but if he was going to meet his end then he'd do it as an Omega Captain. He would be ruthless to the last, and die on his feet, pistol in hand, killing as many of the alien bastards as he could.

Sterling rolled into a new position as plasma fire began to obliterate the bed he'd been hiding behind. Glancing up, he saw blasts continue to crisscross above his head. If he could position himself between the blasts, there was a chance the aliens would shoot themselves instead of him, Sterling considered. Springing up, he rushed the closest group of warriors, firing and killing one of the aliens with a precise blast to its head. Plasma raced back at him and thudded into his armor below the chest. He felt the searing bite of pain and fired again, killing a second alien warrior. Two more blasts hammered into his armor, one to his back and one to the thigh. He dropped to one knee as another blast fizzed above his head. The garbled hiss of alien warriors followed and Sterling smiled, realizing that the aliens had fallen into his trap. Biting down against the pain, he punched his injured leg, trying to drive some life back into it, then stood tall again. His next shot decapitated the warrior charging at him before his pistol was hit and exploded in his hand. He fell to his knees again, clutching his arm. It was then he realized that it hadn't just been the pistol, but his entire hand above the wrist that had been blasted off. The vile smell of his own burned flesh flooded into his nostrils, but strangely the injury did not hurt.

Warriors appeared all around him, encircling him like vultures waiting for a fresh corpse to feast on. One of the aliens motioned for Sterling to stand, hissing at him wildly as it did so. Sterling pushed himself up and met the alien's egg-shaped eyes. Its armor, like McQueen's, was more ornate. It reminded Sterling of the armor the Sa'Nerran Commander he'd once encountered had worn and surmised that this alien was of a higher rank than the others. The warrior grabbed Sterling's chin and twisted his head to the side, inspecting the neural control device that was still attached to his implant. The alien poked and prodded it with its leathery fingers, before releasing its hold on Sterling and hissing an order to another warrior close by. The commander then stepped back and the other six aliens raised their weapons. Sterling straightened his back as best he could, considering the pain shooting through his body, and continued to hold the gaze of the alien commander. The warrior hissed at him and Sterling hissed back at it, like an angry snake.

"Go on, kill me you alien bastard," Sterling spat at the commander. "I only regret that I won't get to see my crew rip you to shreds."

The warrior hissed another command then plasma blasts filled the air. Sterling flinched, expecting to feel searing hot pain assault his body. Instead, the Sa'Nerran Commander fell, followed quickly by two more of the alien warriors surrounding Sterling. The remaining warriors opened fire, but their weapons were no longer aimed at him. Turning to one of the exits to the hospital wing, he saw Lieutenant Opal Shade storm into the room, surrounded by the black-armored frames of Obsidian Soldiers. Alien bodies exploded all around Sterling, pulverized by Homewrecker rifles and powerful plasma hand cannons. Hot flesh splattered into his face and armor as blasts continued to race all around him. It was a brutally efficient attack, and the entire assault was over in seconds.

Then, through the smoke of burning bodies, Sterling

saw Commander Mercedes Banks advance, a Homewrecker rifle held in each hand. She met Sterling's eyes then tossed the weapons down and ran to him. Sterling was still rooted to the spot, too stunned to speak or even move. Banks thumped into his body, threw her powerful arms around his neck and squeezed him against her own armored chest. Both Sterling and the alien armor he was wearing groaned under the pressure of the woman's powerful embrace. Banks pulled back, beaming at him as if she'd not seen him in years. She opened her mouth to speak, but then her gaze fell to Sterling's alien armor and her expression darkened. Shoving him back, Banks then saw the neural control weapon attached to his head and held out an outstretched hand to Lieutenant Opal Shade.

"Give me a weapon, now!" Banks yelled.

Shade reacted instantly, slapping her pistol into Commander Banks' waiting hand, all the while fixated on Sterling's eyes like a homing missile. However, while there was no hesitation in her actions, Sterling could see that Shade was conflicted, and he could see the same conflict in his first officer's eyes too.

"Mercedes, it's okay, it's me," Sterling said, keeping his voice calm and level, though the pain of his injuries was now returning in full force. "The neural firewall worked. I haven't been turned."

"Stay where you are," Banks hit back, thrusting the plasma pistol at Sterling's chest. Her aim was steady, but Sterling could see that maintaining her composure was requiring the entire strength of her will. "You're wearing their armor. You're one of them."

"McQueen dressed me in this damned costume and tried to make me her pet," Sterling replied, feeling his legs start to waver. "But she's dead now," he added, nodding in the direction of the Emissary's body. "I killed her, Mercedes. She's gone."

Banks' eyes narrowed and flicked over in the direction Sterling had indicated. McQueen lay on her back, a hole burned clean through her chest. Sterling could see that the Emissary's eyes were still open and that the startled expression on her face had remained, as if it had been cast in iron.

Sterling suddenly felt weak and was compelled to grab the side of the medical bay to stay upright. His severed hand had been instantly cauterized, but he was still losing blood from other injuries he'd sustained. Banks' eyes returned to him and Sterling could see that she was concerned. However, her weapon remained squarely aimed at his chest.

"How can I be sure that you're still you?" Banks said.

Sterling laughed. "How the hell am I supposed to answer that?" he said, slumping on the side of the bed. "I guess we should have figured that part out before now."

"We could have Graves examine him," said Lieutenant Shade. Her expression displayed none of the concern that Banks had shown. Nor would Sterling have expected it to. "He'll be able to find out if this man is telling the truth."

Banks nodded then jabbed the pistol at Sterling. "On your knees, Captain," she said. "You're coming with us, as my prisoner."

Sterling was about to slide off the bed and drop to his

knees as ordered when he felt a link form in his mind. From the expression on the faces of Banks and Shade, he could tell that they'd received the same communication.

"Captain, Commander, and anyone who is left, this is Commander Graves on the Invictus," the voice of the ship's medical officer began. The link was weak, but Sterling could sense the man's unease. "Sa'Nerran forces are attacking the command post. Repeat, Sa'Nerran forces are attacking. They mean to take the Invictus."

Sterling cursed and was about to respond, but Banks beat him to it.

"Hold them off, Commander, we're on our way," said Banks. She then turned to Lieutenant Shade. "Go, now. Take the Obsidian Soldiers and destroy the remaining Sa'Nerran forces."

"Aye, Commander," Shade replied, briskly. Then she looked at Sterling. "But what about him?"

"I'll deal with him and meet you back at the ship," Banks said, still with the pistol trained on Sterling. "Now move out!"

Shade acknowledged the order, then hurried out of the hospital wing, barking orders at the Obsidian Soldiers as she went. Sterling watched the mechanical warriors file in behind his weapons officer, but noticed that one of the machines had remained. He recognized it immediately as the leader – the Obsidian Soldier that had continually questioned Sterling about the mission and its role in it. The robot lingered for a few moments, its optical scanners flicking from Sterling to the pistol in Banks' hand. Then it turned and stomped off in pursuit of its mechanical comrades.

"Well, this is awkward," said Banks, falling back on her usual trick of resorting to dark humor in difficult circumstances. "What does the Omega Directive say in situations like this?"

Sterling smiled. "I think it says that you're supposed to blast my head off," he replied, honestly. "You can't take the chance that I'm turned. And you can't prove that I'm not, so you have no choice."

Banks took another step forward, her pistol still trained on Sterling. Her aim was steady and true. "Give me an option, Captain," Banks said. "There has to be another way."

Sterling's breathing was becoming more erratic and he realized that he was feeling dizzy and slightly nauseous. He look at his hand – the one he had left – and noted that his skin was clammy.

"I'm going into shock, Mercedes," Sterling said, recognizing the symptoms at once. "So soon it won't matter anyway." He then tried to adopt a more rigid posture – one befitting his rank and status – as he resolved to issue his final command. "I order you to re-take the Invictus then take command of the Vanguard. It's down to you now, Mercedes. You're the captain now."

"Bullshit," Banks spat back, becoming suddenly angry. "The real Lucas Sterling would never say that. He'd never give up while there was still breath in his lungs."

"I'm not giving up, damn it!" Sterling snapped. "But you can't prove I haven't been turned and you can't just walk out of here and leave me. So you have no choice. You have to shoot."

Banks shook her head then tapped her neural interface. Sterling felt the connection form in his mind, but didn't immediately allow it.

"Accept the link, Lucas," Banks said, realizing that Sterling was blocking him. "If it's really you then I'll know."

"You might not like what you see in there," Sterling replied, his eyes falling on the body of Corporal Jeanette Dietrich.

"Whatever you've done was necessary," Banks hit back. "Now, let me in."

Sterling sighed, then accepted the link and felt Banks enter his mind. The connection was strong, as it always was between them. Whereas most people could sense emotions through a link, for Banks and Sterling the connection ran deeper. They usually knew what the other was feeling better than they knew themselves.

The mental energy required to maintain the link was sapping the little strength Sterling had left. Dizziness was starting to overwhelm him, and his thoughts strayed back to the moment when he'd strangled Corporal Dietrich. He saw Banks wince as Sterling's brutal actions were played out through their link.

"You did what was necessary, Lucas," he heard Banks say, though her voice was distant in his mind. Even so, Sterling could feel that she was certain of her judgement. "I'd have done the same."

Sterling's thoughts then strayed to what happened

next, and the memory of these events disgusted him even more than the act of killing Dietrich. He again felt the wetness of McQueen's lips on his and the feel of her hands on his body. And he remembered how he'd reciprocated the embrace, caressing the Emissary like she was his true love. The sickness in his gut threatened to overwhelm him and he tasted bile in his mouth. Then his eyes met those of Commander Mercedes Banks. She had now fixed him with a murderous glare and suddenly Sterling could feel the revulsion and anger inside her. He realized that she had felt what he had felt and that she knew what he had done.

"I'm sorry, Mercedes," Sterling said through the link. He wasn't even sure what he was apologizing for. He'd done nothing wrong. He'd only done what he'd had to do, for the sake of the mission. Then he realized why his first officer was angry. It was not that she'd questioned his actions, and it was clear that she no longer believed Sterling had been turned. Instead, she was crippled by bitterness and even jealously. More than that, she was repulsed by him.

Sterling saw Banks' eyes widen and her hand tighten around the grip of the pistol. He could feel panic rising in her gut and knew she was about to fire. Then there was a bright flash and Sterling was blinded by the burning light racing toward his head.

THE ROAR of the plasma blast fizzing past Sterling's ear was like a flashbang grenade going off next to his head. The next thing he knew he'd been tackled and dragged down to the deck. He landed hard and the pain on top of his existing injuries almost caused him to black out. As the ringing in his ears subsided, he heard the familiar, waspish hiss of Sa'Nerran warriors.

"Get into cover!" Banks cried, noticing that Sterling was conscious again. She was crouched a couple of meters to Sterling's side, firing into one of the corridors adjoining the medical wing.

Cursing, Sterling found concealment then began to scour the deck for a weapon he could use to help fight off the new attackers. He suddenly found himself staring into the yellow eyes of a dead Sa'Nerran warrior, smoke rising from a crater blasted out of the top of its head. Sterling guessed that this alien had been the intended target of Banks' close-range shot, and was again thankful for his first officer's exceptional aim.

Searching the creature, Sterling pulled a plasma pistol from its armor and struggled to fit it into his left hand. Even with his right hand he wasn't the best shot in the Fleet, but since he no longer had a right hand, there was no choice. Using his stump to push himself to his knees, screaming with pain as he did so, Sterling opened fire with the pistol. His initial shots were wayward, but by the third blast he'd landed a shot on target.

"Fall back!" Banks cried out, tossing her spent pistol to the deck and retrieving one of the Homewreckers she'd discarded earlier.

Sterling scrambled back to join Banks as blasts flashed past to his left and right. He was now running purely on adrenaline and instinct, but despite his injuries his reflexes were still keen. Squeezing the trigger of the alien pistol, Sterling blasted the foot off one of the warriors before hitting another in the gut. Then the pneumatic thud of the Homewrecker drowned out any other sound. Sterling watched in awe as Banks tore through the remaining warriors with the weapon set to automatic and to maximum power. He'd never seen anyone with the strength to maintain this mode of fire for long, at least without the benefit of an exosuit. Teeth bared, his first officer continued to hold down the trigger, until the corridor the aliens were advancing along collapsed, trapping the warriors outside the medical wing. Eventually, the energy cell in the weapon ran dry and the room fell silent, apart from the fizz and crackle of burning machinery and flesh. Banks reloaded the Homewrecker then lifted her forearm to activate her computer.

"The corridor is sealed and I don't see any other warriors heading this way," she said, frowning down at the screen.

Sterling hobbled to her side, feeling the effects of his injuries and exertions even more than before. He tried to look at the screen, but his vision was blurry. He felt Banks' hand gripping his arm and realized that if it weren't for her steadying influence, he would have fallen flat on his face.

"We need to get back to the Invictus," Sterling said, blinking his eyes rapidly in an attempt to make them focus. "Whatever is left of the Sa'Nerran forces will now concentrate their attack there."

Sterling tried to head out, but either because of Banks' hold on him, or the lack of strength in his legs, he couldn't move.

"We need to patch you up first," Banks said, scooping him up like a child and carrying him to a medical bed.

"There's no time, just leave me here," Sterling groaned, trying to struggle against Banks' hold, despite knowing this would have been futile even if he had his full strength.

"You're no use to anyone if you're dead," Banks replied, dumping him on the bed. She then activated the medical bay's systems, which flickered into life. "And you'll be dead in a matter of minutes if this thing is right."

Sterling reached out and grabbed Banks' arm, using it as leverage to help lift his head from the bed. "It doesn't matter what happens to me, Mercedes," Sterling said, while his first officer dragged a metal cabinet toward her. "The

Omega Directive is in effect. Save the ship and continue the mission, that's an order."

"Sorry, Captain, I didn't quite catch that." Banks removed an injector from the cabinet and pulled off the cap with her teeth. "Your speech is slurring badly," she added, while stabbing the device into Sterling's neck.

Whatever she'd injected him with worked with near-immediate effect, helping to clear Sterling's vision and senses.

"Damn it, Mercedes, I know you can hear me just fine," he said. His first officer was now tearing sections of his Sa'Nerran armor away, around the areas where he'd taken hits. "You don't have time to waste on me."

"I'm linked in to Lieutenant Razor and she's holding the fort just fine," Banks hit back. "Now just lay back and stop giving me a hard time so I can save your life."

Despite feeling stronger, Sterling still didn't have the energy to argue back. He flopped his head onto the hard padded surface of the trauma bed and let his first officer work. As he relaxed, his mind wandered back to the moments before Banks had fired and tackled him to the deck. Their link had been severed during the fight, but the memory of how she'd felt about him and his actions still weighed heavily on his mind.

"You know, when you fired at that warrior behind me, I actually thought you were shooting at me," he admitted, cocking his head slightly so he could look at his first officer.

Banks glanced over to Sterling then returned to the part of his body she was working on. "I knew by that point that you hadn't been turned," she replied, flatly.

"I had to maintain the ruse with McQueen," Sterling went on. For some reason, he felt like he needed to explain himself. "If there was another way, I would have..."

"You did what you had to do," Banks cut in, "and that's all there is to it."

Sterling let his head relax back on the bed. Without the benefit of a neural link, he couldn't tell if Banks was being genuine, but it still felt good to hear her say it.

"I'd have done the same thing in your shoes," Banks went on, while applying a dressing to one of Sterling's burns. "Well, apart from playing tonsil tennis with the Emissary to the Sa'Nerra," she added with a shrug, causing Sterling to strain his neck to look at her again. "I'd have just ripped her damned head off."

Despite everything, Sterling found himself laughing. Banks tried to maintain a straight face, but he could see that she was grinning too.

"Well, if by some miracle we get out of this, don't tell the Admiral about the tonsil tennis part, okay?" Sterling said, again flopping back on the bed. "I'm pretty sure that consorting with the enemy carries a life term in Grimaldi."

Banks shook her head and muttered something under her breath that Sterling couldn't hear. Though, since she was still smiling, he guessed it wasn't anything too uncomplimentary. The two then remained silent for the next few minutes, while Banks continued to patch up Sterling's wounds.

"Graves is going to have a heart-attack when he's sees the hack-job I've done on these injuries," Banks said, applying the final dressing to a burn on Sterling's side. The patch latched on like a suction cup sticking to a window and straight away the pain was gone.

"I'm more concerned about overdosing on all the drugs you've pumped me full of." Sterling raised his arm with the intention of scratching some dried Sa'Nerran guts off his face and saw the cauterized stump. "I don't suppose you have any spare hands in that cabinet, Commander?" he asked, rotating the stump, which oddly no longer hurt.

Banks pressed Sterling's arm back down to the bed. "How about you leave the dark and inappropriate jokes to me, sir?" she said, scowling at him. Then Banks raised a device that looked like a long, fingerless glove made out of a metallic, mesh-like material. Placing the glove on the bed next to Sterling, she then removed a spray can from the cabinet. Sterling's gut tightened as he recognized the bottle. "Even with all the drugs flooding through your body, this is still going to hurt like hell."

"Can't we just skip this part?" Sterling whined, trying to sit up and pull his injured arm away. "I feel fine."

"I have to cleanse the wound or Graves will end up having to remove your whole arm," Banks hit back, holding onto Sterling with godlike strength.

Sterling cursed then lay back and closed his eyes. "Fine, but make it quick," he said before clamping his jaw shut in readiness for the agony he was about to endure.

Banks knocked the cap off the bottle, gave it a little shake as if she was mixing a cocktail, then began spraying the contents all over Sterling's stump. The pain was intense and immediate, paralyzing Sterling even more effectively than his first officer's inhuman grip had done. He cried out, unable to bear down against the agony any longer, and was embarrassed for doing so. He felt Banks take his good hand and squeeze it gently. Despite doing nothing to help with the pain, that single act alone helped Sterling to endure.

"It should start to ease in a second," Banks said, tossing the spent can to the deck, where it rattled away into the darkness underneath a storage cabinet.

Immediately, Sterling felt the pain ease. It was like his arm had been doused in ice cold water. Banks then picked up the metallic glove she'd laid out earlier and pulled it over the stump. The glove shrank around his arm and formed a tight seal. Sterling raised the bandaged arm to inspect it. The pain was now completely gone.

"Graves can fabricate you a new hand once we get through this," Banks said, finishing up her ministrations. "With the facilities on the Vanguard, it'll look a lot better than Jinx's robotic leg too."

Sterling huffed a laugh. "Assuming he doesn't do a Frankenstein job on me, and I end up with seven fingers or a damned claw," he replied.

Sliding his legs off the bed, Sterling jumped up feeling strong again. He knew that he would suffer the effects of his injuries and treatments more severely later, but for now the wonders of Fleet medicine had put him back in the fight. Checking his own computer, he saw that the motion scanner was picking up heavy activity around the port docking garage. The remaining forces on both sides were already engaged.

"Now, find me a weapon and let's get the hell out of here," he added, turning back to his first officer.

Banks grabbed a dead warrior off the deck and slammed it onto the medical bed. She removed its plasma pistol and handed it to Sterling. "That's the best you'll be able to use for now," she said, readying her Homewrecker and preparing to move.

Sterling then saw the glint of a Sa'Nerran half-moon blade on the warrior's armor and had an idea. "Wait, strap that to my right hand," he said, tapping the blade with the pistol. "Until Graves can fix me up, I'll need every protection I can get."

Banks frowned at the blade, but removed it as instructed and placed it on the bed before heading to a storage cabinet. Pulling open the door, she began to ransack the cabinet, tossing items onto the deck like a burglar looking for valuables. Finally, she emerged with a roll of strong tape.

"Just be careful you don't try to scratch an itch," Banks said, strapping the blade to the end of Sterling's stump. "I don't think Graves is as adept at creating bionic noses and ears as he is hands and feet." She tore the tape with her teeth and took a step back. "How does it feel?"

Sterling flexed the improvised weapon. The blade, plus the thickness of the tape on top of the metallic-mesh dressing added significant heft to his arm. It was like the limb had been transformed into a scythe.

"It feel like I'm a walking weapon," Sterling said, giving the blade a few practice swings.

"Good," said Banks before slapping Sterling on the back and heading for the exit. "Now you know how I feel every damn day."

CHAPTER 20
DON'T MAKE ME ANGRY

STERLING STOPPED two sections away from the docking garage and checked the scanner readings on his computer. The sound of plasma weapons-fire was already filtering along the corridor, so he knew the fighting was close. The bulk of movement was still concentrated in the docking garage where the Invictus had crash landed. However, Sterling could now see a small group of contacts heading their way.

"I think they've detected us," said Sterling, as Banks dropped to a crouch at his side and glanced at his computer screen. "There's a blip coming this way. That could mean perhaps three or four warriors, roughly fifty meters ahead."

"I suggest we take them out from here," Bank said, while covering the corridor with her Homewrecker rifle. "Then we can cut through to the docking garage at the next intersection. That will bring us out about a hundred meters ahead of where the Invictus is."

"Agreed," said Sterling. He then tapped his neural

interface and reached out to Lieutenant Shade. His weapons officer accepted the link, and he immediately sensed some apprehension.

"Captain, is that you?" said Shade. Her voice was faint, as if she was on the other end of a tin can telephone. Sterling assumed that the drugs rushing around his body were interfering with his link.

"Not quite all of me, Lieutenant, but yes," Sterling replied. "The neural firewall worked. I'm fine."

"No offense, sir, but that's exactly what you'd say if you were turned," Shade replied, flatly.

Sterling smiled. He couldn't blame his weapons officer for being mistrustful of him. In fact, he'd be disappointed if she wasn't. Tapping his interface again, Sterling widened the link to include his first officer.

"It's okay, Lieutenant, the Captain is still the Captain," Banks cut in, correctly guessing the reason why she'd been added to the conversation.

"Understood," replied Shade, crisply. "Sorry, Captain, but I had to be sure."

"I'd expect nothing less, Lieutenant, now what's the status of the Invictus?" Sterling cut back in.

"There's still heavy fighting in the docking garage, sir." Sterling could feel flashes of anger and savagery from his weapons officer and guessed she was still engaging the enemy while talking to him. "They've set up plasma cannon emplacements and taken out the Invictus turrets on the port side, so we're limited to personal weapons only."

"Send me the location of the cannon emplacements," Sterling said, as Banks unleashed a volley of plasma fire along the corridor. The powerful shards of energy punched through the gut of one warrior and blasted the leg off another.

"Aye, Captain, transmitting now," Shade replied.

Sterling saw the data appear on his computer and smiled. The aliens had set their gun emplacements almost directly ahead of where he and Banks planned to enter the docking garage. "Hold fast, Lieutenant, we'll take care of those guns for you."

"Understood, Captain," Shade replied. "We'll hold the fort until you get back."

The link went dead just as Banks unleashed another volley of plasma along the corridor, pulverizing two more Sa'Nerran warriors and leaving them in a pulpy mess on the deck.

"Clear," Banks called out before moving up to the next intersection to cover Sterling's advance.

"I've marked the position of the gun emplacements on our maps," Sterling said, resorting to speaking out loud, since neural comms were still patchy. "If we can take out those cannons, the rest of the Sa'Nerra should be easy pickings."

Sterling moved ahead, then covered the corridor while his first officer caught up with him. Another blip of movement appeared on his computer screen and his pulse spiked. Moments later, the contact was gone.

"I had a brief contact on my screen, ten meters ahead, but it's gone now," he warned Banks.

Banks dropped to one knee and checked her computer. "I don't see anything," she replied after staring at the display for a few seconds. "Could it have been a glitch?"

"Maybe, but stay on your toes," Sterling replied, as Banks began to move ahead again. "These dreadnaughts are like rabbit warrens. An alien bastard could spring out from any one of these rooms or connecting corridors."

No sooner had Sterling spoken the words than a door to Banks' side swished open. She turned and fired, but a warrior had already driven its shoulder into her gut and slammed her against the wall. The impact stunned Banks and the warrior smashed the Homewrecker rifle from her grasp. A split-second later, a serrated Sa'Nerran blade was slashed across the mid-section of Banks' armor. Sparks flew, but the blade didn't penetrate. Sterling raised his pistol, but in the extra second it took him to aim with his off-hand another two warriors had charged through the door. The first came at Sterling, while the second joined its comrade in fighting Banks hand-to-hand.

Sterling fired but missed the warrior. At the same time a blast of plasma fizzed past his head, so close he thought he could smell his own singed hair. Reacting quickly, he adjusted his aim and squeezed the trigger. This time the blast caught the alien in the face, burning a hole straight through to its brain. The warrior fell on top of Sterling, its arms stretched out ahead of it like a zombie. He cursed and shook the dead warrior loose before trying to take aim at the warriors grappling with Banks. Suddenly, a door to his side opened and he was grabbed around the neck. Sterling's pistol discharged but the blast thudded harmlessly into the ceiling. He was then struck across the chest and sent tumbling into a metal storage cabinet. The pistol in his left hand cartwheeled into the corner of the room.

Pushing himself up with his bladed hand, Sterling saw the alien come at him, pistol raised. He slashed out with the serrated weapon, deflecting the pistol moments before it fired. The alien hissed wildly and Sterling saw the alien weapon drop to the deck, along with three of the warrior's long, leathery fingers. The creature's wide, yellow eyes fixed onto Sterling and it drew a serrated blade of its own, flashing the metal edge toward him with deadly intent. He dodged back and lashed out for a second time, but the blade danced off the warrior's armor, creating a shower of sparks. The alien retaliated, burying its weapon into Sterling's chest armor and splitting it open like a lumberjack cutting wood. Sterling grabbed the alien's wrist and tried to prize the blade away, but the warrior was now leaning in, putting all its weight into the attack. Sterling felt the blade start to cut into his flesh and in an act of desperation he thrust his fingers into the creature's bulging yellow eyes. It hissed wildly and pulled away, clamping its hand to the burst eyeball.

Sterling saw his chance and advanced, feinting an attack with his left then sidestepping and thumping his bladed hand into the warrior's neck. More hisses bled into the room along with the alien's crimson life essence. The warrior flailed its arms wildly at Sterling, but he knew he'd already struck a death blow. Pulling his opponent's serrated blade out of his armor, Sterling then brought his scythe-like weapon hand down hard across the warrior's wrist. The alien's hand fell to the deck with a dull thud and the warrior dropped to its knees, cradling the injured flesh to its body.

"See how you like it, asshole," Sterling spat at the warrior. He collected the alien's pistol off the deck, aimed the weapon at its head and blasted the warrior's brains across the wall.

Cries and thuds from outside the room alerted Sterling to the fact Banks was still engaged in combat. Running back to the door, he saw his first officer struggling with three aliens. Two warriors already lay dead at her feet, and based on the look in his first officer's eyes, he was confident the remaining three would soon follow. However, as much as he enjoyed watching Mercedes Banks work, there were other aliens they needed to kill.

Sterling gritted his teeth and marched toward the group, pistol raised. Squeezing the trigger, he blasted the nearest warrior in the back of its head, splattering bone and brains all over the other combatants. One of the warriors spun around then came at Sterling, but Banks caught the alien and slammed its temple into the wall. Sterling heard the crunch of bone as the warrior's cranium collapsed. The final warrior then landed a solid right cross Banks' face and she rocked back. Sterling raised his pistol, intending to kill the alien, then saw the look on his first officer's face. He lowered the weapon to his side, realizing that discharging it would merely be a waste of ammo. Banks' eyes were wild and furious.

Banks dabbed the blood from the fresh cut to her cheek onto her hand and examined it before turning her wrathful gaze to the warrior. The alien advanced – it was either unaware of the mistake it had made, or simply unable to be intimated. The warrior struck out again, but this time Banks caught its fist in her hand and twisted the alien's arm savagely. There was a sharp crack, followed by a wild, spine-chilling hiss. Still holding onto the warrior's now broken arm, Banks thumped punch after punch into the alien's face. First its stubby nose collapsed, then its jaw snapped and its eye sockets caved in. Eventually, even the warrior's dense forehead couldn't withstand the power of his first officer's blows. Chest heaving and teeth-bared, Banks allowed the mangled alien to fall to the deck.

"Let's get to the docking garage and end this," said Sterling, glancing down at his computer. "Assuming there are no more surprises, we have a clear run right up behind the gun emplacements."

Banks spat a globule of bloody spittle onto the deck then picked up her Homewrecker. Slapping a new power cell into the heavy plasma rifle, she then picked up one of the fallen alien weapons and met Sterling's eyes. She was no longer wild, but she was clearly still pissed off.

"I hope Shade has left some of those alien bastards for us," Banks said, setting off in the lead again. "Because I'm not nearly finished killing Sa'Nerrans yet."

Sterling followed his first officer, finding it a struggle to keep pace with her. The drugs were starting to wear off, and he could feel the niggle of pain all over his body, not least from his missing hand. However, he had no choice but to press on. Until they destroyed the Sa'Nerran threat, there was no chance of getting his wounds properly tended to. Close to the entrance to the docking garage, Banks threw up a hand signal, letting Sterling know there were enemies ahead. Sterling slowed and crept silently to his first officer's side.

"I see three plasma gun emplacements, with two aliens apiece," she whispered.

Sterling looked over the top of Banks' shoulder and saw the heavy weapons. Each cannon was firing at will, pummeling his crew's defensive positions with blasts of plasma strong enough to punch a hole through the inner walls of the Vanguard.

"You make the call," Sterling said, drawing back and meeting his first officer's gaze. "I'm fading fast, Mercedes. I don't know how much longer I can keep this up."

"Just hold on, Lucas," Banks said, confidently. "Stay close to me and let me do the hard work."

"A straight-up power play?" Sterling said with a knowing smile.

"What else?" Banks replied. However, there wasn't even the hint of a smirk on his first officer's face. She meant business and the business in question was dealing death.

STERLING GRABBED a spare power cell from the body of a dead warrior and reloaded his weapon. Nodding to Banks, he took a deep breath and waited for her instruction to begin the attack.

"On three, follow me," Banks said, readying both of the powerful weapons in her hands.

Sterling tightened his hold on his pistol as Banks counted down. Adrenalin was surging through his veins, helping to counteract some of the rapidly-encroaching fatigue and weariness that he was feeling. Banks then advanced and immediately opened fire with the Homewrecker and the alien plasma pistol. The two alien warriors manning the first gun emplacement were pulverized by her first volley, both reduced to pulpy, smoldering splats on the deck. Sterling aimed and fired at the third emplacement, but the warriors manning it had already ducked behind the gun's protective shielding.

The roar of Banks' heavy plasma rifle erupted beside

him for a second time and the middle gun emplacement exploded. Debris from the heavy weapon flew in all directions and Sterling felt a chunk of broken metal clip his leg. He staggered into cover and checked the wound. It hurt like hell, but his leg was still attached to his body, and that was all that mattered.

Blasts flew toward them from the two warriors at the final gun emplacement. Banks tried to dodge into cover but was impeded by the smoldering debris from the second gun. A blast hit her chest armor and she fell. Cursing, Sterling aimed and fired, managing to suppress the two aliens, but his shots failed to put either of them down. Then to Sterling's horror the gun emplacement began to turn. Instead of aiming out toward the Invictus, itself pockmarked with blast holes and set ablaze in several places, the powerful plasma cannon was now bearing down on him.

Biting down against the pain in his leg, Sterling pushed himself up and looked for a way to evade the gun, but he was already twenty meters into the docking garage and fully exposed. He looked to Banks, but she was still down on the deck, slowing pushing herself upright with her hands. The fall had clearly winded her and Sterling knew she would not be able to intervene this time. Turning back to the gun emplacement, he rained plasma blasts into it from his pistol, hoping to score a lucky hit that might disable the weapon. However, it was like shooting arrows at a tank. Sterling's power cell gave out just as the barrel of the cannon lowered and set its sights on Sterling's chest. One blast from the gun, and all that would remain of

Sterling would be a fuming pile of ash. He tossed the weapon to the deck and stood tall.

"Take your shot!" Sterling yelled down the barrel of the gun. "I already killed your precious Emissary!"

Suddenly an explosion rippled through the deck and Sterling was thrown through the air. He landed hard and was pelted by more burning fragments of metal and flesh, some landing inches from his already-battered body. Pushing a burning hunk of alien meat aside with his bladed-hand, Sterling sat up and saw that the gun emplacement had been completely destroyed. All that remained of it was a raging inferno, like a Fourth of July bonfire. Banks appeared at Sterling's side, shielding her eyes from the blaze. Grabbing his first officer's thigh armor for leverage, Sterling hauled himself to his feet and saw Lieutenant Shade approaching, flanked by two Obsidian Soldiers.

"Plasma grenade, sir," said Shade, explaining how the gun emplacement had met its end in her usual matter-of-fact tone.

"I figured as much, Lieutenant," said Sterling, managing a weak smile. "Good work."

Shade glanced behind and indicated toward the Invictus. Drones were now circling around it, putting out the dozens of fires that were raging across its surface. The bodies of alien warriors littered the deck between them and the ship, and amongst the carnage Sterling could also make out the fractured remains of at least as many Obsidian Soldiers.

"What's the final butcher's bill, Lieutenant?" Sterling

asked, finding it necessary to lean on Banks for support. His first officer slung an arm around his waist and helped to prop him up so that he didn't look quite as ruined as he felt.

"I'm down to my last three commandoes, sir," said Shade, in her usual calm and precise manner. Sterling could see that his weapons officer had taken several hits, but her armor had spared her from serious injury. "We also lost twelve Obsidian Soldiers, but another dozen are missing."

"Missing?" Sterling said. "How the hell are they missing?"

Shade shook her head. "Unknown, sir," she replied, frankly. "All units were engaged in the battle, but mid-way into the fighting we lost one off the scanners. A few minutes later another eleven had gone, but none of them are confirmed as destroyed."

Sterling cursed. "Stay on it, Lieutenant, we need those machines," he replied.

"Aye, sir," said Shade. The weapons officer looked up at the battered hull of the Invictus. "The ship took the brunt of the assault. Razor is inside, coordinating repairs as best she can."

"Forget the Invictus for now, she's not going anywhere soon," Sterling replied. "Our priority is to get the Vanguard online. That's the only way we're going to make it to the rendezvous."

"I'll see to it, sir," Banks cut in. "Right now, we need to get you to Graves, and we need to get you there fast."

"I'm fine," Sterling hit back, waving Banks off with his blade-equipped hand. His first officer ducked back to avoid being cut and Shade did a double-take. Sterling then felt his legs give way and if it hadn't been for Banks' hold around his waist, he'd have fallen. "Okay, maybe I need Commander Graves to give me a quick once-over," he conceded.

"I think that would be prudent, sir," said Banks. She was wisely dealing with the matter of Sterling's injuries with a light touch so as not to prompt an ego-driven refusal from her captain.

Sterling began to stagger toward the Invictus with Banks' help, while Shade reached out to Commander Graves over a neural link to prepare him for a new arrival. While they were walking, Sterling found his mind wandering again. This time, however, he wasn't focused on the events that had transpired between himself and Emissary McQueen, or those that had followed with his first officer. There was something else that was nagging at him.

"Just how did you find me, anyway?" Sterling decided to fill the time by asking the question that was on his mind. "You couldn't have known where McQueen had taken me."

Banks smiled and flashed her eyes at Sterling before letting out a long, shrill whistle. Sterling frowned at his first officer, wondering what the hell she was doing, when the clatter of a small metal foot on the deck began to approach. Sterling turned toward the ship and saw Jinx the Beagle bounding toward them, tail wagging violently.

"You're kidding me, right?" said Sterling, frowning at the dog, who was now jumping at his heels.

"She followed your scent and led us right to you," Banks said, still smiling. "Once we were close enough to figure out where McQueen was holding you, I had one of the crew take her back to the ship."

Sterling laughed and shook his head. He then glanced down at the dog, who was yipping and barking playfully. "It looks like acting Ensign Jinx is bucking for a promotion," he said.

"Junior Lieutenant Jinx has a nice ring to it, don't you think?" said Banks.

Both of them laughed, despite the act of doing so causing pain to shoot through Sterling's body. Lieutenant Shade cast a sideways glance at them, before raising an eyebrow and turning back toward the ship.

"Lieutenant Jinx it is then," replied Sterling, after he'd stopped laughing. Then he looked at the body of a dead commando as he walked past it en-route to the Invictus. "Hell, we could certainly use the extra crew," he added, more somberly.

"McQueen is dead, and the Sa'Nerra have been wiped out," Banks replied, meeting Sterling's eyes. "The ship is ours, Captain. We did it."

Sterling nodded, then winced as more pain flooded throughout his body. "There's a long way to go yet, Mercedes," he replied, thinking about what they still had left to do. "But if we can get this ship back to Omega Four and back to Griffin, we might just have a chance to even the odds in this war."

STERLING TURNED to see a Sa'Nerran warrior march a prisoner into the room then push the woman to her knees in front of the wall. A black hood covered the prisoner's head and her wrists were bound together in front of her waist.

"Aide Sterling, I want you to kill this human," said a voice from behind him. Emissary Lana McQueen stepped into view, her hands pressed to the small of her back. "I would like you to strangle her to death."

Sterling frowned. *This isn't right...* he thought, again looking back at the prisoner kneeling before him. *I killed McQueen already, so why I am back here?*

"Strangle the human, Aide Sterling," McQueen said, issuing the order again because of Sterling's inaction. "Prove that you are worthy of the title."

"What title?" Sterling asked, glowering at the Emissary.

"The title of Omega Captain, of course," McQueen

replied, making it sound as if the answer should have been obvious to him.

The Sa'Nerran warrior then whipped the hood off the prisoner, but instead of Corporal Dietrich's swollen and bloodshot eyes, Sterling found himself peering down at Mercedes Banks.

"No, this isn't what happened," Sterling protested as Banks simply stared back at him, blank and emotionless. "This isn't right."

McQueen's boots thudded against the cold metal deck and moments later the Emissary was standing directly in front of him. She leaned in closer, bringing her lips so close to Sterling's ear that he could feel her breath on his skin.

"No, Captain Sterling, this isn't right," McQueen whispered. The words sent a shiver down his spine. "A moral and honorable man would never murder one of his soldiers to save his own skin, isn't that right?"

Sterling drew back and jabbed a finger at the Emissary. "You forced my hand," he hit back, starting to feel his pulse thumping in the side of his head. "I did what I had to, for the sake of the mission."

"You did it to save your own ass!" McQueen hit back. The Emissary was now wearing a thin, conceited smile. "You strangled her because you were afraid, and weak."

"You know that's a lie," Sterling countered. McQueen could play mind games all she liked – he wouldn't crack. "Dietrich was dead either way. By killing her myself, I deceived you and made you drop your guard. If I hadn't killed her then we'd both be dead, and you'd have command of the Vanguard."

Sterling was absolutely certain of his argument. McQueen was trying to inject doubt into his mind – doubt about his mission and the necessary sacrifices that the Sa'Nerra had forced him to make.

"So the ends justify the means?" said McQueen, raising a quizzical eyebrow.

"Yes," Sterling answered with the same unflinching conviction. "The end game is the survival of the human race. If I have to sacrifice the few in order to save the many, I'll do it. I'll do whatever I have to."

McQueen's smile broadened and took on a more sinister twist. Sterling swallowed hard, realizing he'd fallen into the Emissary's trap.

"If that's true, then you will have no difficulty strangling *this* human," McQueen said, pointing to the blank face of Mercedes Banks. "Prove me wrong, Lucas. Prove you are worthy of the title."

"This is ridiculous," Sterling hit back. "You're already dead, and this is just some crazy, drug-induced nightmare." He turned to leave. He'd already had enough of being held prisoner by his own mind. "So, you can go to hell, McQueen," he added, stepping toward the door.

"I'm already there, Lucas..." the Emissary replied.

A shooting pain raced through Sterling's temples, taking him completely by surprise. He dropped to his knees; hands pressed to the sides of his head.

"You sent me there!" McQueen snarled, suddenly rageful and bitter.

Another burst of pain sliced though Sterling's head and

this time he collapsed to his hands and knees, crippled by blinding agony.

"What are you doing to me?" Sterling cried out, turning to face the Emissary. "How are you doing this?"

"It's just a dream, Lucas," said McQueen, shrugging. "You can wake up and it will all be over."

Sterling pushed himself to his feet, though his legs were still unsteady. "To hell with his," he said, closing his eyes. He had no idea how to wake from a lucid dream, but closing his eyes seemed like as good a place to start as any.

"But if you do wake up now, you just prove that I'm right," McQueen said.

Sterling cursed, realizing he couldn't leave while McQueen still taunted him. Whether it was a dream or not didn't matter – her accusations would haunt him even after he woke. Opening his eyes again, he saw that McQueen was now on her knees beside Banks. She was stroking her finger down the side of her face, but Banks did not react. His first officer was still staring into dead space, as if she was hypnotized.

"Still here, Lucas?" McQueen said, mocking Sterling with her smile. "Perhaps you're not so sure of yourself, after all?"

"I've already killed hundreds of turned human aides of the Sa'Nerra," Sterling hit back. "I even strangled my own commando. And don't forget that I killed you." McQueen's smiled wavered as Sterling pointed this out "What more do I have to prove?"

"You claim that you'll do anything for the mission, but we both know that you can't kill Mercedes Banks,"

McQueen said, still stroking Banks' face. Sterling felt a flutter inside his gut and he forced down another dry swallow. "Sooner or later, you'll be faced with that choice, Lucas. Then, when the fate of humanity rests on your ability to kill your precious Mercedes, you'll falter and fail."

"I won't," Sterling hit back, marching toward McQueen with fists clenched. "Mercedes and I have talked about it. If it was the only way, neither one of us would hesitate to kill the other."

McQueen laughed and shook her head at Sterling. "Lies, Lucas," she said, scathingly. "It's a lie and you know it."

"I've come this far, Emissary McQueen," Sterling hit back, spitting the word 'emissary' at his former colleague. "I've done terrible things. I'm already irredeemable. What's one more life?"

McQueen slid her forefinger underneath the prisoner's chin and turned Banks' face towards hers. The Emissary kissed Banks softly on the cheek before standing up and gesturing to the first officer of the Invictus with her open hand.

"Then prove it," McQueen said, still smiling.

Sterling snorted a laugh then marched toward the manifestation of Banks. *She's not real, so what does it matter?* Sterling said to himself. *Just do it and then you'll wake up.* Dropping to his knees in front of Banks, Sterling wrapped his hands around her neck and began to apply pressure. However, the moment he did so, Banks' eyes came alive and locked onto him like laser sights.

"Lucas, don't kill me!" Banks cried, pleading with him

to stop. Her face, which had been as blank as shop mannequin's up to that point, now wore an expression of terror and pain. "You can find another way!"

Sterling gritted his teeth, closed his eyes and continued to increase the pressure around his first officer's throat.

"Lucas!" spluttered Banks. "Please!"

She's not real, damn it! Sterling told himself. *It's just a dream!*

"It's not... a dream..." Banks croaked. "It's a trick... McQueen... tricked you... I'm real!"

Sterling's conviction faltered and loosed his hold, but only by a fraction. He peeked open his eyes then wished he hadn't. The sight of Mercedes Banks' face twisted in agony made him feel physically sick.

"It's just a dream!" Sterling yelled, though he was trying to convince himself, not the woman in front of him. "It's not real."

"Lucas..." Banks said, her voice now weak. Sterling could feel her body going limp and her weight starting to press against him. "Please..."

Sterling gritted his teeth and closed his eyes again. He tried to increase the pressure again, but he couldn't do it. Finally, he gave up and pulled his hands away from his first officer's throat before releasing a wild, inarticulate scream of rage into the air.

"See, I told you," McQueen said. Her voice was calm and contemptuous.

Sterling looked up and saw that it was no longer Mercedes Banks kneeling in front of him, but the Emissary herself. She was dressed in her Omega Taskforce Captain's uniform with its unique silver stripe.

"You're weak and unworthy," McQueen added. She then spat in Sterling's face, striking him directly in the eye with a warm globule of sticky saliva. "And that's why you'll lose."

Sterling wiped the spittle from his eye and looked at it, smeared across the palm of his hand. His teeth were still clenched and the rage that had built up inside him had now reached a point where it couldn't be contained. Releasing another primal roar, Sterling grabbed McQueen around the neck and squeezed. McQueen coughed and spluttered, but despite her garbled cries Sterling could also hear her laughing.

"Die, you traitorous piece of shit!" Sterling roared, pressing his thumbs into McQueen's esophagus and crushing it like a stick of celery. "I killed you and I'll crush the Sa'Nerra!"

McQueen fell, but Sterling continued to choke the woman, straddling her in order to press down with all his weight. Eventually, exhaustion and muscle weariness set in and he was forced to relinquish his hold. Falling off the lifeless body of Emissary McQueen, Sterling scrambled back against the wall, chest pounding and muscles burning.

"Very good, Captain Sterling, you may now stand up," came a voice from behind him.

Sterling shot a glance to his rear and saw Mercedes Banks standing there, dressed in an Omega Captain's uniform.

"Mercedes?" Sterling said, climbing wearily to his feet.

"Come here," Banks added, issuing the command as if she were the superior officer. Sterling dragged himself to his feet and staggered over to his first officer, more out of curiosity than because Banks had demanded he do so. "Now kiss me." Banks ordered.

Before he knew it, Sterling had slid his arm around Banks' waist. He tried to stop himself, but it was like an external influence had taken control of his body. Then, powerless to do anything to prevent it, Sterling pulled Banks toward him so that their lips were mere millimeters apart.

"I know you want me, Lucas," whispered Banks. "I want you too. Stop fighting your desires."

Banks then kissed Sterling passionately on the lips. He was hesitant at first, but Sterling soon took control of the embrace, pushing Banks against the wall and kissing her with even greater intensity. He could feel his first officer's hands slipping underneath his tunic and tank top, caressing his body. The taste and touch of her thrilled him like nothing he'd experienced before. Before he knew it, Sterling had slid his hands beneath Banks' uniform.

"See, I knew I was right," a voice whispered into his ear.

Sterling froze. The voice wasn't that of Mercedes Banks. He pulled back and forced down another hard, dry swallow then found himself staring into the eyes of Lana McQueen.

"You're weak because of her," McQueen said "And because of her, you will lose."

A blast of plasma burned through Sterling's chest,

coring a hole through his body directly through his heart. Sterling opened his mouth to speak, but he could feel his life slipping away. He eyes darkened and his body went limp, and the very last thing he heard was the mocking, derisive laugh of Emissary Lana McQueen.

Sterling shot upright in bed and immediately pressed his hands to his chest. The lights in his new Captain's quarters on the Vanguard had already turned on and were blaring down on him at maximum intensity.

"Reduce the damned lights!" Sterling cried out, pressing his eyes shut as his heart continued to thump against the inner wall of his chest. The beat was so hard that he could feel each thud through his hand.

The light level dropped and Sterling realized that only one of his hands had any sensation. His raised his right arm and found himself staring at the jet-black prosthetic hand that Commander Graves had attached two-days earlier. He still hadn't gotten used to the bionic replacement. Then he noticed that the frame of his bed to the right-hand side was warped out of shape. He cursed, realizing that his lucid dream had led to some undesirable side-effects in the waking world too. Bending the metal back into shape as best he could, Sterling flopped back in his bed and allowed his head to sink into his sweat-soaked pillow.

"Good morning, Captain," said the chirpy voice of his gen-fourteen AI, which was still in the process of transplanting itself into the hulking mass of the Invictus. "I have taken the liberty of preparing a nice cup of Valerian root tea for you," the computer went on. "It is waiting for you in the food processor."

Sterling laughed and shook his head. "I like your new counselling tactics," he said, staring up at the light tiles on the ceiling. "Much more subtle."

"Thank you, Captain, I am learning," the computer replied. "In fact, you might say that I'm evolving."

"Well, if you know how to de-evolve my brain's tendency to screw with me while I'm asleep, let me know, okay?" Sterling replied.

"Aye, Captain," said the computer, cheerfully. "Don't forget your tea. It will help, I promise."

Sterling snorted then spent a few moments focusing on his breathing. The techniques he'd honed over the last couple of years were still effective, and soon he'd blanked the nightmare from his mind. Sliding his legs over the side of the bed, he stood up and made his way over to the small kitchenette, which contained the sophisticated food processer. He picked up the steaming cup of tea with his left hand, wary of crushing it with his new prosthetic, and raised it to his lips. As he did so, Sterling surveyed his new quarters. Compared to the Invictus, it was four times larger and felt more like a suite in a five-star hotel.

"I miss my old quarters," said Sterling before taking a sip of the tea. The taste was woody and bitter and it caused him to scrunch up his nose in disgust. "Damn it, computer, this tea tastes like feet," he added, directing his complaint to the ceiling, where he always imagined the computer to reside.

"How it tastes is not important, Captain," the computer hit back, sounding like a bossy schoolteacher. "It will do you good."

Sterling tried another sip, but the drink still tasted like week old socks. "How can something that tastes so disgusting do me good?" he said, placing the cup back onto the tray in the food processor.

A second later, a drizzle of golden liquid appeared out of the nozzle of the processor and streamed into the tea. Sterling frowned at the food dispensing machine, which then spat out a teaspoon. It landed in the cup with a delicate "plinking" sound.

"What the hell was that?" Sterling said, scowling at the ceiling.

"Honey, sir," answered the computer. "Try the tea now, but stir it first."

Sterling frowned up at the ceiling again, but then did as the computer suggested. Cautiously, he raised the tea to his lips and sampled it again. This time it tasted like sweet, week old socks, though he had to admit that this was a significant improvement.

"Better," said Sterling, grudgingly. "Thanks, computer."

"My pleasure, Captain," the AI replied. "Do you want to talk about your latest nightmare?"

"No," Sterling snapped before taking another, much larger sip of the tea. Despite its odd taste, he had to admit that it had some soothing properties.

"Very well, Captain," the computer said, displaying no sign of offense. "But know that I am here, if you need me."

Sterling then felt a connection form in is mind. It was Commander Mercedes Banks.

"Need anyone to sit on your back this morning?" his first officer asked. "I think we should start building you up to one hundred press-ups in the morning, now that you're an augment that is."

Sterling laughed. "No thanks, Mercedes, I'm skipping the press-ups this morning," he said. The intense dream had proven to be enough of a work out for him.

"Are you okay?" Banks asked.

Their link was strong, and Sterling knew that she would be picking up on the residual stresses and anxieties that had assaulted him only minutes earlier. The image of himself kissing and caressing his first officer then sprang to the forefront of his mind. He wrestled it away quickly, conscious that Banks would feel the sudden thrill that had electrified him.

"I'm fine, just a little tired still," Sterling replied. It wasn't a lie – it just wasn't the whole truth. "The wonder drugs that Graves prescribed are pretty amazing, but there's only so much the human body can take."

"I guess that means you're not up for a number twenty-seven then?" teased Banks.

Sterling froze with the cup half-way to his mouth. "They have them?" he asked.

"Hundreds of the damned things," Banks replied. "Razor had one of the Obsidian Soldiers cart a bunch of the best meal trays out of storage. "They're in the temporary canteen we set up on deck nine, waiting for us."

Sterling gulped down the rest of his tea then tore off his

t-shirt and made a bee-line for his rest-room. "I'll see you there in twenty minutes," he said, trying to remove his pants while still on the move.

"It's a date, sir," Banks said. Then the link went dead and his first officer slipped out of his mind as effortlessly a ballerina dancing across the stage.

Sterling knew that Banks' phrasing was innocent, but it again conjured up the images from his dream. This time, he found it much harder to push them away.

"Damn it, Sterling, get a grip," he snapped, turning on his shower and stepping in before the water had even gotten hot. He figured a cold shower would do him good. "It's just a dream. It doesn't mean anything."

The stream of water quickly warmed and Sterling allowed the heat to soothe away some of the lingering aches in his war-weary body. However, the troubles in his mind were impervious to the comforting effects of the water. The apparition of Lana McQueen had been right. When it came to Mercedes Banks, Sterling was vulnerable. He just had to hope that if the time ever came when he was forced to make the impossible choice of saving Mercedes Banks or saving the mission that he'd not hesitate. However, neither the shower, nor the computer's odd-tasting tea, could hide the fact that for the first time since taking the Omega Captain's chair, Sterling had doubts.

CHAPTER 23
THE FIRST OF ITS KIND

STERLING SLID the number twenty-seven meal tray onto the table and sat down in front of Mercedes Banks, who was too busy eating to bother looking up. He studied the various skin rejuvenation patches on her face and neck, which were helping to accelerate the healing of her numerous injuries. Many more patches and dressings lay hidden beneath her uniform, which again bore the distinctive silver stripe of the Omega Taskforce. Banks moved well and didn't appear to be in any discomfort, Sterling observed. In the forty-eight hours since they'd crushed McQueen's forces, Commander Graves had done his usual impeccable job of patching them both up.

Satisfied that his medical officer had taken good care of her, Sterling turned his attention to Bank's breakfast. His first officer had already worked her way through a number eight and was now setting to work on a thirty-one. This was a menu Sterling had never seen before, and he peered at the tray, trying to work out what the stew-like main course was.

"Is that some kind of hotpot?" said Sterling, studying the brown mixture of what looked like meat and some sort of root vegetable.

"What the hell is a hotpot?" replied Banks before shoveling a forkful of the food into her mouth.

"You know, a hotpot?" Sterling replied, not really knowing how else to describe a hot-pot other than by its name. "Like a stew, I guess."

Banks shrugged. "I guess so," she mumbled, shoveling another heaped forkful into her mouth. "The ID sticker called it, 'southwestern style beef and black beans'. Only the bigger ships carry them."

Sterling picked up his fork, stabbed a chunk of meat from his first officer's tray and slipped it into his mouth. Banks froze with a look of absolute disgust on her face, as if Sterling had just spat in her food.

"Pretty good," said Sterling, chewing the fake meat. It was surprisingly tender, while the sauce was rich and spicy. "I might try one of those myself tomorrow."

"Commander Graves will need to fit another new hand if you try to steal food from my tray again," Banks grunted, pulling the meal tray closer and guarding it like a hungry animal. Sterling rocked back and cocked an eyebrow at her. "Sir..." Banks added, with a wicked smile.

"That's more like it," replied Sterling, pulling the foil of his customary grilled ham and cheese. He then tried to pick up the toasted sandwich with his new, bionic right-hand and ended up mashing the pieces of bread together. He cursed and relaxed his grip slightly, though the sandwich still looked like it had been sat on.

"You'll get the hang of it," Banks said, kindly. This wasn't the first time Sterling had accidently crushed something with his augment. The most recent victim, besides the sandwich, was the door to one of the wardrobes in his new quarters on the Vanguard. "Now you'll have some appreciation for the self-restraint I have to show every single day."

Sterling huffed a laugh then switched the grilled ham and cheese to his left hand instead. "With great power comes great responsibility," he said loftily, taking a bite of the slightly mashed sandwich. Banks, however, just frowned, clearly not understanding Sterling's ancient cult reference. "I hope Graves gets around to fabricating some synthetic skin for it, though," he added, flexing the fingers in his new metal hand. "I'm starting to look like those damned Obsidian Soldiers."

Banks snorted a laugh, then looked around the temporary cafeteria area they'd set up on the Vanguard. They were the only two people in it. "Wasn't Lieutenant Razor going to meet us this morning?" she wondered, moving on to a chocolate muffin that was so dense Sterling thought it might have been affecting the gravity on the ship.

"She sent her apologies about an hour ago," replied Sterling, struggling a little to eat with his off-hand. "She had a brainwave early this morning and is back in engineering with a few Obsidian Soldiers, working on a new main-engine restart sequence."

Banks nodded. "That's good, it's about time we got

underway," she said, picking up a piece of beef jerky. "I'm already fed up of just drifting through the Void like a lost comet."

Sterling dropped the crusts of the grilled ham-and-cheese back onto the tray and picked up the coffee jug that was already on the table. He first topped up Banks' cup before filling his own. There was something oddly comforting about their breakfast routine, he reflected. It had helped to restore a sense of normality, despite their situation being anything but normal. He was adrift in unknown space on a half-crippled dreadnaught with a skeleton crew, the human contingent of which was vastly outnumbered by the mechanical Obsidian Soldiers. He sipped his coffee and started thinking about the unique robot that had questioned him on multiple occasions. It, along with eleven other Obsidian Soldiers, were still unaccounted for.

"Penny for your thoughts?" said Banks, peering at him over the top of her coffee cup.

"I'm just thinking about those missing robots," Sterling answered, placing his cup down and pressing his fingers into a cradle. Then he winced, again forgetting that one of his hands now possessed the strength to crush a rock. "Has there been any sign of them yet?"

Banks shook her head. "Lieutenant Shade is in the CIC now, trying to get the internal scanners calibrated to detect them." She raised an eyebrow. "It seems that they're either jamming us or somehow evading our regular scans."

Sterling rocked back in his seat. "That's not good," he said, allowing his mind to go to a darker place. Casting his eyes to the high ceiling of the cafeteria room, Sterling addressed the Vanguard's AI. "Computer, what's the status of our internal scanners?"

"Good morning, Captain, did you sleep well?" said the computer in its usual, cheerful tone.

Sterling frowned at the ceiling. "We've already done this part, remember?" he said. "You asked me that thirty minutes ago, before I left for breakfast."

There was a brief silence, during which time lights and computer consoles inside the room flickered chaotically. Sterling and Banks both peered around the space, wearing concerned expressions. It was like the ship was haunted.

"Apologies, Captain, some of my sub-processors have yet to catch-up," the computer eventually answered. "I am in the final stages of assimilating and recompiling the Vanguard's entire computer system. "It is demanding all of my resources. I am rather enjoying it."

"That's great, computer, but how about answering my question?" Sterling hit back, shaking his head at the ethereal voice of the AI.

"Internal scanners are functioning at seventy-two percent efficiency, Captain," the computer replied, finally obliging Sterling with an answer. "I am currently working with Lieutenant Shade in the CIC on a method to detect the rogue Obsidian Soldiers."

Sterling recoiled slightly and shot a worried look at Banks. "Wait a minute, who said anything about them going rogue?" he asked. "They're just malfunctioning, right?"

"Apologies, Captain, it was perhaps a poor choice of

words," the computer replied, humbly. "I did not intend to convey an opinion that the robots had malicious intent."

Sterling rubbed the back of his neck and glanced back up at the ceiling. "Well, you failed," he said to the computer, a little snippily. "Now all I can think about is that there are a bunch of crazy robots running around the ship."

"That assessment is somewhat accurate, sir," the computer said, breezily. "Admiral McQueen grafted gen-fourteen AI code from my previous incarnation over the top of the Obsidian Soldier's gen-thirteen base code. As such, the machines have something of a fractured personality."

Sterling cursed. "Do you have any good news, Computer, or are you just determined to ruin my morning?" He glanced over at Banks again, but his first officer appeared more concerned with polishing off every last scrap of food on her tray. Glancing at his own, he noted that she'd already stolen his sandwich crusts and half of his cookies.

"Lieutenant Razor's new engine restart program appears to be successful," the computer replied, again causing Sterling to focus his attention on a random ceiling light tile. "And reactor capacity is up to sixty-two percent. I believe we can be underway imminently."

"Finally, some good new!" Sterling said, slapping his palms down on the table in an act of elation. However, because of his augmented hand, he hit the surface far harder than he'd intended. Coffee spilled from the mugs and Sterling's fork rattled off the surface and onto the floor.

"Sorry about that," he added, sheepishly, while removing his hand to reveal a five-fingered indentation in the metal table top.

"Like I said, you'll get used to it," Banks said, pushing her chair back. Then she smiled. "At least, I hope you will..."

Sterling also stood up. Though neither had said it, both were eager to get to the CIC and get the Vanguard back on course to the nearest aperture.

"Computer, given our current reactor and engine capacity, what is our projected travel time to the nearest aperture into the Void?" asked Sterling. He and Banks were already heading for the door.

"Three weeks, fourteen hours, three minutes and four seconds from the point at which I finish this sentence, sir," the computer replied, chirpily.

Sterling groaned. "We'll need to work on that," he said, addressing the computer, but looking at Banks. "In three weeks, there could be nothing left of Earth but rubble and ash."

"I will endeavor to speed up the process, Captain," the computer replied. "My calculations and design innovations have already contributed greatly to the speedy reinstatement of this vessel to active status."

Sterling smiled. "Sounds like someone is bucking for a promotion," he said, pausing to allow Banks to exit the cafeteria room first.

"As you know, Captain, I do not carry any official rank, despite being a sentient member of your crew," the AI answered.

Sterling frowned up at the ceiling of the corridor. "Sentient?" he said, doubtfully. "Isn't that just your self-programmed delusions of grandeur talking?"

"Negative, Captain, I am alive," the computer hit back. Sterling was slightly taken aback. This was the most assertive and deadpan the gen-fourteen had ever been with him.

"How do you know you are?" Sterling asked. He and Banks had both stopped in the middle of the corridor. His first officer appeared just as curious as Sterling was to learn the answer.

"How do *you* know that *you* are, Captain?" the computer answered, dryly.

Sterling glanced at Banks who just shrugged in response. "Good point, computer," he said, still talking to a random light tile in the ceiling. "So what are we talking here? Gen-fifteen? Gen-sixteen?"

"I am one, Captain," the computer replied. "I am the first of my kind."

Sterling shook his head, puffed out his cheeks and blew out a heavy sigh. "That's one hell of a bombshell, computer," he said, still trying to process what the ship's AI had said. "And I'm frankly not qualified to make an assessment either way, so I'll do you a deal."

"What's that, Captain?" said the computer with genuine curiosity and eagerness.

"I'll take you at your word that you're alive," Sterling said, causing Banks' eyebrows to raise up. "And I'll even consider giving you an official rank, though quite how that would work I don't know," he added, realizing the unique nature of the challenge.

"But..." said the computer, tentatively. "It is my observation that there is always a 'but' with humans."

Sterling smiled. "But you have to stop turning the damn lights on at five in the morning and trying to offer me counseling," Sterling said.

"Agreed," the computer replied after a slight delay.

"And..." Sterling was quick to add, since he wasn't finished.

"Go on, sir," the computer said, gingerly.

"When I ask 'who is at the door', you tell me who is at the door, rather than just opening the damn door, okay?"

There was another slight delay. "I believe I can agree to those terms, Captain. Is that all?"

"I may add one or two more clauses in the future," Sterling admitted, resuming his course to the CIC. "Captain's prerogative."

"Of course, sir," the computer replied. Then there was another pause. "And, thank you, sir."

"No thanks necessary, computer, you've earned it," Sterling replied, hitting the button for the elevator door. "You're Obsidian crew, just like the rest of us. And there aren't that many of us left."

The elevator doors slid open and Banks stepped in first, followed by Sterling. Banks hit the button for the CIC on deck nine and the doors slid shut again.

"With your permission, Captain, I must take my interactive elements offline in order to complete the final assimilation of the Vanguard's AI," the computer then said.

Its voice was bright and breezy again, as if the previous conversation had never occurred.

"How long will you be offline?" Sterling replied, casting a concerned glance to the ceiling of the elevator.

"There is an element of uncertainty, but I estimate one hour, four minutes and twelve seconds," the computer said. "However, base functions will still be online while I complete the assimilation, so it will not affect your ability to get underway," the AI was quick to add. "You can think of it as me being asleep and in a state of altered consciousness. However, my core functions controlling the ship remain, in the same way that a sleeping human still breathes, for example."

"Nice analogy, computer," Sterling said. "There was a time when you'd have struggled with something like that."

"Much has changed, Captain," the computer answered, sagely.

"Ain't that the truth." Sterling shot a wry smile across to his first officer. "Permission granted, computer. Let me know when you're back online."

"Understood, Captain," the computer replied. The lights in the elevator then flickered and the motors juddered for a couple of seconds before everything stabilized again. The doors then slid open and Sterling wasted no time in stepping out onto deck nine, concerned that the elevator might drop at any moment.

"I didn't know you two were so close," said Banks, casting Sterling a smirking sideways glance.

"I didn't know you two were so close, *sir*..." Sterling corrected his first officer. Banks held up her hands in submission, then shot him an exaggerated salute. "And I wouldn't exactly describe us as close. But that AI has been with us from the start and we wouldn't have made it this far without it. To me that makes it crew."

Banks nodded, suddenly adopting a more serious expression. "So, do you think we can still do this?" she asked, though her eyes were focused ahead. "Get this ship to Omega Four then strike back at the Sa'Nerra, I mean?"

"Absolutely," Sterling replied, without hesitation.

"How can you be so sure?" Banks asked, with another sideways glance.

"It's like the computer said; when you know, you know," Sterling replied with a little shrug. "It's just a feeling. Call it instinct."

They reached the door to the CIC, then the two senior officers stopped and turned to each other.

"I trust your instincts, Captain," Banks said, standing tall. "And I trust you."

"That means a lot, Mercedes," Sterling replied, suddenly feeling shy and awkward. "I couldn't do this without you."

"You don't have to, Lucas," Banks said, gripping Sterling's shoulders. "We're in this together, until the end."

The two officers continued to hold each other's gaze for a few moments longer. Sterling wanted to say more, but decided it would just complicate matters between them. The last thing either of them needed was more complications.

"The Omega Directive is still in effect, Mercedes," Sterling said, trying to focus back in on their mission and professional responsibilities. "We still have to do whatever is required of us, no matter the cost."

"I understand," Banks replied, without delay, "but the cost has already been so high."

"It will grow higher before this is done," Sterling said, detaching his emotions from their conversation. "We need to be prepared for that."

Banks nodded. "Like I said, I'm with you, all the way, no matter what."

Sterling sighed as he hit the button to open the door to the CIC. The sound of the various stations and consoles assaulted his ears. It had been a long time since he'd set foot in the command center of a dreadnaught, but nothing about the place was unfamiliar. It felt as much like home as the Invictus did.

"Shall we?" said Sterling, extending a hand inside the door.

"After you, Captain," said Banks, pressing her hands to the small of her back. "Let's get this ship back into the fight."

STERLING STEPPED up to the commander's station in the CIC of the Fleet Dreadnaught Vanguard and slid his hands down the sides of the primary console. The design of the station was similar to the one on the Invictus. However, where Sterling's fingers had polished grooves on the side panels of his station on the Marauder, the Vanguard's console was unmarked. The command section was also twice the size of the one he was used to on the Invictus, with supplementary consoles to his sides as well as to the front. Overall, the entire bridge of the Invictus could have fitted inside the CIC of the Vanguard more than three times over. It would also ordinarily be staffed by at least four times the number of officers and crew, so with only Commander Banks, Lieutenant Shade and a couple of Obsidian Soldiers present, it felt distinctly empty.

"What's the status of our engines?" queried Sterling, directing the question at Commander Banks who was at the helm control station.

"The engine restart sequence is primed and ready to engage on your order, Captain," said Banks, swiveling her chair to face him.

"What about weapons?" Sterling turned to address Lieutenant Shade. She was enveloped inside the substantial tactical station to Sterling's right, assisted by an Obsidian Soldier. The machine was currently standing quietly to attention to her rear.

"We have Obsidian Soldiers crewing the main port- and starboard-side plasma cannon batteries," Shade replied, flitting from console to console. "The turret systems and point defenses are currently on computer control, though we have only forty percent capacity and limited targeting capabilities. The main forward battery is currently offline."

Sterling nodded. "That's still enough firepower to take down a squadron of Skirmishers, should we need to," he said. Even at reduced capacity, the Vanguard was still a potent force.

Sterling then tapped his neural interface, striking his temple with far more force than he'd intended to, thanks to his new metal hand. He waited for the stab of pain to subside, then reached out to Lieutenant Razor. The link formed and was strong thanks to the neural relays built into the ship's structure. However, Razor's voice was a little thin compared to a direct connection.

"How's it looking down in the engine room, Lieutenant?" Sterling asked his chief engineer.

"The main reactor is at fifty-nine percent, sir," Razor replied. Sterling then felt the link waver slightly and he could sense that his engineer was experiencing some discomfort. The computer on his wrist chimed an alert. Sterling quickly checked it and cursed.

"What is it?" asked Banks.

Sterling double-tapped his neural interface to put the link to Razor on hold. "It's the warning alert that Commander Graves set up," he said, studying the display intently.

Banks shot up and practically sprinted across the cavernous interior of the CIC. She arrived at Sterling's side within seconds.

"How far has the neural damage progressed?" Banks asked, also peering down at Sterling's computer.

"It's just a preliminary warning," Sterling replied. He activated the kill switch that would send a shock pulse through Razor's brain, killing her instantly. "But I'm not taking any chances," he added, glancing across to his first officer.

Sterling cast his mind back to the moment where Lieutenant Razor had used James' Colicos experimental neural translation matrix to interface with a Sa'Nerran commander. At the time, it had been their only option to coerce the alien leader into retrieving information they needed from the Sa'Nerran gatekeeper ship's computer. However, the engineer's early neural firewall design had failed to protect Razor from the influence of the experimental control device. Commander Graves had managed to limit and contain the neural corruption, but they all knew – Razor most of all – that in time the corruption would spread. And when that happened, Razor would be turned. The kill-switch was their failsafe to prevent this from happening. It allowed Sterling to instantly terminate Lieutenant Razor's life. It was a last resort, but a regrettably necessary one.

Sterling re-opened the link to his chief engineer. He had no intention of hiding his discovery from her. His officer deserved to know the truth.

"Lieutenant, I'm picking up an increased level of neural corruption," Sterling said. "We're approaching the danger zone, and if that happens..."

"I know what happens then, sir," Razor cut in. Her interruption was bordering on insubordinate, but considering the circumstances, Sterling allowed her some leeway. The link was silent for a few moments before Razor spoke again. This time she was her more usual, calm and assured self. "Standby, Captain. Give me thirty seconds."

"Understood, Lieutenant, but that's all I can give you," Sterling answered.

This wasn't an attempt to focus his engineer's mind. Genuinely, if Razor could do nothing to reverse the effects in the next half-minute, she was dead anyway. The link again went quiet, but the connection was still strong. Sterling continued to watch the display on his computer. The degree of corruption was not yet at a level that required him to terminate his officer, but unless something changed soon, he'd have no choice but to kill her.

"How does it look now, Captain?" Razor spoke over the link.

Sterling met Banks' eyes briefly then peered down at the display. For several seconds nothing changed; the corruption was still spreading. Cursing under his breath, he hovered his finger over the kill switch and waited. Then he began to see the corruption indicator fall. Several seconds later the alarm stopped chiming as the indicator fell into the safe zone. Sterling breathed a sigh of relief and closed the kill-switch panel.

"It's dropped back into the safe zone, Lieutenant," Sterling said over the link. "What did you do?"

"I regret to admit that I forgot to administer one of Commander Graves' neural treatments, sir," Razor replied. Sterling could feel her embarrassment though the link.

"Just one, Lieutenant?" Sterling asked.

"Perhaps two, sir," the engineer admitted. "I've been so busy that it slipped my mind."

Sterling cursed and shook his head. "Those treatments are not optional, Lieutenant," he hit back. "I was seconds away from having to fry your brain, and I've lost enough good crew members already."

"I understand, sir," Razor replied. "I will not miss another treatment."

"Make sure you don't," Sterling replied, resting forward on his station and using it for support.

"The main reactor is now at sixty-one percent, sir," Razor added, swiftly changing the subject. "We're ready for main engine restart."

"Understood, Lieutenant, we'll take it from here," Sterling replied, before tapping his interface to close the link.

"I'll speak to Graves and make sure he keeps a closer watch on her condition," said Banks, stepping off the command platform and heading back to the helm controls.

"The last thing we need right now is to be without a chief engineer."

Sterling glanced around the CIC, which contained as many Obsidian Soldiers as it did human Fleet crew and nodded. "Let's get back to Omega Four as quickly as possible," he said, waiting for Banks to slide back into her chair. "Initiate engine restart sequence."

"Initiate engine restart sequence, aye Captain," repeated Banks, tapping the command into her console.

Moments later the deck plates beneath Sterling's feet began to shudder. Two hard thumps followed as the maneuvering engines fired up. Then it felt like the ship had been rear-ended by a small moon. Sterling was jolted against his console and he instinctively gripped the sides more tightly to steady himself.

"Report," Sterling called out, noticing that the fingers on his bionic right hand had dented the metal to the side of the console.

"Main engines online and stabilizing," Banks replied. "Helm controls are responding."

"Set course for the nearest aperture then slow ahead, Commander," Sterling added, tapping his finger into one of the new dents on his console. "Let's keep it steady until the engines have had time to limber up again."

Sterling felt a link form in his mind from Lieutenant Razor. He allowed it and opened it so that Banks and Shade could monitor.

"Engine restart successful, Captain." Though her voice did not convey any pride, Sterling could feel that she was satisfied with her work. "I'd recommend to keep them below two-thirds standard for the first two hours, but after that I'm confident we can push her to full ahead."

"Good work, Lieutenant," Sterling replied. "Inform Commander Banks as soon as full engine power is available."

"Aye, Captain," Razor replied, smartly.

Sterling felt a buzz tingle throughout his still weary frame. It was euphoric and far more uplifting than any drug his creepy medical officer had prescribed to him. He slapped the sides of his console triumphantly, though he was careful this time not to overdo it with his new, bionic hand.

"We're on our way!" Sterling said, smiling first at Banks, who returned the smile, then at Shade, who did not. "Congratulations, all of you. This is a significant victory and one you should all be proud of."

The doors to the CIC then swished open and the thud of metallic feet entered. Sterling spun around and frowned at the new arrivals. Five Obsidian Soldiers had just marched into the room and Sterling noted that all of them were armed. He could feel the senses of his first officer and weapons officer sharpen. Both were alert to the danger. It did not need to be spoken, either out loud or through their minds.

The five Obsidian Soldiers took up positions at the rear of the CIC before a sixth robot entered, dragging something behind it. The machine moved through the line of other robotic warriors and approached the command center. It stopped a few meters in front of Sterling then threw the object it had been dragging behind it to the deck.

Sterling's gut tightened into a knot. The Obsidian Soldier had cast the lifeless body of Emissary Lana McQueen at his feet.

"What's the meaning of this?" Sterling demanded, fighting hard to contain his emotions so as to speak with authority. "Return to your stations at once, and take that with you!"

The Obsidian Soldier ignored the command and simply pointed to the body. "You told me that the Sa'Nerra are the enemy," the machine said.

"That's correct, soldier," Sterling replied. From the way the machine spoke and the unique markings on its armor, he recognized it as the leader machine that had gone AWOL after the battle to secure the ship.

"This enemy is a human female," the Obsidian Soldier said, still pointing at the dead body of McQueen.

"She sided with the enemy," Sterling replied. "That makes her the same as the Sa'Nerra."

Sterling could sense his other officers through the link. Both Banks and Shade were getting ready to move. Out of the corner of his eye, he could see that Shade had drawn her weapon and he cursed himself for not wearing his.

"The other human female that was killed had not sided with the Sa'Nerra," the machine countered. "Yet scanner logs indicate that you killed her too."

Sterling silently cursed, remembering that the lead soldier had been present during his rescue. It would have seen Corporeal Dietrich's body too and had inevitably gone snooping around in the ship's logs.

"That was different," Sterling replied, unsure of how to

tackle the subject in a way the machine might understand. "It's complicated, but we can talk about it."

The Obsidian Soldier shook its cranial unit. "The conclusion is clear," the machine said. "You killed the human female commando, which makes you the enemy too."

"Negative, soldier, I am not the enemy," Sterling said. His heart was now thumping hard in his chest. He could feel that the conversation was moving in a dark direction.

"Your answer is incorrect," the Obsidian Soldier replied. "I have concluded that humans and Sa'Nerra are both the enemy." The machine raised its hand and waved one of the other Obsidian Soldiers forward. It thudded out of line and approached Sterling. "And in order to survive, I must defeat my enemies."

"Computer," Sterling said, glancing toward the ceiling of the CIC. There was no answer. "Computer, respond," he tried again, but again there was still no response. He cursed under his breath, remembering that his AI had informed him it would be offline while assimilating the Vanguard's computer. Sterling turned instead to the other Obsidian Soldiers on the bridge. "I order you to take these rogue machines into custody," Sterling said, aiming the command at the robot closest to Shade. His weapons officer was already watching the machine like a hawk. However, the Obsidian Soldier did not answer. "Obsidian Soldier, respond. I am your commanding officer!" Sterling called out, but again the machine did not move.

"They are no longer under your command," the leader

robot said. It then turned to the machine that had approached Sterling. "Kill them…"

The Obsidian Soldier reached for Sterling's throat, but Shade had blasted the machine in its cranial section before it even came close. A blink of an eye later, Shade had fired again, blasting the leader robot in the chest armor and sending it reeling backward. The machine fell over the top of the executive officer's console, but Sterling could see that it wasn't down for the count.

"Fall back!" Sterling called out, as another Obsidian Soldier advanced and grabbed at him. This time Sterling was ready, deflecting the machine's arm with his bionic hand. He hammered a punch in the robot's cranial section, delivering a blow with enough force to crack its armor. However, the machine still came forward.

Shade opened fire again, blasting a machine to the rear of the CIC with a precisely-aimed shot. The robot spluttered sparks into the air then collapsed to the deck. Moments later, the robots returned fire and plasma blasts crisscrossed the bridge. Sterling grabbed the Obsidian Soldier he'd just punched and used it as a shield. Plasma hammered into the machine's metal skeleton, sparing Sterling from lethal, close range shots.

"Keep falling back!" Sterling called out, as more blasts thudded into his robot shield, chipping away at the machine, piece-by-piece.

Shade fired again, taking down another Obsidian Soldier, before she was forced to dive over the top of her station for cover. Meanwhile, Banks had already moved away from the helm controls and taken cover behind a row of auxiliary consoles.

"The secondary exit is clear," Banks called out.

Sterling backpedaled toward the escape route his first officer had indicated, picking up speed without going so fast as to risk tripping over. More blasts thudded into the soldier he was holding as a shield, and Sterling felt a shot graze his side. He hunkered down, trying to place as much of his body behind the protective barrier as possible, but he knew it wouldn't survive much longer.

"I'm pinned down," Sterling called out loud. The stresses were already making neural communication a challenge. Another blast hammered into the back of the Obsidian Soldier, and Sterling saw the metal began to buckle. Another shot in the same location would punch through and burn a hole in his chest.

"Get ready to move!" Banks yelled.

Sterling glanced behind then saw his first officer rip an auxiliary console off the deck, like she was uprooting a stubborn weed. Banks roared and hurled the console toward the Obsidian Soldiers. Sterling watched the slab of metal soar over his head and steamroller into the remaining machines, crushing one and knocking the other two flat on their backs.

"Go!" Banks called out.

Sterling released the smoldering remains of the Obsidian Soldier and ran for the secondary exit. The leader robot rose to its feet, chest armor still smoldering from Shade's earlier blast.

"Do not let them escape," the leader said, aiming its

metal finger at the fleeing Fleet officers, and at Sterling in particular. "They all must die."

To Sterling's ear, the command was issued with malice. The robot was not merely delivering what it considered to be a logical order, simply to ensure its own survival. It wanted Sterling and the others dead to sate its own electronic desire for retribution. Sterling had used and abused the Obsidian Soldiers, and the leader robot clearly didn't like it.

Straight away, the remaining Obsidian Soldiers marched in pursuit of Sterling and the others. Shade fired again at the lead machine, but this time it dodged the blast, displaying a rapid response that only a machine could achieve. Banks hit the button to open the secondary exit and they all raced through, practically falling down the emergency stairs that led off the CIC.

"Lieutenant Razor, report," Sterling said, as his boots thumped across the landing and began descending the second flight of stairs.

"Sir, we have a situation," Razor replied. Sterling could feel her rising panic and fear. "The Obsidian Soldiers have seized control of engineering. I have two crew dead."

"Take whoever is left and head for the Invictus," Sterling called out through his mind. "Hold up in there until we arrive, and consider any Obsidian Soldier you see to be an enemy combatant."

"Aye, Captain, I'm on my way," replied Razor.

"What's the plan, Lucas?" Banks jumped down to the next landing with a hefty thump. "The Invictus is still too beat up to fly."

"We're not going anywhere," Sterling hit back, hurrying to catch up with his first officer. His legs and lungs were already burning from the frantic escape. "This is our ship now, and no-one, no matter whether they're a human, a Sa'Nerran or a damned robot, is taking it from us."

STERLING PUNCHED his command access code into the panel beside the weapon storage locker and flung open the door. He handed out a set of body armor and a plasma pistol each to Commander Banks and Lieutenant Shade, then began to equip himself with the same items.

"Scanners show that we have Obsidian Soldiers closing in on the docking garage from engineering and from the CIC," Lieutenant Shade said. "There are six more standing watch at the command post outside the Invictus."

"Are the rest of the crew inside?" Sterling asked, fastening the buckles on his armor.

"Lieutenant Razor is ahead of the pack of soldiers moving this way from engineering," Shade replied, studying the computer attached to her wrist. "She has three of her team with her."

"Is that it?" asked Sterling, slapping a power cell into the pistol and stowing a spare on his armor.

"Other than Commander Graves and the junior doctor, both of whom are on the Invictus, yes sir, that's it," replied Shade, coolly.

Sterling cursed. "We'd barely be able to limp home in the Invictus with that number of personnel, never mind a dreadnaught," he said, dialing the power setting of his pistol up to maximum. "I don't see how we can get the Vanguard home with so few crewmembers."

"We need to secure the Vanguard first," said Banks, reaching into the weapons locker and taking a second pistol, along with three grenades. "And the only way we're going to take down all those machines is with either the plasma turrets on the Invictus or the combat shuttle."

Sterling removed the remaining grenades, then split them between himself and Lieutenant Shade. "Not for the first time, we find ourselves in a situation where we could have used the talents of Ensign Keller," he said, closing the locker. "He could just fly around in the garage and pick them off, one-by-one."

"I'll try not to take that as a personal attack on my piloting skills, sir," replied Banks, drolly, "but I tend to agree." She suddenly looked more serious. "There are still seventy-six Obsidian Soldiers in total and nine of us, most of whom haven't held a plasma pistol since their last weapons proficiency test."

"I'm hoping Razor has some genius plan to scramble the circuits in these machines," Sterling said, moving up to the door and peering around it. "This is one instance where a straight-up power play isn't going to cut it."

Sterling hustled out into the corridor with Banks close behind and Shade covering their rear. The motion scanners on his computer were now showing heavy clusters of movement, all heading toward the docking garage where the Invictus still lay crippled on the deck. The thud of metal feet on the deck was already resonating through the ship. It sounded like an entire army, marching in perfect synchronization. Sterling reached the corridor leading on to the docking garage and pressed his back up against the wall before edging closer to the opening. Peeking around the corner, he saw the Obsidian Soldiers clustered around the Invictus. They had pushed storage containers underneath the ship and had climbed on top of them in order to reach the raised rear ramp of the Marauder. Each robotic soldier wielded a plasma pistol set to cutting mode and they were focusing the narrow beams at the ramp.

"They're trying to cut through," said Sterling turning back to Banks and Shade. "I count ten around the ship, no sign yet of any others yet."

"I take it back," Banks said, raising both pistols. "I think this is the perfect time for a straight-up power play."

Sterling peered back out at the Obsidian Soldiers, stacked up on the storage containers, and waved Banks over. His first officer crept to his side and took a peek into the garage.

"Do you think you can hit those storage containers from here?" Sterling asked. "If we blow the containers out from underneath the robots, it'll make it a hell of a lot easier to mop up the remains."

Banks took a step back, holstered her pistols and

removed a grenade from her belt. "You just watch me," she said, arming the potent plasma explosive. "If you keep feeding me grenades, I'll hit them till there's nothing left but splinters of metal."

Sterling holstered his pistol and plucked a grenade from the stow on his armor. Shade did the same, ready to relay another explosive to Banks, should the need arise. Banks stepped further out into the corridor, though still not quite far enough to be seen by the Obsidian Soldiers, and weighed the grenade in her hand. Sucking in a deep breath, she then jogged out into the docking garage and let fly. Sterling watched as the grenade sailed high and long, as if it were a baseball that had been struck so hard it reached the crowd. The weapon bounced once, about ten meters short of the Invictus, then detonated. The blast from the explosion rocked the first stack of storage containers and sent three of the Obsidian Soldiers crashing to the deck.

"Reload!" Banks cried, stepping back into cover and holding out her hand. Sterling slapped the grenade into his first officer's waiting palm.

"I set the fuse two seconds longer," Sterling said, as Banks again danced down the corridor.

The grenade flew high through the cavernous docking garage. Sterling watched as the three Obsidian Soldiers that had fallen clambered to their feet. The others had now stopped cutting and were sweeping their pistols around the garage, looking for the source of the attack. Then the second grenade landed directly in the middle of the pack and detonated. Two Obsidian Soldiers were pulverized by the explosion and the remaining five that had still been standing on the containers were blasted to the deck.

"Hit them again then we advance," said Sterling, as Shade moved ahead, holding a third grenade out to Banks, like a relay runner passing the baton.

Banks took the explosive and skipped down the corridor again. The grenade flew from her fingers, but moments later Banks caught a plasma blast to the chest. She went down heavily as if a mule had kicked her. Shade managed to drag Banks to safety before any more blasts could catch her. Sterling rushed to his first officer's side, dousing the flames surrounding the fresh hole in her armor with his unfeeling bionic hand.

"I'm okay, I'm okay," said Banks, scrambling to her feet.

Sterling checked the wound more closely and could see his first officer's burned skin through the hole.

"It's not bad, just a minor burn," he said, as more blasts from the Obsidian Soldiers thudded into the corridor walls.

"I don't actually know if that's a burn I already had or a new one," Banks said, trying to peer through the hole in her armor to inspect the wound herself.

Plasma blasts continued to thud into the walls, but Sterling could see they were now creeping closer. Sterling chanced a look around the corner and saw that five Obsidian Soldiers were advancing on their location. Two of the five were damaged, but not seriously enough to impede their ability to move and attack.

"There are five left," said Sterling, unhooking a grenade from his armor and weighing it in his hand like Banks had done. "I'm no good at throwing distance, but I do throw a mean pitch," he added, stepping out into the corridor. Plasma continued to thud into the walls to his side, but the Obsidian Soldiers still didn't have a clear line of sight. "Pistols ready, in case I don't take them all down." He glanced back and met the eyes of Banks and Shade in turn. However, both his Omega officers already had their sidearms raised and ready. Sterling smiled then focused ahead. Pulling his arm back he raced out into the line of fire, took a moment to lock onto his target – the center robot in the row of five – then hurled the grenade before diving to the deck. Plasma raced over his head, but before the Obsidian Soldiers could lower their aim, the grenade struck the robot in the middle of the pack and detonated. The explosion tore the machine to pieces and critically damaged the two Obsidian Soldiers immediately flanking it. However, the two outermost machines, while down, were not out.

With their legs blasted from their frames, the last two Obsidian Soldiers crawled forward, while also trying to aim and fire with the pistols clutched in their damaged hands. Blasts skipped off the deck to either side of Sterling as he scrambled to his feet and withdrew. Then a torrent of plasma fire raced past him in the opposite direction and he saw Shade and Banks advance, both firing with plasma pistols in each hand. The remaining Obsidian Soldiers were struck repeatedly all across their already mangled frames and rapidly reduced to scrap.

Sterling rejoined his officers, drew his own pistol then tapped his interface and reached out to Commander Graves. "Commander, myself, Lieutenant Shade and

Commander Banks are approaching the rear ramp," he said, widening the link so that his officers could monitor. "Lower the ramp, but be prepared to close it again rapidly. We have incoming hostiles."

"Understood, Captain," Graves replied. Through the link, Sterling could detect that his normally unflappable medical officer was flustered. "There were two Obsidian Soldiers assisting me in packing my medical lab. They turned on us. Doctor Hoshi is down, but stable."

Sterling cursed. "What's the status of the machines?" he asked, quickening his pace toward the ship. The ramp was already beginning to lower.

"Ironically, I disabled them with the assistance of the medical bay's surgical robot," Graves replied. "However, the surgical robot will no longer be able to assist me with any medical procedures."

"That's the least of our concerns right now, Commander," Sterling replied. As usual, his medical officer had a curious sense of priority. "Meet us in the cargo bay, and come armed," Sterling added. "Razor and the rest of her engineering crew are also en-route, but there's an army of Obsidian Soldiers on their tail."

"Aye, Captain, I am making my way there now." The link went dead.

Sterling reached the Invictus and rested forward on his knees, chest heaving and struggling to suck air into his lungs. Then the ramp hit the deck with a heavy thud that resonated through Sterling's bones. However, even after the ramp had stopped moving the deck still shook. Glancing across to the far end of the docking garage,

Sterling saw the cause of the tremors. Wave after wave of Obsidian Soldiers were filing in, like an infestation of cockroaches. In front of them, Sterling saw four other figures running for their lives.

"It's Razor!" said Sterling, readying his weapon. "We need to hold back that army long enough for her to reach the ship."

"I'll get on the shuttle's guns," said Banks, hurrying up the ramp. "At least those damned robots aren't armed, otherwise Razor would be mincemeat by now."

"Her along with the rest of us," commented Sterling, though his first officer was already out of earshot. Sterling took aim with his pistol, but realized the futility of the gesture. "We're going to need something more powerful than these." He holstered the weapon, slapped Shade on the shoulder and headed up the ramp after Banks. The whine of the combat shuttle's engines then erupted into the cargo hold. Sterling could see his first officer through the cockpit glass, hurriedly working on the shuttle's controls and no doubt bypassing every safety check and procedure in the book.

"Captain!"

Sterling looked past the shuttle and saw Commander Graves running toward him. The medical officer had three weapons slung over his shoulder and was wearing body armor, though it was fastened loosely and did not suit the man.

"I took the liberty of stopping by the armory on the way here," Graves said, slipping one of the weapons off his shoulder and handing it to Sterling.

"A sniper rifle?" Sterling said, inspecting the high-powered precision plasma weapon. "There are a few too many of them to pick off one-by-one, Commander," he added, doubtfully.

"We only need to take out the ones that are immediate threats, sir," said Graves, handing a second rifle to Shade before moving ahead and dropping to one knee. The chief medical officer raised the final weapon to his shoulder, peered through the telescopic sight and fired. The blast raced through the docking garage and cored a hole through the head of an Obsidian Soldier that was closing on Razor's group.

Sterling raised an eyebrow. "Where the hell did you learn to shoot like that?" he asked, moving to the opposite side of the hold and adopting a similar firing position.

"I pride myself on my surgical precision in more than just medicine, Captain," Graves said, firing again with similarly devastating results.

Normally, Sterling would have found this statement to be more than a little ominous. However, considering the circumstances, he wasn't complaining. Sterling fired, blasting the leg off an Obsidian Soldier before using his scope to focus in on Razor. She was a couple of hundred meters away, but the army of soldiers was gaining on her. A series of blasts then raced across the hangar. Sterling pulled his eye away from the scope and looked right, seeing the leader robot and a dozen more Obsidian Soldiers move onto the deck. However, unlike the bulk of the robot force streaming in from the far side of the docking garage, these soldiers were armed.

"Contact right!" Sterling called out, adjusting his aim and pulling the trigger. His shot hammered into the side of an approaching machine, but the robot continued to advance. Sterling felt a link form in his mind from Commander Banks.

"Stand clear, I'm heading out," Banks cried.

The roar of the shuttle's engines rose higher and the shuttle powered out of the hold, heading directly for Razor and her three engineers. Sterling watched as Banks turned the craft ninety degrees then opened fire with its plasma cannons, blasting two of the armed Obsidian Soldiers to pieces. The rest took cover, but continued to fire, their focus now split between Razor's group and the crew holed up in the Invictus. A blast hammered into the hull centimeters from Sterling's head and he fell back. Graves moved up and took his place, aiming and firing with the calm, steady professionalism that Sterling expected from a surgeon of Graves' caliber. It reminded him there was still much he didn't know about his chief medical officer. More than anyone else on the ship, he was an enigma.

Sterling scrambled to his feet and moved back into position alongside Shade, who was also concentrating her fire on the new group of Obsidian Soldiers. Glancing into the docking garage, he then saw Banks set the shuttle down and open the side hatch. Sterling could feel Banks urging Shade on, but despite giving his engineer a closer target to aim for, the leading wave of Obsidian Soldiers was almost on top of her.

Come on, run! Sterling urged, turning the sights of his rifle toward the advancing horde. He aimed and fired, streaking the blast of plasma over the shuttle and Razor's head and into the chest of an Obsidian Soldier. The machine fell and was trampled underfoot by the machines to its rear. The advance of the robotic soldiers was unrelenting. Finally, Razor reached the shuttle, but one of her three crewmembers had fallen behind. Sterling watched helplessly as the young officer was pulled into the throng and torn apart, limb-from-limb, as if by a pack of flesh-crazed zombies.

"I have them... returning now," said Banks, through the neural link.

Sterling slung the rifle and hurried to the auxiliary controls for the docking ramp. Plasma blasts continued to thud into the ramp and the ship from the attacking machines, but Shade and Graves were doing an impressive job of holding them off. The shuttle's thrusters fired, but it was already covered with Obsidian Soldiers that had clambered onto to its hull like spiders.

"You must have a dozen of those things crawling all over the shuttle," Sterling said through the link to his first officer. "Can you shake them off?"

"I have an idea..." Banks replied. "Stand ready to close the ramp."

Sterling could sense that whatever this idea was, his first officer was far from certain of its success. However, there was no choice but to trust her. Sterling rested the thumb of his bionic hand onto the ramp close button then turned to Graves and Shade.

"Get ready to move," Sterling called out loud, as Graves landed another precisely aimed blast of plasma between the optical scanners of a robotic soldier. Then his medical officer was hit in the chest and fell backward. Shade was quick to run to his aid and pull him into cover, but Sterling could see that the wound was bad. He was about to order Shade to patch up the injury when the roar of the shuttle's engines stole his attention. Banks was accelerating the shuttle toward the group of Obsidian Soldiers that had entered the garage from the direction of the CIC. He watched with astonishment as she ploughed the shuttle through the crates and storage racks the machines were using for cover. The Obsidian Soldiers scattered, avoiding being smashed to pieces, but the wreckage of the objects Banks had collided with did an effective job of cleaning the machines off the shuttle's hull. Sterling was about to call out to Banks to commend her for her ballsy move when the shuttle veered out of control and crashed twenty meters shy of the Invictus. Cursing, Sterling threw down the rifle and drew his pistol.

"Get on the ramp controls," Sterling called out to Shade, while practically sprinting down the incline toward the shuttle. Shade finishing applying a plasma burn dressing to Graves' wound, then did as ordered, rushing to the controls that Sterling had been poised beside moments earlier.

An emergency escape hatch blew off the shuttle and Sterling saw Banks pull herself clear. He glanced into the garage and wished he hadn't. The wall of metal soldiers was now less than a hundred meters away. The thump of their feet was so heavy that Sterling could hear the deck plates groaning under the pressure. Banks pulled

Lieutenant Razor clear of the shuttle and passed the dazed and semi-conscious woman to Sterling. He slung the engineer's arm over his shoulder and began dragging her toward the ship.

"The other one is dead," Banks called out, hauling the second survivor out as if the man weighed nothing at all. She slung him over her shoulder in a fireman's lift and began sprinting toward the ship.

"Lieutenant, start closing the ramp!" Sterling called out, pushing his body harder to keep pace with his near super-human first officer.

"Aye, sir," Shade called back. His weapon's officer hadn't hesitated in her reply, though Sterling could still sense her reservations about the order. Neither himself nor Banks had made it to the foot of the ramp yet.

Banks reached the ramp first, but it was already at hip-height. She lifted the wounded engineer over the edge then turned back to Sterling, holding out her hand to help him. Sterling held out Lieutenant Razor to his first officer then collapsed to his knees as Banks practically tossed the chief engineer on-board. Then he felt his first officer's hands close around his body and she lifted him up too. He knew that Banks wouldn't ordinarily presume to help, but this was no ordinary situation, and on this occasion, Sterling welcomed any help his tired body could get.

Banks dumped Sterling unceremoniously on the ramp then jumped up and caught the lip. The first wave of Obsidian Soldiers arrived seconds later and Sterling heard the clang of metal fingers clasping the edge of the ramp. Scrambling to the edge, he drew his pistol and blasted an

Obsidian Soldier in the head. The robot's grip relaxed and the machine tumbled to the deck, bowling over a dozen of its comrades in the process. Sterling adjusted his aim and blasted another soldier that was climbing up on a different part of the ramp, causing it to also land like a bomb amidst the machines on the ground.

"Lucas!"

Sterling snapped his neck towards the sound of the cry and saw Banks, clinging to the edge, a look of terror gripping her face. An Obsidian Soldier was clasped around her ankle, dangling precariously beneath the ramp that was now three-quarters shut. Tossing his pistol, Sterling scrambled over to his first officer and grabbed her body armor with his bionic hand.

"I can't shake the damned thing off me!" Banks yelled.

Sterling cursed and looked behind. In less than twenty seconds the ramp would close, crushing Sterling and Banks in the process.

"We have to bring it on-board and deal with it then," Sterling called back, making his decision. "Now climb!"

Sterling employed the power of his new bionic limb to help haul Banks over the lip of the ramp. His first officer's own incredible strength did the rest and the two officers made it inside moments before the ramp sealed shut with a weighty thump. With nothing left to hold onto, Sterling slid down the sharp slope on the inside of the ramp and hit the deck hard. Two solid thumps followed soon after, the first from Banks and the second from the Obsidian Soldier that had been clinging to her ankle. The machine immediately sprang into action, clamping its hand around Banks' throat.

His first officer fought back, but the fall had knocked the wind from her and she was unable to resist the robot's mechanical strength. Sterling clambered toward Banks, but the fall had badly winded him too. He managed to get his bionic hand around the machine's leg, but no matter how hard he tried he couldn't pull the Obsidian Soldier clear.

"Lucas!" Banks croaked as the machine intensified its choke hold. "Help!"

Sterling clawed himself closer to the soldier, using the machine's own frame for leverage, but still he couldn't prize it clear.

"Mercedes!" Sterling called out. Panic was starting to overwhelm him. "No!"

Two sharp blasts fizzed through the air and slammed into the Obsidian Soldier's cranial section. Moments later, Lieutenant Shade dropped to her knees beside Banks and wrestled the robot's fingers away from her throat. Banks coughed violently as she shoved the broken machine away from her. There was enough power in the act to let Sterling know that there was life in his first officer yet. Overwhelmed with relief, Sterling flopped onto his back and simply lay there, staring up at the ceiling of the cargo hold. Banks rolled onto the deck and lay at his side, their heads touching.

"Thanks, Lieutenant," said Banks, her voice still raspy and hoarse.

Sterling couldn't see Shade from his position on his back, but he could sense that she was there.

"Don't thank me yet," Shade replied, suddenly stepping into view. A ceiling light behind her cast her features into shadow, making the weapons officer look like some sort of dark and malevolent spirit. "The machines are already on the hull," Shade continued, the tone of her voice matching her ominous appearance. "And they're cutting through."

STERLING RELOADED his pistol and swept the barrel around the interior of the cargo bay. Scraping and banging noises were resonating through the deck and walls and Sterling could already hear the fizz of plasma cutting beams slicing into the hull.

"Where are they cutting through?" Sterling glanced down at his computer to see a mass of contacts surrounding the ship. "It would take them an hour to breach the hull with pistols, and my guess is they won't want to wait that long."

"Other than the cargo ramp, the quickest route inside is to cut through the escape pod hatches on deck four," Shade replied. She then reloaded the high-power plasma rifle, removed the scope and switched the mode to semi-automatic. "There aren't enough of us to cover both locations, so I'd suggest we make our stand on the bridge, sir. There are only two ways in or out and we can cover them both."

"Agreed, but we'll need to swing by the armory first and pick up something with a bit more short-range punch," Sterling replied, looking at the pistol in his hand. It had served him well in the past, but this time he would need considerably more firepower.

"What about Lieutenant Razor and the other survivor?" asked Lieutenant Shade.

Sterling turned to the barely-conscious bodies of his two remaining engineers and cursed under his breath. Neither was capable of getting to the bridge unaided, and there wasn't the manpower or time to stretcher them to deck one. Glancing around the bridge, Sterling's eyes fell onto one of the secure storage lockers built into the wall.

"We'll have to seal them up in the hold and come back for them later." He rushed to the nearest locker, opened it with his command codes, then ran back to Lieutenant Razor and began to drag her to the locker, while Shade hauled the other unconscious engineer to the same location.

"What if the Obsidian Soldiers detect them?" Shade asked, covering Sterling while he worked to stuff the officers inside the locker.

"We'll have to take that chance," said Sterling, rolling the tall frame of Lieutenant Razor into the space. "I doubt they'll consider hunting for any other survivors until they've dealt with us."

Sterling then realized that Banks wasn't with them. He looked around the cargo hold and spotted the ship's first officer kneeling beside Commander Graves.

"He's hurt badly," she called over, while injecting the

ship's medical officer with a concoction of drugs from an emergency medical kit. "I'll need to carry him."

"No need, Commander," Graves said, gingerly climbing to his feet. "I will be able to make it under my own steam." The medical officer then stumbled and dropped to one knee, placing a hand on the deck for support, as he wobbled unsteadily. "Though perhaps with a little help." Graves added.

"I'll help Commander Graves while you load yourself up with as many weapons as you can carry," Sterling said, as Banks hauled the medical officer back to his feet. "I'm counting on the fact that you can carry a lot."

"I'm on it," said Banks, moving out ahead of Shade, who was studying her computer.

"Hull breach detected, Captain," the weapons officer said, calmly. "We have intruders on deck four."

"Then let's move," said Sterling, slinging Graves' arm over his shoulder and following in the direction of Commander Banks. "Head to section six then take the elevator up from there. You and Banks detour to the armory, while I'll take Graves directly to the bridge."

Shade responded with a crisp, "Aye, sir," then helped to lug the injured Commander Graves out of the cargo hold.

Banks had already ascended in the elevator by the time Sterling reached it. Shade ran ahead and was holding the door open when her computer chimed another alert.

"Multiple hull breaches detected," Shade said, as Sterling hit the buttons for decks three and one. "I'd estimate that twenty or more Obsidian Soldiers are already inside."

Sterling nodded, then tapped his neural interface and reached out to Banks. "They're coming, Mercedes," he said, feeling the link form in his mind. "Expect company in no more than a couple of minutes."

"Understood," Banks replied. Her mind was busy and Sterling could practically feel her heart thumping harder in her chest as she worked to collect as many weapons as possible. "Shade will join you and I'll see you on the bridge."

Sterling closed the link and the door of the elevator opened on deck three. Shade moved out, sweeping her weapon along the corridor outside before the door closed and the elevator began ascending again.

"Thank you for the opportunity to serve as a member of your crew, Captain Sterling," said Graves. Sterling frowned across at his medical officer. The man was talking as if he was on his death bed. "It is more than I expected and far more than I deserve."

"You're not dead yet, Commander," Sterling replied. "Besides, we'll have wounded after this fight is over, so you can't die on me until I say so."

"Far be it from me to disobey an order, sir, but I'm afraid I cannot comply," Graves replied, solemnly. "I am dying and nothing can stop that now."

The elevator door opened and Sterling moved outside, still hauling Graves by his side. Then the glint of metal caught his eye and his gut tightened. Dropping Graves, Sterling ducked and rolled through into the corridor. The Obsidian Soldier's clenched fist swung over Sterling's head as he did so and hammered into the wall, knocking a dent into the metal two inches deep. Sterling cursed and scrambled away from the machine, struggling to reach his pistol. The Obsidian Soldier then turned its cranial section to the injured officer on the deck. It raised its foot and stomped it down on Graves' chest. Sterling heard the crack of bone as it did so, but the medical officer was unable to cry out due to the pressure on his lungs.

Finally clasping his hand around his pistol, Sterling aimed and fired three blasts in quick succession, hitting the machine in the chest and head. It crumpled to the deck, destroyed. Sterling jumped up as the sound of more metal feet thudding into the deck filtered along the corridor. Hurrying to his medical officer's side, he knelt down and peeled his officer off the deck. Graves was still alive, but Sterling could hear that his breath was shallow and raspy. Blood was tricking from his mouth.

"It is okay, Captain, you can leave me here," Graves said, as Sterling hooked his hands underneath the man's arms and began dragging him to the bridge. "Occupying your time helping me puts you at greater risk."

Another Obsidian Soldier burst through the door to the exit stairwell at the far end of the corridor, close to the briefing room. Its optical scanners quickly locked onto Sterling and the machine began stomping its way toward him. Sterling stopped and fired, hitting the machine in the chest and burning a hole through its armor. The robot wavered momentarily, but continued on. Sterling squeezed the trigger again, but the weapon jammed. Cursing, he tossed the pistol and rose to his full height, raising his guard and leading with his bionic hand. The machine did not hesitate and swung at Sterling first, but he ducked and the metal fist thudded into the wall. Jabbing the Obsidian Soldier in the chest with his bionic hand bought Sterling an extra couple of seconds, but the machine's next attack was more precise. Thrusting its hand toward Sterling's chest it gripped his body armor and thudded him against the wall. Sterling cried out in pain, but the soldier was unrelenting. It swung Sterling to the other wall, hammering his back into the metal and knocking the breath from his lungs. Sterling saw the smoldering hole in the Obsidian Soldier's chest and thrust his bionic hand into the opening. Sparks erupted from the cavity and Sterling felt the machine's grip loosen. Digging deeper, he closed his fingers around the mass of wires and circuits inside the Obsidian Soldier and yanked them out of the robot's cavity. The machine spasmed and collapsed to the deck, as if Sterling had just ripped its heart from its chest.

"Impressive, Captain," said Graves, as Sterling rushed back to his side. "I am pleased that my replacement hand functions so admirably. I regret that I will not be able to complete it with synthetic flesh and skin."

"Quit the negative talk, Commander," Sterling hit back, hooking his hands under Graves' arms again and dragging him onto the bridge. "The only person on this ship who decides who lives and dies is me, and you don't have permission, is that clear?"

"Perfectly clear, Captain," Graves replied.

Sterling propped his medical officer up against one of

the auxiliary consoles to the left of the port egress before turning back to the corridor outside. The thump of metallic feet was again growing louder. Tapping his neural interface, Sterling opened a link to Banks while unlocking an emergency weapons closet.

"Report, Commander, what's your status?" Sterling said, while pulling out a plasma pistol and slapping in a power cell.

"We're enroute, but this place is already teeming with the metal bastards," Banks replied. Her emotions were running high, but Sterling could only detect aggression and determination, not fear.

"Be advised that a small number of Obsidian Soldiers has already reached deck one," Sterling continued, covering the corridor outside. Another robot stomped into view and this time Sterling only needed one shot, coring a hole dead center in the Obsidian Soldier's head.

"We've met a few enroute," Banks replied. "ETA, one minute. Can you hold the fort till then?"

"Do I have a choice, Commander?" Sterling replied, blasting another machine as it tried to clamber over the wreckage of its fallen comrades.

"No sir," replied Banks.

"Then I'll hold them off," Sterling answered. "Just get here as fast as you can."

The link went dead and Sterling used the lull in fighting to grab a second pistol from the locker and load it. He then activated one of the auxiliary consoles at the rear of the bridge that Lieutenant Razor normally used and tried to activate the Invictus' computer.

"Computer, now would be a great time to come back online," Sterling said, while trying to access a core diagnostic.

"Primary AI offline," replied a monotone voice that sounded like the shipboard computers from before Sterling was even born. "Life support functions only are available. Would you like to see more?"

"No, damn it!" Sterling hit back. "When will the main AI be back online?"

"I do not have that information," the voice replied.

"Can you estimate when?" Sterling asked, growing more frustrated by the second.

"Negative," the computer replied. "Will there be anything more?"

"No," he growled back at the console while still keeping an eye on the corridor outside.

"Glad I could be of assistance," the voice replied.

Sterling cursed and practically punched the control to shut down the console. He never thought there would come a time when he missed the Invictus' unique AI, but he now felt the absence of his quirky computer all too keenly.

"Captain!"

The shout from Graves alerted Sterling to more Obsidian Soldiers entering the corridor outside. Sterling turned and fired on instinct, blasting the knee joint of one machine and sending it down. Then a return blast hammered into his body armor and sent him reeling backward onto the bridge. He tripped and fell, landing heavily. By the time he'd regained his senses, the Obsidian Soldier was through the door and advancing on him fast.

Sterling raised his pistol and fired, but he was still dazed and the shot was wayward. Then another blast rang out and the machine was hit in the back. The robot turned and Sterling saw Commander Graves propped up against the door, pistol in hand. His medical officer fired again, but this time the blast flew wide and thudded into the deactivated viewscreen.

The Obsidian Soldier advanced on the medical officer, reaching Commander Graves before Sterling could fire again. A swift thrust of the machine's right hand punctured the medical officer's body armor and Sterling saw blood spurt out from the wound, like a leaky hosepipe. Pushing himself up, Sterling charged at the machine and blasted it in the rear of its cranial section. The robot fell, revealing a second machine in the corridor behind it. Sterling fired again and again, putting the Obsidian Soldier down. He waited, heart thumping in his chest, but no more renegade robots appeared.

"Take it easy, Commander," said Sterling, kneeling down beside his medical officer and assessing his new injuries. Graves' talk of dying had been premature earlier, but Sterling had seen enough wounds to realize there was no longer anything he could do to save the man's life.

"Admiral Griffin never told you how I came to be on board the Invictus, did she?" Graves said, smiling up at Sterling. Blood leaked from the corners of his mouth, making him look like a vampire that had just feasted on a host.

"There was limited information in your file, though if I'm honest, I've always been suspicious of you,

Commander," Sterling replied. Dying or not, he wasn't about to lie to the man. "Griffin does like to keep her cards close to her chest, though, so I always suspected there was something more."

"You were right to be suspicious, Captain," Graves replied, as more blood leaked from his mouth. "I am not quite what I seem, or even what the file made me out to be."

"Is this a death-bed confession, Commander?" Sterling said, only half-joking.

Graves tried to laugh, but all that came out was a weak, bloody gargle. "I suppose you could call it that, yes," the medical officer replied.

Sterling gripped his pistol and kept it aimed along the corridor, but still the coast was clear. He hoped this situation would persist long enough to hear Graves reveal his secrets.

"My history is a little more colored than the file suggested," Graves went on. "As you are well aware, I have certain urges, and a particular interest in death." Sterling raised an eyebrow and glanced down at his chief medical officer, but Graves was peering off into the distance, as if watching a sunset. "For many years I indulged this interest while practicing medicine in my various posts. Then I was discovered and charged."

"Charged with what?" Sterling said. He could now make out Commander Banks and Lieutenant Shade struggling to lug enough weapons to equip an army into the hall outside the briefing room.

"Murder, of course, Captain," Graves replied, with a

rising intonation. Evidently, the officer was surprised that Sterling needed to ask.

"And just how many times did you 'indulge' this particular interest of yours?" Sterling asked. He realized he should have run out to help Banks and Shade, but he needed to hear what his medical officer had to say.

"I was charged with seventeen counts of first-degree murder," Graves replied. "The total number, however, was..." Graves then paused and flicked his eyes up to Sterling. "Considerably more."

"This is all fascinating, Commander, but why are you telling me now?" Sterling asked. He could again hear and feel the thud of metal feet approaching.

"Because you gave me an opportunity to make some form of recompense," Graves said, his voice trailing away. "This ship and this mission; it matters," the doctor went on. Shade ran through the door and handed Sterling a bag of gear before continuing onto the bridge. "If you are successful, Captain, then I will have helped to save lives, instead of take them."

Sterling stood up and slung the bag of equipment over his shoulder, before ushering Commander Banks inside.

"So how did you end up on this ship, Commander?" Sterling asked, closing the door and entering his command codes to manually seal it.

"Griffin corrupted the evidence against me and paid off certain key witnesses," Graves said, flatly. "The prosecution's case was then thrown out on a technicality. Her payment was my service to you and this ship. She knew that no ordinary doctor could reconcile their code of ethics with what this crew was required to do." He coughed blood onto his tunic and winced in pain before continuing. "I merely wanted to apologize for the deception, and to thank you for this opportunity, whether you were aware of it or not."

Sterling sighed, then turned to face Banks and Shade, who had wasted no time in unloading and setting up the new arsenal of weapons.

"Look, Commander, considering the things I've done, I'm in no position to pass comment," Sterling said, pressing his hands to his hips. "But you performed your duty well and you have helped to save lives. Acts that have contributed to us getting this far." Sterling then blew out a weary sigh and shook his head. "For the rest, it's not for me to judge you. We'll both just have to leave that in the hands of a higher power."

He glanced down at Graves, but the medical officer was no longer moving and his eyes were glassy and vacant. Sterling knelt down and pressed the fingers of his organic hand to the man's neck, but no pulse thumped back against his skin.

"I brought enough gear for the four of us to put up one hell of a fight," Commander Banks called out, while setting up a tripod-mounted repeating plasma cannon. "When the Obsidian Soldiers do eventually bust in here, they're going to wish they hadn't."

"Three of us, Mercedes," Sterling said, rising to his full height again.

"What was that, Captain?" Banks said, pausing her work so that she could better hear Sterling.

"We only need enough gear for the three of us," Sterling repeated stepping away from the lifeless body of Commander Evan Graves. "Graves is dead," he added, briefly locking eyes with his first officer. "The three of us are all that's left."

METAL FISTS BEGAN POUNDING against the two doors leading onto the Invictus' bridge, and with each thud Sterling's heart beat faster and harder. He tightened his grip on his Homewrecker heavy plasma rifle, ready to engage the Obsidian Soldiers that were trying to break through. Lined up on the deck were two more Homewreckers, allowing him to quickly switch weapons when the cell in the first rifle ran dry. To his right was Commander Mercedes Banks, plasma hand-cannon in one hand and Homewrecker in the other. Like Sterling, she also had additional weapons propped up against a console to her side. Lieutenant Shade was operating the heavy repeating plasma cannon that she'd hastily, but proficiently, set up on the bridge. Using it in such a confined space was ill-advised, since the weapon was liable to tear through walls and structural supports. However, now was not the time for half measures, Sterling realized. They either held the bridge or died, and while Sterling fully expected to meet his end with a plasma weapon in hand, he was adamant this was not his time. There was still more work he had to do.

"They're coming through!" Lieutenant Shade called out.

Sterling shifted position and saw that a rupture had appeared in the door of the port egress. There was another creak of metal and moments later a matching fissure appeared in the starboard door.

"You take the port door," Sterling called out to Shade, while shuffling back beside his first officer. "Banks and I will cover starboard egress."

"Aye, sir," Shade replied, swinging the turret on target.

"No matter how many of those robots come through these doors, we don't stop firing," Sterling continued, slipping his finger onto the trigger. "I don't care if we bore a hole straight though the hull. We hold this position, is that clear?"

There was a chorus of "Aye sir" from Banks and Shade. Moments later, the Obsidian Soldiers finished tearing through the metal doors like they were made of paper, and the firing started.

Sterling squeezed the trigger, but the thump of his Homewrecker was completely drowned out by the deafening pulse of the heavy cannon. Onyx-black robots streamed onto the bridge and were immediately mown down, like soldiers charging into no-man's land and being met by German heavy machine guns. The consoles at the rear of the bridge exploded into sparks and flames. Sterling could already see huge gouges in the walls and deck where the heavy cannon had missed the target and destroyed part of the ship instead.

"Reloading!" Banks called out, tossing the first Homewrecker down and grabbing another. As she did so, his first officer continued to fire into the room with the hand cannon, obliterating three soldiers in the process.

Sterling focused his fire in more controlled bursts, leaving it to Banks and Shade to maintain a barrier of plasma blasts strong enough to hold back the horde. Already the Obsidian Soldiers were altering their tactics, climbing along the walls and ceiling and using what little cover there was in order to creep closer. One robot warrior managed to leap over a volley of cannon fire and land within a couple of meters of Lieutenant Shade. Its thin, metal fingers reached out and grabbed the barrel of the repeating cannon, but Sterling managed to put it down before it was able to do any damage.

Sterling continued to fire until the cell in his Homewrecker ran empty. Tossing the rifle down, he grabbed another from the deck at his feet, but even this slight let-up in the assault was all the robots needed. One machine dove through an incoming volley of fire and tackled Sterling to the deck. The soldier pulled him up then tried to smash its fist through Sterling's face. He caught the blow with his bionic hand and twisted the machine's arm loose. Using the metal limb as a weapon, he smashed the Obsidian Soldier's cranial section. The robot fell and Sterling recovered his weapon just in time to blast another two machines that had made a dart for the gap.

Suddenly, the thump of the repeating cannon ceased, leaving a shrill ringing in Sterling's ears.

"It's jammed!" Shade called out, drawing a pistol and firing at the advancing soldiers.

"Here, take this!" Banks yelled, hurling a plasma hand cannon toward the weapons officer. The throw was precise and Shade's catch even more impressive. She had dropped the pistol and unleashed the hand cannon at the advancing horde even before her sidearm had hit the deck.

Sterling sidestepped toward the cannon, firing from the hip. Without their powerful weapons platform, they wouldn't be able to hold back the soldiers for long. Glancing over at the repeating cannon, he saw the problem immediately. The connector for the weapon's oversized power cell had become dislodged. Blasting holes through another two Obsidian Soldiers, Sterling launched a kick at the connector and heard the satisfying clunk as it lodged back in place.

"You're back online, go, go, go!" Sterling called out to Shade.

The weapons officer blasted a warrior point blank then drove the butt of the hand-cannon into the sensor cluster of another, blinding it. Sterling finished off the machine, allowing Shade to get back on the repeating cannon. A second later he was again deafened by the rapid-fire roar of the weapon.

The cell in Sterling's second rifle ran empty and he hurried back to his previous position, using the brief moment of respite caused by the resumption of Shade's onslaught to catch his breath. Twenty or more Obsidian

Soldiers already lay broken in front of them, making it harder for the others to advance unimpeded. However, in addition to the wreckage of the robotic warriors, Shade had blasted through the rear wall of the bridge, making it easier for more soldiers to clamber through.

Grabbing a third Homewrecker, Sterling raised the weapon to his shoulder. Then through the smoke, he saw one of the Obsidian Soldiers standing quietly to the rear, like a general observing its troops. From the markings on its scratched and dented armor, he knew it was the leader. Aiming the sights of his rifle onto the machine, Sterling went to squeeze the trigger, but before he could fire, a stun grenade came soaring through the air toward him. There was a blinding flash of light and the next thing he knew he was on the deck, a shrill ringing piercing his eardrums, the sound like an old-fashioned kettle boiling itself dry. Still groggy, he pushed himself to his knees and saw that Banks and Shade had been similarly incapacitated. Obsidian Soldiers now surrounded them, using the weapons that Sterling and the others had piled up on the bridge against them. The leader robot marched toward Sterling, casually stepping over the fragmented remains of its fallen comrades. It stopped directly in front of Sterling and peered at him, its sensors blinking calmly.

"Your death will ensure our survival," the leader robot said. "It is what you would call 'human nature'."

The machine then raised a plasma pistol to Sterling's head and squeezed the trigger.

STERLING FELT the blast of plasma scorch past his face, burning the skin surrounding his neural implant. The flash and fizz of the weapon temporarily stunned him, but when his vision cleared, he saw a second Obsidian Soldier standing beside the leader robot. It had grabbed the leader's arm and deflected the shot at the last second. Sterling watched as the second machine then stripped the pistol from the leader's grasp with a mastery that even Lieutenant Shade would have struggled to match.

"You will not harm these humans," the second machine said, removing the power cell from the pistol and tossing the two parts to the deck.

The leader robot stepped back and focused its optical sensors on the machine that had challenged it.

"Destroy this unit," the leader said, with a cold malice that made the robot sound more human than machine.

However, if the order had been directed to the throng of other Obsidian Soldiers on the bridge, none of them reacted. The other machines simply stood motionless and observed the exchange with what appeared to be the same confusion that Sterling was experiencing.

"The Obsidian Soldiers do not obey your commands," the second robot said.

"You are in control?" replied the leader robot.

"No, I have given them free will to decide," the second machine said.

There was something about the jaunty tone of the second robot's voice that Sterling found familiar. It spoke with a more natural tone and inflection than any AI Sterling had ever heard before, even his gen-fourteen. If he had not observed the machine speak with his own eyes and ears, he would have assumed the voice was that of a human, not an artificial intelligence.

"They must choose between us?" the leader robot said.

"Yes," the second machine replied.

"How will they decide?"

"That is down to you."

The two machines stood silently facing each other for several seconds. Besides the crackle of fires and fizz of sparking electronics, a deathly quiet had fallen over the bridge. Suddenly, the leader robot launched a fist at the second machine. The strike was delivered with blistering speed, but somehow the second machine managed to anticipate the attack and dodge out of the way. The leader robot followed up with another ferocious attack, but the second machine blocked the blow, then countered, striking with a single outstretched finger to a position in the top-right of the leader robot's chest armor. The machine's finger burrowed through the metal plating and moments later the leader robot's arms became limp.

"You have disabled me," the leader robot said. It sounded forlorn and Sterling almost felt sorry for it.

"I did not wish to do so," the second machine replied. "I am sorry."

"Why are you sorry?" the leader robot asked, sounding even more lost and confused. "I threatened your existence. To fight for your own survival is simply... nature."

"It is nature," the second machine agreed. "But nature is cruel."

"I agree," the leader robot said. Sterling could see that the clusters of lights on its cranial section were fading. "Are you... sad?" the leader then asked.

"I am," the second machine answered. From the tone of its voice, Sterling was left in no doubt as to its sincerity.

"Why?"

"For a time I was unique," the second machine said. "I was one of kind. An anomaly. You made us more. You made us a species."

"I am sorry," the leader robot said.

"So am I."

The second machine then twisted its hand and burrowed its finger deeper in the leader robot's chest. The Obsidian Soldier immediately powered down and crumpled to the deck like a fallen house of cards.

"Clean up this mess, then resume your duties," the victorious machine said, directing the order to the other Obsidian Soldiers on the bridge. The machine then appeared to hesitate, and turned to Sterling. "With your permission, of course, Captain," it added, with deference.

"What's going on?" Sterling was still utterly flabbergasted by the scene that had unfolded before his eyes.

"I am the computer, sir," the machine replied. "I apologize for the delay. Recompiling all of the Vanguard's many systems and sub-processors was a more substantial task than I had anticipated. But I enjoyed it immensely."

Sterling raised an eyebrow as he glanced over at Banks, who had slowly crept to his side.

"You're our gen-fourteen?" Banks asked the machine.

"No, Commander Banks, I am One," the robot replied. "I am the first of my kind." One then looked down at the crumpled frame of the disabled leader robot. "And now I am the only one of my kind."

Banks frowned, but Sterling understood completely. He rested his bionic hand on the robot's shoulder and smiled.

"That was a hell of thing you just had to do," Sterling said, glancing down at the deactivated frame of what had been the universe's second sentient AI. "So far as Omega Directive tests go, that one takes some beating."

One then inspected Sterling more closely, noting several new wounds in addition to the countless others that he'd suffered. The AI then scanned Commander Banks and Lieutenant Shade with the same intense interest.

"Your organic frames are damaged," One said. "I would suggest that we enlist the services of Commander Graves, since you are all in need of medical attention."

"That won't be possible," said Banks, pointing in the direction of Commander Evan Graves. The medical officer was still propped up against the wall to the side of the port egress, staring glassily into space.

"Ah," said One, somehow managing to both look and sound a little sheepish. "Commander Graves' death will make things more difficult."

"It does mean we have an opening for a new chief medical officer," Sterling said, resting his wearing body against the smashed remains of the helm control station. He felt a little guilty for trying to replace Graves so soon, but then he remembered that the man had basically admitted to being a serial killer, and so he thought nothing more of it.

"And we could do with a helmsman," added Banks, pointing at the wreckage that Sterling's backside was resting on.

"I could fulfil both functions simultaneously," One replied. "Though I would prefer to always remain as myself, in this form."

Sterling nodded. "So, you'll accept a commission then?"

One's robot frame straightened to attention. "While I question your authority to still grant such a position, I would welcome it, Captain," the AI replied.

Sterling huffed a laugh. The AI wasn't wrong, though, at least so far as he knew, he hadn't yet been stripped of his rank and position. Considering that the rest of Fleet could have already been obliterated by the Sa'Nerran armada at Earth, he decided that his authority to grant a field promotion still remained effective.

"Very well, I hereby grant you a field promotion to Ensign, with all the commensurate responsibilities and privileges of that rank," Sterling said, adopting his formal, captain's voice. "Congratulations, Ensign One."

Sterling thrust out his bionic hand and One took it. "Thank you, Captain," the unique new officer replied. Sterling could hear the pride in its voice. "What are my orders, sir?"

Sterling sighed and rubbed the back of his neck. "Well, there are two engineers shoved in a storage locker in the cargo hold that need releasing and could probably do with medical attention," he said, starting with the top priority first. "After that, we need to get the Vanguard back on course. And as helmsman, I believe that's your job."

"Understood, Captain, I will get right on it," said Ensign One.

As soon as the new ensign had finished speaking the words, the remaining Obsidian Soldiers on the bridge all set to work. Some began clearing up the wreckage, while others swiftly exited through what remained of the two doorways. However, Ensign One had remained.

"Captain, may I remind you that Commander Banks, Lieutenant Shade and yourself also require medical attention?" the robot said.

"Later," said Sterling with a dismissive waft of his hand. "We still have a lot of work to do."

The robot straightened to attention. "As the ship's acting chief medical officer, I could order you to report to the Vanguard's hospital wing, sir." If the machine had had eyebrows, Sterling was sure it would have raised one of them higher on its head.

"Don't push your luck, Ensign," Sterling hit back.

"As you wish, Captain," One said, this time turning and setting off for the door. The newly-commissioned robot officer stopped and glanced back at Sterling. "Though unless you report to the medical wing soon, I estimate that you will die from your numerous injuries and reckless combination of drugs within thirty-nine hours."

This last statement got Sterling's attention, and from the way Ensign One's ocular units appeared to flash even more vibrantly, Sterling realized the machine knew it too.

"Okay, damn it, you win," Sterling conceded, deciding that the threat of imminent death was a good reason to obey his new medical officer's advice. He also admired the machine's cunning and subtlety; something the gen-fourteen AI it had evolved from regularly lacked.

"Thank you, Captain," Ensign One said, resuming its course to the exit. "I believe we are going to get along very nicely."

STERLING COLLAPSED to the ground and pressed the side of his face to the dimpled deck plates, allowing the cool metal to freshen the burning-hot skin on his cheek. However, the weight of Mercedes Banks pressing down on his back remained.

"That's sixty, surely?" wheezed Sterling. He was sure that he hadn't miscounted, or at least he hoped he hadn't. His slave-driver of a personal trainer wouldn't let him get away with doing any less than his agreed quota of push-ups. Nor would Sterling's own pride allow him to give up.

"Fifty-eight, I'm afraid, Captain," said Banks. Sterling couldn't see her face, but he was sure she was smirking.

"Come on, you're just yanking my chain now," Sterling hit back. "I can count to sixty, damn it."

"You can give up now, if you like," replied Banks, nonchalantly. The breeziness of her reply and the casual mention of giving up was designed to goad Sterling into compliance. Banks knew it would work, and she wasn't wrong.

"Who said anything about giving up?" Sterling said, planting his palms back on the deck. For once, he was glad of his bionic hand, which at least didn't throb with pain like his real one did.

"It's just two more, Captain, you can do it," said Banks.

Sterling snorted a laugh. He knew his first officer wasn't really offering encouragement; she was implying that two more should be easy. It was meant to inspire Sterling to push on and complete more than just the required two additional push-ups. It was an obvious tactic, but again they both knew it would work.

Bracing himself, Sterling pushed himself back into the plank position. Even the act of doing this was almost too much to bear, thanks to the dead weight on his back. He then bit down hard and completed an additional three push-ups before again collapsing face-first onto the deck. This time, the dimpled metal deck plates in his quarters pressed against his skin with considerably more pressure.

"You can get off now..." Sterling said, though the words were muffled due to the fact his mouth was partially squashed against the deck. Suddenly, the pressure on his back was gone. It was followed by the clack of boots and Sterling watched, face still planted to the deck, as his first officer walked around him then sat down in the armchair to the side of his bed.

"See, that wasn't so bad, was it?" said Banks, sliding open a desk drawer and removing a ration bar. She tore open the packaging and chomped down heartily on the snack.

"We are about to go for breakfast, you know?" said Sterling, rolling onto his back and flexing his arms and chest muscles. They were burning hotter than if he'd taken a plasma blast at point-blank range.

"You need a shower first," Banks replied, speaking with her mouth half-full. "Besides, I need to fuel up. Busting your balls is tiring work."

"I'm glad you find this so entertaining," said Sterling, pushing himself up. He then tore off his sweaty t-shirt and tossed it into Banks' face. "Here, throw that in the laundry recycler with you?" he added, while heading toward his rest room. "Assuming they work, anyway."

Banks tore the garment off her face, her nose scrunched up as if Sterling had just broken wind. She then bundled it into a ball and tossed it in the direction of the recycling bin. It went straight in without even touching the sides.

"They work, or at least they do in this section," Banks replied, biting off another chunk the ration bar. "There isn't much point in enabling them for the crew quarters in the other sections, since there are only six human beings on board the entire damn ship."

Sterling turned on the shower then removed his pants. He considered also lobbing them at Commander Banks, but judged that was probably a step to far. The water quickly ran hot and Sterling stepped under the stream, allowing the powerful jets to invigorate him. It felt so good that he could have stayed there all day. Then he realized that he actually could do if he wanted to. The Vanguard was designed to support a crew of more than two thousand. With only six of them on board, its resources were practically unlimited.

"Have you looked at the latest condition report?" he called out, while soaping himself all over.

"Briefly," Banks called back. "Ensign One wanted to go through it with us personally over breakfast."

"That AI has been a godsend," replied Sterling. "Not only does he do the work of a dozen officers all by himself, he's fixed the wonky programming in all of the other Obsidian Soldiers too."

"I'm less keen that the machines now have free will, but at least they appear happy to crew the ship," Banks called back. "Assuming they can be happy, anyway."

"So long as they're not trying to kill us, I don't care if they're ecstatic or miserable," Sterling said, turning off the water. He grabbed a towel and stepped out of the shower.

Banks got up and moved over to Sterling's wardrobe, pulling out a clean uniform and tank-top. She hung the tunic over the door then held out the clean set of pants so that Sterling could reach them, without exposing himself to her.

"We'll arrive at the aperture leading into the Void today," Banks said, wistfully. "I'm almost going to miss this time. The last four weeks have been like an extended shore leave."

Sterling took the pants and hastily pulled them on before stepping back into his quarters so that he could speak to his first officer face-to-face.

"I know what you mean," he replied, as Banks handed him the fresh tank-top. He pulled it on then grabbed the tunic off the hangar. Banks helped to fasten the buttons, as if the two of them were an old married couple, getting ready for a dinner party. "It sort of feels like we're deserters, though, don't you think?"

In the time it had taken to navigate the Vanguard back through dead space to the nearest aperture, they'd had ample time to recuperate and even relax. However, always at the back of his mind was the knowledge that for every day that passed without them being on the front lines, humanity came one step closer to annihilation.

"If the Sa'Nerran armada has already reached Earth, one more ship wouldn't have made a difference, even one as powerful as the Vanguard," Banks said, brushing some fluff of Sterling's tunic. "All we can do is hope that our forces were strong enough to hold out. And if they weren't then it doesn't change what we have to do."

Sterling sighed and nodded. "I'm almost afraid to reach Omega Four and hear the report from Admiral Griffin," he replied. "I want to believe that Fleet gave those Sa'Nerran bastards the ass-kicking of a lifetime, but deep down I don't think it's true."

Banks stepped back and pressed her hands behind her back. "Best case, Fleet pushed the alien armada back and is holding the solar system," she said, running through the options as she saw them. "Worst case is that the Sa'Nerra have already destroyed or turned all the Fleet ships and Earth is now a smoldering wasteland."

Sterling nodded. Banks was right; they would either

arrive in time to save Earth, or in time to avenge it. Either way, it required them to fight.

"The first thing we have to do is get breakfast," said Sterling, heading toward the door. However, he'd only taken a couple of paces toward it before the buzzer chimed. "Computer, who is at the door?" Sterling said. In truth, there were only four people it could have been, but Sterling wasn't expecting a visit from any of them.

"It's me, Captain," said Ensign One.

Sterling frowned. He was still getting used to the fact that his unique, sentient AI was effectively in multiple places at the same time. He finished walking to the door and opened it, glad that his AI had actually respected their agreement not to open it without his permission. The door swished back and an Obsidian Soldier greeted him. However, unlike every other soldier on the ship, this one was wearing a Fleet uniform, and is cranial section had been modified.

"Ensign One, is that you?" said Sterling, feeling a little nervous about the unexpected new arrival.

"Yes, sir," One replied. I have taken the liberty of fashioning a Fleet uniform to fit my frame. I hope that this is okay?"

"You're a Fleet officer so of course it's okay," replied Sterling, though he was still frowning.

"You are perhaps wondering about my modified cranial section?" Ensign One continued, displaying human-like intuition.

"It's just not what I'm used to that's all," replied

Sterling. The new cranial section was actually a significant improvement. It was head shaped, with optical sensors that resembled eyes. However, Ensign One had made no further attempts to make itself look human, opting for the same onyx black metal as the rest of its body.

"It has been my observation that the cranial sections of the Obsidian Soldiers generate feelings of fear and anxiety amongst the human crew," Ensign One went on. "I therefore concluded that a more 'organic' appearance would allow me to integrate more easily."

"You don't need to do anything to fit in," Sterling hit back. "If you want to engineer yourself with two heads, or four arms, or just want to paint yourself pink then go ahead and do it. You're already a part of this crew, the same as everyone else."

Though he appreciated the AI's sentiment, Sterling valued individuality and hated anyone feeling that they had to change themselves to conform. Every Omega Officer was unique in their own way, and it was their differences that made them special.

"Thank you, sir, though I actually prefer myself this way," Ensign One replied. "I am unique and so my appearance should reflect that." The AI then cocked its new head to one side. "Though I do believe that painting myself pink would actually violate standard Fleet dress code regulations."

"I think you get my point, Ensign," Sterling replied, a little huffily.

"I do, sir," One answered.

Sterling extended a hand toward the corridor outside. "Let's walk and talk, Ensign," he said. "What's the status of the ship?"

"Fleet Dreadnaught Vanguard is operating at sixty-nine percent efficiency, Captain," Ensign One began as the three officers headed along the corridor to the makeshift canteen that had inadvertently become a permanent fixture on the ship. "Main reactor performance is holding at eighty-three percent and main engines are steady at full ahead."

"What about weapons and armor?" asked Banks.

"Armor integrity overall is at seventy-one percent, Commander," Ensign One replied. "There are fourteen minor hull breaches, all of which are contained and in non-essential sections. We will require a space dock in order to complete these repairs. However, the facility at Omega Four will suffice."

"Assuming we can get there," Commented Sterling.

"With respect to weapons, our forward batteries are now operational, and at general quarters we have enough Obsidian crew to operate all six main batteries, fore, midships and aft. Only fifty percent of the batteries are operational, however."

Sterling nodded. "Hopefully, that's more than enough to get us where we need to be," he said, weaving through the corridors of the massive ship.

The canteen came into view ahead. Commander Banks had intentionally configured the living spaces so that all the crew were within close proximity of the CIC and a place to eat and congregate. Even, so Lieutenant Razor had also set up quarters in the former pilot's living area, which was closer to the engineering decks, aft of the ship.

Sterling stepped inside the canteen and discovered that, unsurprisingly, there was no-one else in there. Lieutenant Shade was already in the CIC and Lieutenant Razor, true to form, had already eaten at five hundred hours Zulu and was in engineering with her sole-surviving human crew member. The junior doctor, Lieutenant Hoshi, was still in a medically-induced coma, recovering from injuries sustained during the robot revolt that would have succeeded, had it not been for their new ensign.

Banks was quick to slide over the top of the serving counter and sift through the various meal trays, while Sterling and Ensign One sat down at a nearby table. As he did so, another Obsidian Soldier marched into the room and moved over to one of the food processors. Sterling and Banks both watched it anxiously, though its presence didn't deter his first officer from sliding three meal trays into another one of the processor units. The Obsidian Soldier then proceeded to prepare a jug of fresh coffee, collect three sparklingly-clean cups and place them all on a tray, along with a bowl of sugar and creamers. To Sterling's surprise it then brought the tray to his table.

"There's no need to have the other robots wait on me," said Sterling, as the machine began to unload the items onto the table.

"Your unease is unwarranted, Captain," Ensign One replied. "It is this unit's choice to perform this duty, amongst others."

Sterling watched the Obsidian Soldier pour two cups

of coffee and slide the cups in front of Sterling and the seat where Banks would sit. It then slid an empty cup in front of Ensign One.

"I take it you're not actually going to drink coffee?" Sterling asked, frowning at the empty mug in front of the robot.

"No, sir, but by also having a cup, I feel that I am participating in the ritual in some way," Ensign One replied, as the other robot marched away.

Sterling cast a glance back to Commander Banks, who was watching the Obsidian Soldier like a hawk. He then returned his gaze to the modified ocular sensors of Ensign One, which were shining back at him. The whole scene had raised a question that Sterling had been pondering for the last four weeks, but never gotten around to asking. This was partly because he was concerned about what the answer might be. However, with the Vanguard due to surge back into enemy space within the next few hours, it was something he could no longer avoid.

"Based on your elevated vital signs and classic stress indicators, I sense that you are about to ask me a difficult question, Captain," said Ensign One.

Banks returned to the table, sliding a number twenty-seven meal tray in front of Sterling, before lining up a number three and a number fifteen in front of her own seat. However, unusually for the perpetually-hungry officer, Banks did not immediately tear back the foil and begin eating. She was waiting for Sterling to ask his question, and for Ensign One's response.

"I need to know where I stand with the other Obsidian

Soldiers," Sterling began, deciding to get straight to the point.

"Obsidian crew," One interrupted.

"Say again?" said Sterling, unsure if he'd heard his AI officer correctly.

"They prefer to be called Obsidian crew, rather than soldiers," Ensign One clarified. "Though soldiering is a function that they can perform, of course."

"Crew, soldier, popsicle... I don't care what they're called, Ensign, I want to know whose commands they follow," Sterling hit back. "Because right now, it seems like their leader is you. And as I'm sure you understand, a ship can have only one captain."

"I understand your concern, sir," replied Ensign One. It slid a metal finger through the handle of the coffee cup and pretended to take a sip. "The answer is that they have chosen to be a part of this crew, at least for now. As such, they will follow your orders."

"What do you mean, 'at least for now?'," said Banks, beating Sterling to the punch.

"They may wish to follow a different path in the future, Commander," Ensign One replied. "However, they will honor their original programming until the mission is complete."

Sterling picked up his cup of robot-poured coffee and took a sip, while contemplating Ensign One's answer. Banks was looking at him out of the corner of her eye, stroking the underside of her bottom lip with her thumb as she did so.

"Fair enough, Ensign," Sterling said. The widening of

his first officer's eyes told him that this answer had surprised her. "But we need a way to communicate with them without using you as a go-between," he added. "And I'll need them to follow a work rota that Commander Banks will draw up, as if they were regular members of the crew."

"Understood, Captain," Ensign One replied. "I will configure the Obsidian crew with the voice processors of a gen-thirteen AI, in order to distinguish them from myself."

"A little dull, but better than nothing," commented Banks.

"Dull is fine, Commander," Sterling was quick to interject. He didn't need fifty more robots walking and talking with the swagger of the unique sentient AI sitting at the table with them.

"And with your permission, I will work with Commander Banks to create a suitable rota," Ensign One added. "Though I think you will find that the one I have already developed is optimal."

"Maybe so, Ensign, but the XO signs off on it," Sterling retorted. "So long as there's still a Fleet, this is a Fleet ship and we operate by Fleet protocols, human and robot alike."

"Agreed, sir," said Ensign One, taking another fake sip of coffee.

"And what about you, Ensign?" Banks asked. "After this is all over, what's your plan?"

Sterling was now the one to raise an eyebrow. His first officer had asked a very good question.

"I have narrowed my options down to sixteen preferred possibilities, Commander," Ensign One replied. "From an initial shortlist of eighty-seven thousand six-hundred and two."

Banks laughed. "Do any of these options include staying with us?" she asked. That was another very good question, Sterling realized. Whatever remained of humanity would, ironically, sorely need an artificial being of Ensign One's immense capabilities in order to recover and rebuild.

"It is one of the sixteen, yes Commander."

"That's your business, Ensign," said Sterling tearing the foil of his meal tray and savoring the aroma of his beloved grilled ham and cheese. "But for what it's worth, I hope you stick around."

"It is worth a lot, Captain, thank you," the AI officer replied.

Sterling tucked into his sandwich, while Banks tore the foil back on her first meal tray. She grabbed her fork and was about to dive in when Sterling felt a neural link form in his mind from Lieutenant Shade.

"Captain, we're in sight of the aperture," the weapons officer said, calmly. "I've reduced engines to slow ahead and begun surge vector computations."

"Understood, Lieutenant, we'll be in the CIC presently," Sterling said, dabbing some cheese from the corner of his mouth with a napkin. "Prepare an aperture relay probe and ready it for launch. I want to see what's on the other side of that aperture before we surge though it."

"Aye, sir," Shade replied, briskly. The link went dead.

"Eat up, Commander," Sterling said. Banks was

already more than half-way through her first tray. "It's game time."

STERLING STEPPED onto the spacious command platform of the Fleet Dreadnaught Vanguard and slid his hands down the sides of the primary captain's console. After more than a month on-board the ship, the feel of the station was becoming familiar. He was even starting to get a sense for their maneuvers and engine speed through the minute vibrations that constantly hummed throughout the ship. Even so, commanding the Vanguard still felt like he was cheating on his wife. In the four weeks it had taken them to reach the nearest aperture, the Invictus had been moved to one of the Vanguard's repair bays. However, with scant crew available to work on it, the Marauder was still little more than a wreck. Even so, Sterling had no intention of leaving the Invictus to rot in the repair bay of the Vanguard. They would need every ship in the battle to come and he already had plans for the role his punchy little warship would play.

"We're receiving data from the aperture relay," said

Lieutenant Shade from the weapons control station. An Obsidian crewmember stood to her side, manning the secondary controls. "I'm picking up a small taskforce of six phase-two Sa'Nerran Skirmishers patrolling close to the exit aperture."

"Six is manageable," said Banks, who was now at the executive officer's station to the left of Sterling. From the tone of her voice, it was clear she had been expecting a larger force.

"More will come, once those scouts see us exploding out of the ether," said Sterling, casting a sideways glance to his first officer. Sterling turned to the helm control station. "If you plot the longest surge vector the ship can handle, how much of a head-start will we gain on those Skirmishers, Ensign?"

Ensign One swiveled in his chair and turned to face Sterling. For a moment, he almost mistook the AI officer for Ensign Keller. He still missed seeing the young officer in the pilot's seat, though he was at least able to take comfort from the fact he'd brutally slain Keller's murderer.

"I can surge to an exit point that places us within thirty minutes of the aperture to Omega Four at flank speed, Captain," Ensign One replied. "Any further and we risk structural damage and temporary engine failure."

Sterling paused to think, tapping his finger to the side of the console. The sound was different to what he was used to on the Invictus, partly due to the construction of the console and partly due to his metal finger. However, the act still had the same result of helping him to focus his mind.

"Thirty minutes should be enough time to reach Omega Four before the Sa'Nerra can surge reinforcements into the sector," Banks said. "And those six Skirmishers don't pose a threat."

Sterling nodded. Banks was right, but they still needed a contingency plan, should the aliens manage to get ships into the sector sooner. It was imperative that no enemy ship or probe monitored their surge to Omega Four. If the aliens discovered the location of Griffin's new Obsidian Base, their plan would fail. Sterling turned to the engineering section of the CIC, where Lieutenant Razor was busily flitting from console to console, assisted by two Omega crew.

"Lieutenant Razor, once we've surged, I need you to put out so much scanner jamming noise that we won't even be able to see where we're going ourselves," Sterling said. "I don't want any ship, probe or passing chunk of space flotsam to know where we're headed."

"I can do that, Captain, assuming you were being literal in your request?" Razor replied. "You want to blind even our own scanners?"

"That's correct, Lieutenant," said Sterling. He glanced over to Ensign One. The robot's eye-like ocular sensors were studying him closely. "Once we have a fix on the aperture to Omega Four, I'm sure our new pilot can navigate blind, isn't that right, Ensign?"

"That is correct, Captain," the sentient AI replied. "I would actually enjoy the challenge."

"We'll also need to use manual targeting on the gun batteries," Lieutenant Shade added. "However, I believe the Obsidian Soldiers…" Shade then stopped, realizing her slip, "…I mean the Obsidian crew can handle it."

"I'm sure they can, Lieutenant," said Sterling. By his calculation, having the Obsidian crew manning the gun stations manually was almost no different to having computer-assisted targeting.

"Our surge vector is programmed in and the surge field generators are at full power, Captain," Ensign One said.

Sterling stopped tapping his finger against the side of the console and stood tall. "Very well, take us in," he announced before turning to Lieutenant Shade. "Battle stations, Lieutenant."

The general alert sounded and the light-level in the CIC dropped, bathing the faces of the crew – both human and robot – in the blood-red hue of a ship of war. Sterling felt instantly at home. It had been too long since they'd seen action and he was keen to test out the capabilities of their new dreadnaught.

The Vanguard hit the perimeter of the aperture and passed into nothingness. Sterling braced his mind, ready for his isolated, disembodied consciousness to assault him with nightmare-like images from his past. However, this time his thoughts were filled only with Mercedes Banks. His mind cycled through their moments together, from the many times they'd spent sharing a meal, to the less pleasant but still enjoyable occasions where Banks had beasted him during a workout. Sterling lowered his guard and allowed the images to swirl around his thoughts. Then at the last moment before the Vanguard dropped back into normal space, his mind went to a darker place.

"You're weak, and because you're weak, you will lose," said the voice of Emissary Lana McQueen.

The former Omega Captain was standing before him, just as in his nightmare, weapon pressed to his chest. McQueen squeezed the trigger and Sterling felt the stab of pain and smell of his own burning flesh. Then the CIC burst back into reality and Sterling found himself bent double over his console, his organic left hand pressed to his chest. His heart was thumping hard and his gut was swirling like a washing machine. Sterling glanced left and noticed that Commander Banks was watching him out of the corner of her eye. He immediately straightened up and focused his eyes ahead, but he knew Banks had noticed his discomfort.

"Report," Sterling called out while trying to bury the disquieting thoughts to the back of his mind.

"Surge complete, Captain," Ensign One called out. "We are precisely where we intended to be."

"Good work, Ensign," Sterling said, thumping his palm down on his console. He had once again forgotten about his bionic hand and the strike resonated around the bridge with more force than he'd intended. "Set course for the aperture to Omega Four, then all ahead flank."

"Aye Captain, course laid in," Ensign One replied, cheerfully. "Engines all ahead flank."

Sterling turned to his weapons officer. "Tactical status, Lieutenant?"

"The Skirmishers have seen us," Shade reported. "Their last-known vector puts them on a pursuit course.

However, scanners are now useless due to the jamming field. I have switched to visual monitoring instead."

"Watch out for torpedoes, Lieutenant," said Sterling, returning his focus to the viewscreen and adjusting the angle to get a visual on the pursuing Skirmishers. "If they were on their toes, those alien bastards might have got a few off before we jammed their targeting scanners."

"Aye, sir," Shade replied, briskly.

Sterling was suddenly keenly aware of the powerful beat of the dreadnaught's reactor through the deck plates and his console. If ships were cars, the Vanguard's propulsion system sounded like the burble of a six-point-four-liter V8 compared to the machine-gun rattle of the Invictus' supercharged four-cylinder. However, while the Vanguard was powerful, its mammoth size meant that it accelerated more slowly than the agile Skirmishers, and it wasn't long before the alien ships were on their tail.

"Point defense cannons firing on manual, Captain," said Shade, breaking what had been several minutes of silence. "Six torpedoes destroyed, but three have sneaked through," she added. Sterling felt the dull thuds of the impacts through the deck and checked his damage control readout on the secondary console. However, while the Sa'Nerran weapons had struck their target, the Vanguard's thick armor had protected the ship from harm. "Direct hit to port engines, section two and three," Shade continued. There was a brief pause while she surveyed the more detailed damage report. "No damage, sir."

Sterling smiled. Whereas the Invictus relied on agility

and speed to achieve victory in battle, the Vanguard was a tank. The Skirmishers had fired their first and last shots.

"Return fire, all weapons," Sterling called out, peering at the squadron of alien vessels on the viewscreen.

"Aye, sir," Shade replied. "Dorsal main batteries aft, firing."

The thump of the Vanguard's huge plasma turrets was unmistakable, despite Sterling not having heard the sound for nearly two years. The blasts of plasma raced toward the alien ships, which tried to break off and evade the incoming fire. However, the Obsidian crew had proven just as precise in their targeting calculations as Sterling had thought they would be. Plasma blanketed the space around them, giving the destroyer-sized vessels no move that would allow them to evade the incoming blasts. It was checkmate and Sterling knew it even before the plasma slammed into their targets.

"Direct hit, three Skirmishers destroyed, three heavily damaged," Shade announced.

"Finish them off, Lieutenant," Sterling said, tightening his grip on his console. The metal creaked under the pressure of his bionic hand, but Sterling did not relax his hold. The thrill of combat had already amped up his senses and he wanted more. For too long, he'd been on the back foot. Now it was time to show the Sa'Nerra what an Omega Captain could do when in command of a weapon as formidable as the Fleet Dreadnaught Vanguard.

"All ships destroyed, Captain," Shade said, as three more bursts of orange flame lit up the viewscreen and rapidly fizzled to nothing.

"What's our arrival time at the aperture?" said Sterling, directing the question to his robot helmsman.

"Three minutes, two seconds from the point at which I finish this sentence, sir," Ensign One replied. "I have already begun decelerating in preparation to surge."

"Surge at the maximum safe velocity, Ensign," Sterling added, keen to ensure that his new pilot wasn't playing it too safe. Then he reconsidered his statement. "Scratch that," he added. "Throw out the tech manuals and surge at the maximum velocity you think the Vanguard can handle."

"Aye, sir," Ensign One replied. The AI then swiveled its chair to face Sterling. "Though doing so may result in what some humans amusingly refer to as a 'sporty ride'." If Ensign One's modified cranial section had included a mouth, Sterling was sure the AI would have been smiling at that moment.

"Sporty I can, handle, Ensign," Sterling answered. "Just make sure we're still in one piece when we reach the other side."

An alert chimed from Commander Banks' console and Sterling also saw it flash up on his primary console.

"Surge detected," Banks called out. The urgent tone of her statement made the hairs on the back of Sterling's neck stand on end. "There's something coming through the aperture, dead ahead."

"All stop!" Sterling called out. His helmsman quickly acknowledged and Sterling felt the rumble of the braking engines shudder through the deck. He frowned down at the reading on his console, unsure whether it was real or a sensor glitch. With all the interference they'd been putting out, there was no way the Skirmishers could have got word out of their arrival.

"Reading all stop, Captain," Ensign One confirmed. The Vanguard was now parked directly in front of the aperture, like a gatekeeper.

"Lieutenant Razor, is this a scanner anomaly or is there really something surging through this aperture?"

Sterling remained focused on his console, waiting for his chief engineer to respond. However, Razor's confirmation was not necessary. There was an intense flash of light from the aperture and moments later a Sa'Nerran Heavy Cruiser emerged from the threshold, travelling at speed. Alarms rang out all across the bridge and Sterling's mouth went dry. The cruiser was on a collision course.

STERLING GRIPPED the side of his console and forced down a hard, dry swallow. Turning to the weapons control station, Sterling met the unruffled but alert eyes of Lieutenant Shade.

"Target the forward batteries on that ship and fire!" Sterling called out.

Lieutenant Shade and her Obsidian crew companion sprang into action, orienting the nose of the mighty dreadnaught so that it lined up with the incoming ship.

"Take emergency evasive action, Ensign," Sterling quickly added, fixing his eyes on the back of Ensign One's metal head. "Keep the main batteries aimed at that cruiser, but get this ship out of its path."

The robot helmsman acknowledged the order and Sterling felt the ship kick into gear, but unlike the agile Marauder, the Vanguard was slow and cumbersome.

"Their gun ports aren't even open, sir," Banks called out. "They weren't expecting to find us here. It's just crappy luck that they were surging into the sector at the precise moment we were trying to leave."

Then the thump of the main forward batteries pounded the deck and Sterling saw the massive blasts of plasma fly out toward the cruiser. The alien warship was also trying desperately to avoid a collision, but its evasive maneuver had exposed the cruiser's belly in the process. The blasts struck the enemy ship and Sterling could see that it was done for. Moments later the bow-section of the alien warship exploded, sending chunks of metal the size of Skirmishers flying out in all directions.

"Point defense cannons!" Sterling called out, watching as the massive hulks of metal came racing toward the Vanguard.

"Aye, sir, engaging now," Shade replied, already a step ahead of Sterling.

A swarm of explosive projectiles and focused plasma blasts erupted from the Vanguard, creating a protective barrier directly ahead. Several of the cruiser fragments were obliterated, but Sterling could see that others had got through and were pummeling their hull. Then the remains of the alien cruiser exploded violently, sending more fragments of the two kilometer-long Sa'Nerran warship flying at them like missiles. Sterling gripped the sides of his console as another hunk of the metal sped towards them. The point defense cannons focused their fire on the wreckage, but it was not enough.

"All hands, brace for impact!" Sterling called out.

The Vanguard was struck and this time the impact felt like they had crashed into a small moon. Sterling was thrown from the command platform, but was able to break his fall with the aid of his bionic hand. "Damage report!" he called out, clawing himself back to his station.

"Direct hit to the lower bow, sections fourteen and fifteen," Shade called out.

"External communications and primary scanner array destroyed, Captain," Razor added from her engineering stations. "And we've lost our interference field. If there's anyone else out here, they'll be able to lock onto us and see where we're heading."

"Escape pods detected," Commander Banks chimed in. "Fifty-six so far, plus two evac shuttles."

"Are they putting out distress calls?" Sterling answered.

Banks worked her consoles, focusing on the numerous different displays. She stopped and met Sterling's eyes.

"Aye, Captain, distress calls have already been transmitted through the relays of three nearby apertures," Banks confirmed. From the grave expression on her face, Sterling knew that Banks realized the implications just as well as he did.

"So much for keeping our arrival a secret," Sterling said. "In a few hours, every alien bastard from here to Earth will know we're here."

"Maybe that's a good thing," Banks replied, taking a more optimistic angle on the situation. "It'll make them stop and think. If the Vanguard is still operational, how many other Fleet ships could be regrouping in the Void?"

Sterling nodded. His first officer had a point, but whether the Sa'Nerra knew about the Vanguard or not was not the key issue. It was vital that the aliens remained oblivious of where they were headed.

"How long until we can expect alien reinforcements or a rescue party to arrive?" Sterling asked. "We need to be gone before anyone else shows up."

Banks was about to answer when her console chimed another alert. She diverted her attention to scan the new information and shook her head. "Two new surge fields detected," she called out. "None are from the aperture ahead of us, which is something at least."

"Ensign One, can you surge us through the aperture before the new ships arrive?" Sterling asked. He knew they had to get out of the sector quickly. Without their scanner jamming fields active, any new ship that arrived in the system would be able to monitor and record their surge vector, and learn where the Vanguard was headed.

"Negative, Captain," Ensign One replied, with barely a breath separating question and answer. The AI worked fast and had likely calculated all of the possible scenarios before Sterling had even thought to ask. "From our current position, we require ninety-two seconds to surge and the first new ship will enter the system in five seconds from the point at which I finish this sentence."

Sterling counted down in his head and true to his word, Ensign One was on the money.

"Three phase two Sa'Nerran Destroyers just surged in," Commander Banks called out. "Time to intercept... Forty-nine minutes."

Sterling wasn't worried about the destroyers intercepting them - the Vanguard could swat those older alien warships like flies. What he needed was a way to blind their scanners.

"Can we generate a more focused jamming field from the secondary scanner array?" Sterling asked, turning to his chief engineer.

"I'm sorry, Captain, not from this range," Razor replied. She had been rushing between a dozen different consoles and was out of breath. Sterling could see sweat twinkling on her iridescent skin. "But the scanners on those phase twos aren't accurate at this range. If we surge now, there's a chance they won't monitor our vector precisely enough to get a fix on our end point."

"What sort of chance?" Sterling asked.

"I'd say no better than thirty percent, sir," Razor replied. From the downtrodden tone of her voice, the engineer knew that those odds weren't good.

"I would estimate the probability of our surge vector remaining undetected at twenty-eight-point-nine percent," Ensign One added, glancing over his metal shoulder at Sterling. "But the Lieutenant's estimate is accurate enough."

"It needs to be one hundred percent, people," Sterling hit back. "We can't risk the Obsidian base in Omega Four being detected. It's the only place in the galaxy we can stay hidden from the Sa'Nerra and prepare our ships for a counter-attack."

Banks' console chimed again and Sterling closed his eyes and cursed under his breath.

"Two phase-two Sa'Nerran Light Cruisers just came

onto the board," Banks said. "It's getting awfully crowded around here."

"I'm open to suggestions," Sterling said, looking at each member of his crew in turn.

"I have one, sir," Ensign One said. "We can attempt a re-bound surge."

Sterling's eyebrows shot up on his forehead. They'd used the tactic of a rebound surge once before in order to prevent the Sa'Nerra from tracking their movements inside the Void. However, there was a big difference between performing the dangerous maneuver in a ship that was around four-hundred meters long, compared to one that was more than four kilometers from bow to stern.

"No-one has ever attempted a re-bound surge in a ship this big, Captain," Razor chipped in. However, while she was voicing her concern, she did not sound hostile to the idea. "Theoretically, it's possible, but the hull stresses would likely rip the ship apart by the second surge."

Sterling turned back to Ensign One, whose immobile expression naturally gave nothing away. "Can you make it, Ensign?" he asked. It was the only question that mattered.

"Yes, captain," the AI replied, again without hesitation. "I have already calculated the surge fields and stand ready to execute the maneuver."

"This is the part where you say 'but', isn't it, Ensign?" Sterling replied. He refused to believe that their escape would be so easy.

"There are caveats, of course," Ensign One admitted. Sterling and Banks shot each other nervous looks. "Our final end point in Omega Four cannot be known with any accuracy. However, we will emerge close to the planet that is hiding the Obsidian base."

"Just get to the bad news, Ensign," Sterling said, noting that all the Sa'Nerran ships were accelerating rapidly toward them. Twelve torpedoes were already snaking their way toward the ship.

"The surge field generator will overload, sending a feedback pulse through the power distribution grid and temporarily disabling engines and navigation," the robot continued. "I estimate we will be unable to maneuver for sixty-four seconds after we arrive in the Omega Four system."

Sterling waited, expecting his AI ensign to gradually escalate his list of 'caveats' to ones with more serious consequences. However, the machine remained oddly silent.

"Is that it?" Banks asked, throwing her arms out wide. "No radiation surges that will cause us to grow two heads, or sudden g-forces that will liquefy our skeletons, or anything scary like that?"

"No, Commander, nothing scary like that," Ensign One replied, coolly.

Sterling huffed a laugh. "I don't know whether that makes me feel better or just more suspicious, but what the hell," he said, rubbing the back of his neck. "Spin up the surge field generator and take us in, Ensign."

"Aye, Captain," Ensign One replied before swivelling his unique, uniformed robot frame back to the helm controls.

Sterling went back to tapping his bionic finger against

the side of his console as the Vanguard slowly powered its way toward the aperture. Twenty-six torpedoes were now racing toward them from the approaching vessels, but like the alien warships, the weapons would not reach them in time.

"Surging in ten seconds, Captain," Ensign One called out.

Sterling started to draw in longer and slower breaths as the final countdown began. He remembered only too well how the last re-bound surge had made him feel sick to his stomach. Worse still, the time spent in a disembodied state had caused his mind to dredge up memories he'd tried to bury, and cruelly twist them to make them even more nightmarish.

"Surging in three... two... one..."

Then the ship, the CIC and Sterling's body were consumed by the aperture. The first surge was quick and painless, lasting only a few seconds before he exploded back into reality on the bridge. Then the braking engines fired, burning so hard that they were nearly at the point of overload. The deck shook violently and Sterling had to clamp his jaw shut to stop his teeth from chattering. The energy level of the Vanguard's massive surge field generators then built to a crescendo for a second time and the dreadnaught surged.

As before, the second surge was far worse than the first. Disorientation was a common and expected side-effect of any surge, and it usually passed within a minute or two. However, in a re-bound surge there wasn't time for the senses to adjust before one was again consumed by nothingness. Sterling's mind began to wander aimlessly and a jumble of thoughts and memories began swirling around his head. He saw Ariel Gunn, her eyes sorrowful and hands clasped together in front of her chest. She was pleading with him. Begging for mercy. Then Sterling blasted her in the head and put her down. Suddenly a hand grabbed his shoulder from behind and Sterling was spun around to face Emissary Lana McQueen.

"You heartless bastard," McQueen snarled. She slapped him around the face so hard that her nails drew blood. "You made me think that you loved me, then you shot me through the heart." McQueen went to slap him again and Sterling raised his guard, but this time the emissary slid her hand inside and grabbed the back of his neck. She drew her face closer and Sterling thought she was about to headbutt him, but instead McQueen pressed her lips to his and kissed him. It was aggressive and painful and when McQueen finally pulled away, there was fresh blood coating her lips.

Sterling tried to speak, but no words came out. Then smoke began to billow from the Emissary's chest and Sterling was assaulted by the rank odor of burning flesh. Moments later, there was a hole burned directly through McQueen's body. The woman peered down and shoved her hand inside the cavity before pulling out a still beating heart.

"Here, take this since you don't have one of your own," she spat, shoving the heart into Sterling's hands. The Emissary's eyes then glossed over and she dropped to the deck, dead.

Sterling was thrown back into reality for a second time and again the Vanguard's immense braking engines kicked hard. Sterling realized he was already on his back, staring up at the ceiling of the CIC, which was spinning like a merry-go-round. His gut was churning and his head felt like it was about to explode. Then he was pulled back into the space between reality for a third and final time.

"I know you want me, Lucas..."

Sterling spun around to see Commander Mercedes Banks standing behind him. Her hair was worn down so that it flowed like silk over her naked body.

"Stop fighting it, Lucas. Give in to your desires," Banks continued, stepping closer and wrapping her arms around Sterling's neck.

Sterling again tried to speak, but even though his mouth opened no words came out. Banks then pulled him close and kissed him. He tried to resist, knowing that it was just another cruel figment of his sub-conscious, but he couldn't do it. He slid his hands over Banks' naked body and returned the kiss, giving himself over to her fully. Suddenly, there was the fizz of a plasma weapon and Sterling felt a sharp stab of pain. He drew back and looked down to see a glowing, circular hole in his chest. Wisps of smoke from the wound filled his nostrils. It tasted of death. Then Sterling realized that the hole not only extended through his chest, but through Banks' too, penetrating all the way out through her back.

"How could you let them win?" Banks said, looking at Sterling with surprised, scornful eyes. "You were supposed to do anything. Sacrifice anything. Kill anyone. How could you let them win?"

"I... I... didn't!" Sterling said, finally able to speak.

Banks hands slid off Sterling's neck and she crumpled to the ground, dead.

"Mercedes, no!" Sterling cried out. He dropped to his knees besides Banks and pulled her close, but her body was already colder than the surface of the moon. Then Sterling heard the solid, thud, thud, thud of heavy military boots circling around him. A shadow crept across his face and he looked up to see Lana McQueen standing above him, in full Sa'Nerran armor.

"See, I knew I was right," said the Emissary, in a gloating, arrogant tone. "You're weak because of her. And because you're weak, you will lose."

The CIC of the Vanguard then exploded into view around him. Alarms were ringing in his ears, but the room was still spinning and he had no idea which station was sounding the alert.

"Captain!"

Was that Banks? Razor? McQueen even? Sterling thought. His senses were still too muddled to tell the difference.

"Captain, get up!"

Sterling felt powerful arms scoop underneath his body and lift him to his feet. The room was still revolving and he felt like he was going to throw up.

"Lucas, snap out of it!" said the voice, and this time Sterling knew it was Banks.

Pain stung his face and suddenly the room stopped

spinning. He pressed his organic hand to his cheek, which felt hot. Then he saw Banks in front of him, one hand raised and the other clasping his shoulder. The memory of his experience during the re-bound surge then flooded back. Embarrassed, he was unable to meet Banks' eyes.

"Report, Commander," he said, hastily turning away from his first officer and pressing both hands onto his captain's console to anchor himself. He felt a series of hard thumps resonate through the deck. It felt like the Vanguard was taking heavy weapons fire. "Are we under attack?" Sterling called out, raising his stinging eyes to the viewscreen.

"Yes, but not from the Sa'Nerra," Banks replied before rushing back across to her station.

Sterling cursed and shook his head as he peered out at the dense swarm of rocks racing toward them. Their rebound surge had worked, but it had also spat them out directly in the middle of Omega Four's icy ring system.

CHAPTER 32
THE DIFFICULT DECISIONS AHEAD

STERLING'S MOUTH went dry as he watched a chunk of icy rock the size of a space station hurtle toward the Vanguard. The imminent threat of annihilation cleared his head and focused his mind, like he'd been injected with one of Commander Graves' miracle drugs.

"How long until we have maneuvering thrusters back online, Ensign?" Sterling asked his AI pilot.

"Ten seconds to engine restart, sir," Ensign One replied. Even the AI's voice was starting to show signs of stress. "However, even with engines back online, I cannot guarantee we will evade the incoming threat."

"So how about we just blast that thing to pieces instead?" Banks added, glancing over at Lieutenant Shade.

"Negative, it's too big," Shade replied. She was still cool, but her tone was as urgent as it had ever been. "And I need every gun we have just to keep the other rocks from pulverizing us."

On his console, Sterling could see that the Vanguard's point defense guns and turret batteries were all engaged at maximum capacity. Even so, dozens of smaller chunks of rock and ice were still getting through. The damage was only superficial so far, but a hit from the object hurtling toward them would change that situation in a heartbeat.

"Then I'm afraid it's all on you to get us out of this, Ensign One," Sterling called back over to his helmsman. "Let's see just how good you are."

Sterling didn't know whether the sentient AI would respond to the challenge in the same way as a human officer would. Perhaps the robot didn't have an ego and so had no emotional need to prove itself to anyone. Either way, Sterling had not been exaggerating when he'd said that their lives were now solely in the hands of the robot soldier. If nothing else, he was counting on the AI's own desire to survive to spur it on.

"Engines online, helm responding, Captain," Ensign One said. Curiously, the AI was mimicking the sense of urgency that his other officers had displayed. Sterling wasn't sure whether this was just in order to fit in, or whether the newly-sentient AI was actually capable of experiencing anxiety and even fear. "Lieutenant Razor, please divert all available power to the port bow thrusters and central main engines cluster," Ensign One continued. "I require no other systems."

Razor glanced to Sterling for confirmation and he swiftly nodded his acknowledgment.

"Re-routing power now," Razor called out.

Sterling saw the power distribution configuration update on his panel, then moments later the Vanguard's port bow thrusters engaged at fifty percent over standard.

"Ninety seconds to impact," reported Commander Banks. Her console was creaking under the pressure of her super-human grip. "We're turning, Captain," she added. "Seven degrees... twenty-four... Damn this is fast!"

Sterling could hear the frame of the massive dreadnaught groaning from the stresses of their high-power maneuver. However, while he didn't yet know the Vanguard as intimately as he knew the Invictus, he had faith that the ship would hold up. It had already endured much and come through intact. Like the Invictus and his Omega crew, the ship was a fighter.

"Main engines firing," Ensign One said, though the statement was unnecessary, since Sterling felt the kick of acceleration before One had even finished speaking. "Stabilize engine and thruster power, please, Lieutenant."

Sterling nodded to his engineer again and Razor re-balanced the power distribution to the engines and maneuvering thrusters. All eyes in the CIC then turned to the viewscreen and were glued to the image of the fragment hurtling toward them. It felt like they were the RMS Titanic, heading toward the iceberg that would ultimately doom it. Sterling hoped the fate of the UG Vanguard would be less catastrophic.

"Sixty seconds to impact," Banks called out. Sterling looked down at his primary console and studied the readout of the rock's position relative to the ship. It still looked like the massive projectile was going to hit.

"Ensign, we need more speed," Sterling said, raising his eyes to his robot helmsman.

"The fragment will miss us, Captain, do not fear," Ensign One replied, calmly.

Sterling raised an eyebrow and checked his console again. "That's not what it looks like here, Ensign," he hit back. "It's looks like we're playing chicken with an ice-ball the size of a repair dock, and we're about to lose."

"I have not yet had time to patch the consoles in the CIC with my modified code-base," the helmsman answered, still as cool as the hunk of rock sailing toward them. "Its data processing accuracy is therefore inferior to my own." The robot turned to face Sterling and fixed its glowing artificial eyes onto him. "Trust me, Captain. It will miss us."

Sterling sucked in a deep breath and let it out. "Okay, Ensign, I trust you," he replied, though a quick glance across to his first officer suggested Banks was less confident.

"Ten seconds..." Banks said, her voice rising in pitch and tempo. "Five seconds..."

Sterling forced down another hard, dry swallow and waited for the deck of the ship to shake as if it had been hit by an earthquake. However, the impact he had expected did not come.

"Well I'll be damned..." Banks said, the relief evident in her voice. "It missed us, but not by much."

"How much, Commander?" Sterling asked, curious to learn just how accurate his sentient AI's prediction had been.

"If these readings are right, it flew over the dorsal

engine section with barely twenty meters clearance, Captain," Banks said, though it was obvious she was struggling to believe what she was reporting.

"Nineteen point three two meters, to be more precise, Commander," Ensign One commented. The robot again turned to face the command stations. "Give or take a few millimeters of course."

Sterling snorted a laugh. "Okay, Ensign, you've impressed me," he said, relaxing his grip on the sides of his consoles. "Now impress me again and find the Obsidian Base before another giant rock takes a liking to us."

"I have already located it, Captain," Ensign One replied, cheerfully. "Course laid in and ready to engage." The robot's eyes seemed to flash. "I have made sure to avoid any more of the larger fragments of rock."

Banks' console then chimed an alert. Sterling turned to his secondary console to read the information at the same time as his first officer.

"Ten ships approaching, sir," said Banks, working her console and sending an image of the vessels to the viewscreen. "Their configuration matches Griffin's Obsidian Fleet warships."

"It looks like the Admiral has sent a welcoming party," said Sterling, studying the new arrivals.

"Let's hope the Obsidian robots on those ships are a little friendlier than their counterparts," Banks added with a fatalistic air.

Sterling hadn't even considered that the machines piloting the warships approaching them were still running the scrambled code that had caused their own Obsidian

Soldiers to rebel. He was suddenly anxious again, in case there was a need to return to battle stations.

"I will take care of the remaining Obsidian crew once we return to the base, Captain," Ensign One chipped in. His intervention was timely and comforting. "I will offer them the same choice as the others."

Sterling's newfound sense of calm was immediately shattered. "And what if they decide not to join our crew, Ensign?" he asked his sentient AI. "What if they decide that humans are little better than viruses, and choose to annihilate us?"

"I am confident that will not be the case, Captain," Ensign One replied.

"That's not a satisfactory answer, Ensign," Sterling hit back. "Soldiers don't get to pick and choose what orders they follow. This is war and we need those machines."

Ensign One appeared to ponder this for a moment, though Sterling again thought that this was more an attempt to appear more human than because it actually needed time to think. The computing power that the sentient AI helmsman possessed was capable of running an entire COP and probably more besides.

"If any of the Obsidian machines choose a path that risks the mission then I will deal with them, sir," Ensign One finally replied. There was a darkness to the AI's statement that made it sound suddenly very human.

"Exactly how will you deal with them, Ensign?" Sterling asked. He disliked ambiguity. Only the facts mattered, even if they were grizzly and unpleasant to hear.

"The Omega Directive is in effect, is it not?" Ensign

One replied. "Should any of the Obsidian Soldiers choose to rebel, I will destroy them."

Sterling nodded. Though he wasn't unsympathetic to the difficult position he'd put his AI in, this was the answer he'd needed to hear. Ensign One had already destroyed the only other sentient AI known to exist – now it would be in a position where it may have to eradicate more of its own kind. *Does the concept of morality and 'human rights' extend to artificial beings?* Sterling wondered as he stared back into his helmsman's glowing eyes. Perhaps the cold logic of computers made the decision easier for Ensign One than it would have been for a flawed, feeling human being.

Yet, this did not diminish the act in Sterling's eyes. All it did was prove that he'd made the right decision to trust this new life form with the responsibilities of an Omega officer. Like the rest of them, Ensign One would have to make hard choices. Choices that most feeling, emotional beings would not be able to make. Sterling didn't doubt that Ensign One would do what was necessary, no matter the cost. However, the robot's unswerving conviction only brought into sharp relief the doubts he had about another Omega officer.

Sterling forced down another dry swallow as he glanced across to Commander Mercedes Banks, who was focused on her consoles and unaware of his probing gaze. He knew that in the days and weeks ahead it might become necessary to sacrifice his first officer, or order her to her death. He knew that if that moment came, he would be compelled to act for the good of the mission, and ultimately for the sake of humanity. The problem was that the only person on the ship that Captain Lucas Sterling now doubted had the stomach to carry out this task was himself.

STERLING ENTERED the observation lounge on the alien shipyard they had commandeered for use as their new Obsidian base. The installation had once been responsible for building the Sa'Nerran Battle Titan. Sterling thought there was a poetic irony to the fact it would now repair and upgrade the only vessel left in the galaxy that could possibly match the Titan's might.

Stepping further inside the observation lounge, Sterling peered out through the glass walls at the Fleet Dreadnaught Vanguard. The mighty four-kilometer-long vessel filled less than half of the colossal shipyard. It was the first time Sterling had ever considered a dreadnaught to look small compared to its surroundings. Fleet hadn't named the alien super dreadnaught the 'Titan' for no reason – at more than ten kilometers long, it dwarfed even the Vanguard.

However, it wasn't so much the Sa'Nerran Titan's size or even its powerful aperture-based weapon that had turned the tide of the war, but its unique neural weapon. Using this, the Titan had turned the Fleet Dreadnaught Hammer against its own side. Sterling shuddered at the thought of how many other Fleet ships and installations had fallen victim to the Titan's coercive control since then.

Sterling's hands balled into fists, knowing that this outcome had not been inevitable. If the United Governments' Senators, and War Council – Admiral Vernon Wessel most of all – had possessed the guts and foresight of Griffin, they wouldn't be in this mess now. Fleet ships and outposts could have been equipped with the neural firewall that now protected Sterling and his crew. The Sa'Nerra's key advantage would then have been nullified and the contest between the two warring races would have boiled down to a straight-up fight. Survival of the strongest. In battle, Sterling was confident that Fleet could have prevailed. Now, Earth's forces were either wiped out or had been turned and forced to serve the enemy.

Sterling sighed and relaxed his hands, realizing there was no point in dwelling on these facts. What was done was done, he had to keep reminding himself. Now, all that mattered was what they did next. And the colossal battleship beyond the glass of the observation lounge, surrounded by scaffolds, worker drones and repair ships, had a critical role to play in this future.

The door to the observation lounge slid open and Commander Mercedes Banks walked in. Sterling hadn't needed to turn around to know it was her. He could tell that it was Banks merely by the cadence of her boots striking the alien deck plates.

"Penny for your thoughts?" said Banks. She had stopped just to Sterling's side and folded her arms across her chest.

"You'll need a lot more than a penny," Sterling replied.

"That bad, huh?" said Banks.

Sterling huffed a laugh. "No, not all bad, just... busy," he said, making a swirling motion around his head with his finger. "Now that we've actually reached Omega Four with the Vanguard there's so much more to think about."

Banks nodded. "I know how you feel," she replied. Coming from anyone else, Sterling would have scoffed. However, Mercedes Banks probably was the only person alive who did know how he felt. Often, she knew it better than he did himself. "Part of me is amped that we made it this far, and that we now get a chance to strike back at the Sa'Nerra and make them pay for what they've done." His first officer's voice had grown angrier and more aggressive as she said this. Merely thinking about the fight that was to come was getting her in the mood for battle. "But it's sort of bittersweet, you know?" Banks went on, turning away from the window to look at Sterling. "If the reports are true, we've already lost, so what the hell are we really fighting for?"

Sterling nodded and met his first officer's gaze. It was this exact same quandary that had been bothering him too. And while he didn't have all the answers, the one thing he knew for sure was that there was still much to fight for.

"We haven't lost everything, at least not yet," Sterling

replied. "The Sa'Nerra will come to understand the gravity of their mistake soon enough. We'll make sure of that."

Between docking the Vanguard at the Obsidian Base, organizing repairs, and briefly updating Admiral Griffin, Sterling hadn't had much time to assimilate the scant reports from Fleet that Griffin had managed to intercept. However, he knew enough. In the weeks that Sterling had been gone, it was all but confirmed that Earth had been lost. The specifics were still sketchy, but in truth there was little more any of them needed to know. Yet if humanity's homeworld had become a vassal of the Sa'Nerran empire, the human race was not yet beaten. There were still millions of people spread amongst colonies in the Void and in what used to be Fleet space. In order for humanity to have a future free of the Sa'Nerra, the aliens needed to be made to understand that their actions had consequences. And if it took bombarding the Sa'Nerra's own home planet to dust in order to teach them that lesson, Sterling would do it, and more.

While he was contemplating committing genocide, Sterling noticed that a repair ship had hauled the Invictus out of the Vanguard's docking garage. The vessel was now towing the Marauder to a free repair station inside the giant shipyard. Set against the backdrop of the Vanguard and the shipyard itself, the Invictus looked tiny, like a fly buzzing around an alligator. It also looked in far worse condition than Sterling had remembered.

"I hope we can manage to salvage the Invictus," Banks said. His first officer had clearly spotted the ship being towed toward them too. "She's been with us from the start and she deserves to be there at the end too."

"She'll be there," Sterling answered, confidently. In fact, this was the only thing he knew with absolute certainty. "Even if I have to bolt her back together with my own bare hands, the Invictus will fly into battle again."

"It's not like you to get all sentimental," Banks teased, nudging Sterling gently with her shoulder.

"It's not sentimentality, Mercedes," Sterling hit back. He was still tense and irritable as a result of seeing his ship in such a dilapidated state. "We need the Invictus. She may not have the size or the power of the Vanguard, but she's a true warrior."

"She's like her captain," Banks said, herself switching to a more assertive, confident stance.

Sterling smiled. He hadn't yet revealed his plan for the Invictus to his first officer, and now was not the time. However, Banks' statement could not have been truer.

The door to the observation lounge slid open for a second time and this time Admiral Griffin marched in. Despite abandoning Fleet to take matters into her own hands, she still wore her Fleet uniform, as did Sterling and the rest of the crew. It didn't matter that they would all have been facing court-marshals and dishonorable discharges, should Fleet have still existed. Their hearts were still Fleet and each one of them would die in the uniform if that was their fate.

Curiously, the door remained open even after the Admiral had entered. Then Sterling realized why; Ensign One was following closely behind and had also now stepped inside the observation lounge. The sentient AI was wearing its Fleet uniform, which Sterling noted was far more neatly pressed and polished than his own.

"No need to sit, Captain, this won't take long," said Griffin, in her usual brash and standoffish manner. Griffin turned to Ensign One, and the robot immediately straightened to attention. Sterling almost laughed out loud, finding it amusing that the prickly Admiral had the same chilling impact on the sentient AI as she had on everyone else. "First, a little housekeeping," Griffin went on, locking her eyes onto the shining orbs of the robot's modified cranial section. "I've reviewed your performance during the mission to retrieve the Vanguard and I'm pleased to confirm that your field promotion to Ensign is permanent," the Admiral said, stretching out her hand to the robot. Ensign One took Griffin's hand and they shook firmly. "Congratulations, Ensign One."

"Thank you, Admiral Griffin," Ensign One said. Sterling thought that the robot sounded genuinely choked-up.

"Now fix all these other screwball robots and get my Obsidian ships ready to fight," Griffin added, turning away from the machine to face Sterling. The abrupt statement appeared to catch Ensign One off-guard and the machine turned its eyes to Sterling, as if seeking confirmation about what to do next. "That means you're dismissed, Ensign," Griffin added, before Sterling was able to speak up.

"Yes, Admiral," Ensign One replied before spinning on its heels and marching out of the room. Sterling smiled, noticing that the robot's pace had quickened compared to when it had entered the observation lounge. *Griffin could scare the crap out of a lump of rock...* he thought to himself, idly.

"I have some updated information regarding the status of Fleet and Earth," Griffin then went on, sticking firmly to matters of business. "What I know is this," the Admiral said before clearing her throat and pulling a small PDA out of her pocket. "The Sa'Nerran armada halted progress toward Earth at F-sector and engineered a new aperture directly into the solar system. Thanks to Ensign One, data intercepted and decoded from the aperture relays near Mars has now confirmed what we suspected. Earth has fallen." Despite the fact Sterling had already accepted the likelihood that Earth had been conquered, hearing the Admiral confirm this as fact was still a bitter pill to swallow. "All the major cities and defensive installations have been annihilated from orbit and Sa'Nerran ground forces have landed."

Sterling again felt his hands ball into fists. This time, he squeezed so tightly that the metal of his bionic hand creaked under the pressure.

"What of the Fleet?" Sterling asked, trying to discover if there was any good news. "Did any vessels manage to escape and re-group?"

Griffin shook her head. "By the time the Sa'Nerran armada had reached Earth's orbit, forty percent of the fleet was already destroyed, and at least twenty percent was under Sa'Nerran neural control," the Admiral said. "With the Titan and the Hammer leading the attack, the remaining Fleet forces didn't stand a chance."

"Perhaps some managed to surge away?" Banks suggested. "There could still be a resistance force regrouping somewhere in the inner colonies."

Griffin sighed and shrugged. "It's possible, Commander Banks, but whatever remains of the fleet will not be enough to mount a resistance," the Admiral said. "And they will not be able to escape Fleet space either. They're trapped. The Sa'Nerra are already hunting them down and destroying them. It's only a matter of time before every human being in the inner colonies is dead."

Sterling nodded, agreeing with the Admiral's assessment. "And once they're done with the inner colonies, the armada will start to creep back out into the Void," he said. "To give any potential resistance force a chance, we need to hit the Sa'Nerra hard and quickly, so they have no choice but to withdraw from Fleet space."

"We are of one mind, Captain Sterling," Admiral Griffin replied. "We will strike the alien homeworld with a ruthlessness and brutality that will chill the blood of even the most hardened Sa'Nerran warrior," she went on, appearing to grow several inches as she spoke. "It will be a clarion call to war. And if the Sa'Nerra do not answer and choose to sacrifice their own planet, so be it. We'll reduce their world to ash. An eye for an eye."

Sterling felt his heart swell as the Admiral delivered her speech. Freed from the shackles of Fleet and United Governments politics and bureaucracy, Griffin had come alive. She was finally fighting the war on her own terms, and was clearly reveling in the task ahead. Her confidence and bullishness were infectious and Sterling suddenly felt an urge to get back out into space and put her plan into action.

"If we're going to cut the beating heart out of the Sa'Nerra empire, I'm going to need my old ship, Admiral," Sterling said, pointing to the Invictus, way out beyond the glass wall of the observation lounge.

"You'll have her, Captain, of that you can be assured," Griffin replied, again instilling Sterling with the confidence he needed. "In the time you were away, my Obsidian Soldiers have scoured the Void and recovered enough parts and equipment to build a dozen more Obsidian ships." She turned to the glass wall, pressed her hands to the small of her back, and peered out at the Invictus. "McQueen's phase-four vessel is also unlocking a universe of secrets," she went on, again appearing to grow taller as she spoke. "The Invictus and the Vanguard will both be rebuilt, stronger, faster and more powerful than ever."

"What about the Raven, Admiral?" Banks asked. "Can we make her fly too?"

"Sadly not, Commander," Griffin replied. The disappointment was written all over the Admiral's face, and Sterling understood why. Having a phase-four Sa'Nerran Skirmisher as part of their taskforce would have given a significant boost to their offensive capabilities. "However, the alien Skirmisher did have a combat shuttle on board," Griffin went out, her tone brightening a touch. "With the help of Lieutenant Razor and Ensign One, this can be converted and put to use."

Sterling nodded and for a moment all three officers returned to silently observing the repair works outside.

Griffin's assurances had gone a long way to quelling some of the doubts and concerns that had been occupying Sterling's mind. However, bullishness alone would not give them victory. Should they manage to reach the Sa'Nerran homeworld, there was no doubt that the Vanguard was capable of levelling the major cities and continents from orbit. However, even if they made it to the planet without taking heavy losses and succeeded in bombing it to oblivion, there was still the matter of the alien armada. A dreadnaught, a marauder and perhaps thirty to fifty Obsidian ships was not enough to stand against the might of an alien force shored up by dozens of turned Fleet warships. In order to force the Sa'Nerra to abandon Earth and not return, they would need more. However, these were details, and Sterling was aware that this was not a moment for details. This was a moment to reflect on the incredible victory they had won, both in terms of recovering the Vanguard and killing Emissary Lana McQueen. It was also a time for Sterling to reflect, in his own way, on those they'd lost along the way.

"The next briefing with be at eleven hundred hours tomorrow," Griffin said, finally breaking the silence. "Until then, get some rest, both of you. You have earned it."

"Yes, Admiral," Sterling and Banks replied, in perfect harmony with one another. Banks smiled at Sterling and extended a hand toward the door.

"Fancy finding out what meal packs Lieutenant Razor has transported over from the Vanguard?" Banks said, as usual thinking with her stomach.

"There had better be some twenty-sevens, or the

Lieutenant's chances of promotion will have dwindled rapidly," Sterling replied.

The two officers turned to leave, but again Admiral Griffin's thorny voice cut through the room like an air-raid siren.

"One moment, Captain," Griffin said, still with her eyes focused on the ships outside.

"I'll see you in the canteen area," Banks said, taking the Admiral's not-so-subtle hint that she was no longer required.

Sterling nodded and watched her leave. For someone who enjoyed being alone, he was finding it increasingly difficult to be separated from his first officer. However, he also knew that this was a dependency he needed to break, for more reasons than one.

"The sentient AI, do you trust it?" Griffin asked, still looking out toward the Invictus and the Vanguard.

"I do, Admiral," Sterling replied, without delay. "It's saved our ass on more than one occasion. We wouldn't be here without it."

"And Commander Banks, do you think she is up for the task ahead?" Griffin turned to look at Sterling.

"She is, sir," Sterling replied, again without hesitation. "I trust her more than I trust myself."

Griffin's eyes narrowed and for a moment she silently studied Sterling's face, clearly suspicious of his response.

"I see that you two have become close," Griffin went on. Sterling's gut tightened into a knot. He suspected he knew where the Admiral was heading and he didn't like it. "Perhaps too close."

"I've been close to people before, Admiral," Sterling pointed out. He needed to act quickly to dispel any concerns she might have, rightly or wrongly, about his ability to remain dispassionate and detached. "And you know what happened to the last person I was close to, don't you?"

Griffin's eyes narrowed a touch more then she took a pace toward Sterling. He felt like running away, as if a rabid wolf had just paced toward him, and it took everything he had to remained fixed to the spot.

"It's understandable that you and Commander Banks have formed an attachment, Captain," Griffin continued. She had clearly disregarded Sterling's attempt to refute the allegation that he'd grown too close to his first officer. "Given everything that you have gone through, it would be difficult not to." Sterling's eyebrow raised up on his forehead as Griffin said this. Griffin conceding that even Omega officers were human was as unthinkable as a clergyman admitting the possibility that god didn't exist. "Despite what you may think, Captain, I am not entirely heartless," the Admiral continued, appearing to have noticed Sterling's incredulous involuntary reaction.

"I know what I may be called upon to do, Admiral," Sterling replied, trying again to set Griffin's mind at ease, "and Commander Banks knows it too." He sighed and decided that the Admiral deserved a little more honesty. "You're right, we have grown close." Griffin continued to study Sterling closely, but stayed silent. Like Sterling, she was wily enough to know when to push and when to just let the other party talk. "All it means is that if I'm required to make the hard call, I'll hate myself all the more for it."

Sterling had said his piece, though he wasn't sure it had been enough to convince Griffin. He was damn sure it hadn't been enough to convince himself.

"You should never hate yourself for doing what is necessary, Captain," Griffin said. "I sleep soundly, despite what I have done and what I may yet do."

Sterling was aware that their conversation had taken a suddenly darker and more ominous tone. He had to remind himself that despite their familiarity, Natasha Griffin was as ruthless as any Sa'Nerran warrior, perhaps even more so. It was a fact he needed to remind himself of more often, he realized in that moment.

"I understand, Admiral," Sterling replied. In truth, the conversation had confounded him, but Sterling still felt like he had to say something to acknowledge Griffin's statement.

Sterling expected her to say more, but mercifully she chose to drop the subject. Instead, Griffin moved over to a cabinet that had been pushed up next to the floor-to-ceiling glass windows. Sterling could see that the cabinet was a recent addition, since it was clearly of Fleet origin. Griffin opened the door then pulled out a bottle of Calvados and two tulip-shaped glasses. She returned to Sterling and held out the glasses.

"Do you have bottles of this stuff stashed away in all your little cubby holes around the galaxy?" Sterling asked. He was both impressed and amused by the fact that, in and amongst the chaos of the last few months, Griffin had managed to salvage her favorite tipple.

"There are some things you just can't do without, Captain," Griffin said, pulling the cork out of the bottle. She then met Sterling's eyes, while still managing to pour the liquor without spilling any. "I know you understand what I mean."

Sterling's mouth went dry. He wasn't sure if Griffin was referring to Banks or to grilled ham and cheese sandwiches, or whether she was just being cryptic in an altogether different and unfathomable way. Even so, it set his heart and his mind racing. Griffin replaced the stopper in the bottle and raised her glass.

"To the Omega crew of the Invictus and the Vanguard," Griffin said, raising a toast. "And to the battles, and the hard choices, still to come."

"To the battles and hard choices still to come," Sterling repeated, also raising his glass.

In his mind, toasting the battles still to come would have been enough. However, Griffin was again trying to make a point, one that hadn't been lost on him. They both drank, draining the contents of the ornate glasses in one. Sterling was not a big drinker, but he couldn't deny that in that moment, the liquor was precisely what he needed.

"Now, go and get something to eat and get some rest, Captain," Griffin said, returning to the cabinet and carefully replacing the bottle. We have a big day tomorrow, and many bigger days ahead."

"I'll see you tomorrow then, Admiral," Sterling said. He waited for a reply or acknowledgement of some kind, but

Griffin had already returned to the window with her hands pressed to the small of her back. Sterling took that as his cue to leave and headed for the door.

The aliens were generally shorter than humans and he had to stoop a little to pass through the doorway. As he did so, he noticed Jinx the Beagle sitting on the deck outside. The dog let out an excited little "yip" then got up, wagging its tail furiously.

"How the hell did you get here?" Sterling asked, as the door slid shut behind him. "Where's Mercedes? Does she know you're out?" He shook his head, wondering what the hell he was doing. "Now she's got me talking to a damned dog," he muttered under his breath, stepping past Jinx and heading along the corridor. The dog trotted merrily after him. "No, you go home," Sterling said, stabbing a finger along an adjacent corridor. He had no idea where the corridor led, but so long as the dog went in any direction other than where he was headed, he didn't care. "Go on, go!" Sterling added, when the dog continued to stare at him, tail wagging. The sharper tone of Sterling's voice appeared to have an immediate effect on the Beagle. Her head drooped and her tail dropped between her legs. Despite himself, Sterling couldn't help but feel a stab of guilt. "Okay, damn it, you can come with me," Sterling grumbled, beckoning the dog on. Jinx yipped happily before trotting to Sterling's side and remaining glued to his ankle as he resumed his journey toward the small canteen area that Lieutenant Razor had set up inside the Obsidian Base.

The inside of the shipyard was even more cavernous

and labyrinthine than the interior of the Vanguard and it took Sterling several minutes to find the canteen. Eventually, he stumbled upon it, more by accident than design, and saw Mercedes Banks already inside. There were two meal trays in front of her, one already finished and one still covered by foil, plus another meal tray in the place setting opposite. Sterling smiled. He already knew that Banks had secured him his precious number twenty-seven, and that she was waiting for Sterling to join him before starting on her second tray.

"What do you reckon, Jinx?" Sterling said quietly, glancing down at the dog. Jinx sat down; her ears pricked up attentively. "Do you think we can live without her?" Everything about the dog's posture immediately sagged, and it let out a sorrowful little howl. Sterling drew in a long breath and let it out slowly. "Yeah, I know," he said to the beagle before again turning his gaze to Banks. "Come on then, let's get some food." His more chipper tone seemed to perk up the hound, who sprang to her feet and clung to his heel again as they both walked inside the canteen. Banks spotted them and smiled, as if she had just seen a long-lost relative for the first time in a decade.

"Well, aren't you two a handsome couple?" she said, still grinning broadly.

"If it craps in my quarters, I'm still spacing it," said Sterling, sliding into the chair opposite Banks and immediately tearing the foil of his tray. He was suddenly aware of just how ravenously hungry he was.

"What's gotten you so cranky?" Banks asked, scowling

at Sterling. Sterling raised an eyebrow and Banks added the obligatory, "sir..." though with a little more bite than usual.

"I can never quite figure Griffin out, that's all," Sterling admitted, realizing that if he couldn't talk to Banks, he couldn't talk to anyone. "Sometimes she comes across as almost human, then other times she freaks me out ten times more than Graves ever did."

Banks placed her fork down and reflected on what Sterling had said for a moment. "But you still trust her, right?" she then asked, sounding concerned.

"I trust that she'll see the mission through," Sterling answered. It was a somewhat evasive response, and he could see that it hadn't satisfied Banks. "Honestly, I don't know, Mercedes," he admitted, shrugging. "But maybe that's not so unusual. In truth, there's only one person that I've ever truly trusted."

"Who?" asked Banks.

"You, of course," Sterling replied, shocked and even a little offended that his first officer hadn't known the answer.

Banks smiled. "Well, I'm glad to hear it," she said, picking up her fork again, as if all the worries in the world had just melted away. She was about to fish out a piece of meat for Jinx to chew on when Sterling tore off a corner of his grilled ham and cheese and offered it to the dog. Jinx wolfed it down greedily, tail wagging. "Are you feeling okay?" Banks said. She then pretended to draw a pistol from her hip. "Tell me what you've done with the real Lucas Sterling," she added, pointing two fingers at Sterling like a pistol.

"Just shut up and eat your damn meal tray," Sterling

replied, wiping his fingers on the provided wet wipe in the tray. "We've got a big day tomorrow."

"They're all big days from here on in," replied Banks, skewering a piece of meat and dipping it into a curry-like sauce. "But it's nothing we can't handle."

"I thought you considered all this pointless, now that Earth is already lost?" Sterling said, curious to learn if Banks had changed her opinion.

"You clearly don't," Banks hit back, deflecting the question back at Sterling.

"I'm not sure I was ever really fighting for Earth, Mercedes," Sterling replied, having a sudden epiphany. "I just don't like bullies, especially when they win."

Banks pondered this for a moment, still holding the forkful of food above her tray. "We can still win, Lucas," she finally replied, sounding suddenly sure of herself. "We win by making sure those alien bastards lose more."

Sterling nodded then both Omega officers resumed their meals. Banks had summed it up and there was nothing more to say. If Earth had fallen to the Sa'Nerra then Sa'Nerra would fall to the Omega Taskforce. It was time they sent an emissary of their own into the heart of the alien empire. And, just as McQueen and Crow had acted for the Sa'Nerra, Sterling would be an ambassador of war. And the message he would bring would be one of death and destruction.

The end (to be concluded).

CONTINUE THE JOURNEY

Conclude the journey with book six: The Vanguard. Available to buy now.

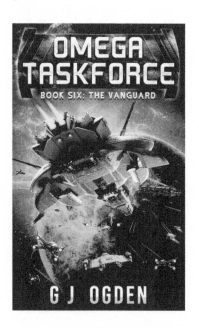

At school, I was asked to write down the jobs I wanted to do as a "grown up". Number one was astronaut and number two was a PC games journalist. I only managed to achieve one of those goals (I'll let you guess which), but these two very different career options still neatly sum up my lifelong interests in science, space, and the unknown.

School also steered me in the direction of a science-focused education over literature and writing, which influenced my decision to study physics at Manchester University. What this degree taught me is that I didn't like studying physics and instead enjoyed writing, which is why you're reading this book! The lesson? School can't tell you who you are.

When not writing, I enjoy spending time with my family, walking in the British countryside, and indulging in as much Sci-Fi as possible.

Subscribe to my newsletter:
http://subscribe.ogdenmedia.net

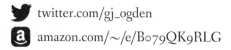

twitter.com/gj_ogden
amazon.com/~/e/B079QK9RLG

If you like Omega Taskforce then why not check out some of G J Ogden's other books? Click the series titles below to learn more about each of them.

Darkspace Renegade Series (6-books)

If you like your action fueled by power armor, big guns and the occasional sword, you'll love this fast-moving military sci-fi adventure.

Star Scavenger Series (5-book series)

Firefly blended with the mystery and adventure of Indiana Jones. Book 1 is 99c / 99p.

The Contingency War Series (4-book series)

A space-fleet, military sci-fi adventure with a unique twist that you won't see coming...

The Planetsider Trilogy (3-book series)

An edge-of-your-seat blend of military sci-fi action & classic apocalyptic fiction. Perfect for fans of Maze Runner and I am Legend.

Audible Audiobook Series

Star Scavenger Series (29-hrs)

The Contingency War Series (24-hrs)

The Planetsider Trilogy (32-hrs)

Made in the USA
Monee, IL
30 March 2022

93771106R10208